DOGLANDS

DOGLANDS

Tim Willocks

RANDOM HOUSE NEW YORK

Text copyright © 2011 by Tim Willocks
Jacket art copyright © 2011 by Angelo Rinaldi

Visit us on the Web!
www.randomhouse.com/teens

Educators and librarians, for a variety of teaching tools,
visit us at www.randomhouse.com/teachers

Library of Congress Cataloging-in-Publication Data
Willocks, Tim.
Doglands / Tim Willocks. — 1st ed.
p. cm.
Summary: Furgul, a half-greyhound puppy, escapes a cruel dogtrack owner and sets out in the hope of finding his father and the fabled Doglands, later returning to try to free his mother and the other abused dogs.
ISBN 978-0-375-86571-8 (trade) — ISBN 978-0-375-96571-5 (lib. bdg.) — ISBN 978-0-375-89604-0 (ebook)
[1. Adventure and adventurers—Fiction. 2. Greyhounds—Fiction. 3. Dogs—Fiction. 4. Animals—Treatment—Fiction. 5. Supernatural—Fiction.] I. Title.
PZ7.W68368Do 2011 [Fic]—dc22 2009033328

Printed in the United States of America
10 9 8 7 6 5 4 3 2 1
First Edition

This book is dedicated to:

GRACE AMERLING for choosing FEARGAL
GRANT AMERLING for writing "FURGUL"
and
ESTHER COX for being the first to read it.

CONTENTS

The Doglands are everywhere and nowhere
Because dogs are everywhere and nowhere

They live in a world they do not rule
But sometimes
With the winds
A dog will run

This is his tale . . .

PART ONE

BRAVEDOG

CHAPTER ONE

THE CAMP

Once upon a time in the Doglands, a blue greyhound gave birth to four pups in a prison camp that the dogs called Dedbone's Hole. The blue greyhound's name was Keeva and she named her firstborn Furgul, which in dog tongue means "the brave." Keeva loved Furgul from the moment she saw him, but as she licked his newborn body clean and gave him her milk to drink, her heart was filled with fear. Furgul had been born with a terrible secret. And she knew that when the masters discovered his secret, they would take him away.

Dedbone's Hole was a greyhound farm, where the masters made the rules and where no dog was free. Furgul was born in one of the whelping cages, whose floor was hard and cold and damp, but Furgul and his three sisters kept one another warm.

Keeva gave them milk and love. And for the first few weeks of their lives, the pups were happy. Yet as Furgul learned how to walk and talk, and as his eyes, nose and ears grew keen, he realized that Dedbone's Hole was ruled by boots and teeth and chains.

Every dawn he heard the voices of the masters, harsh and angry and mean.

"Shout! Shout! Shout!" they roared. "In! Out! Here! There! Everywhere!"

Every day he heard the squeals as greyhounds were beaten down.

"This isn't fair!" cried the greyhounds. "We haven't done anything wrong!"

Every night he heard the murmurs of dogs who were hungry, frightened and sad.

"There is no justice here," they whispered in the dark. "But what can we do?"

To keep her pups happy, Keeva crooned sweet songs and was always cheerful and kind, but every time he snuggled up against her body to go to sleep, Furgul could sense the hidden fear pounding inside her heart. He was too young to understand very much, but he knew that this fear was wrong. He wanted to make it go away. He wanted to make it right, but he didn't know how.

When the pups no longer needed Keeva's milk, they joined the other hounds in the exercise yard and Furgul got a better look at Dedbone's Hole. A lot of greyhounds lived here, in a compound surrounded by a high wire fence. Outside the fence he saw a junkyard and some shacks. Inside the compound the greyhounds were locked in crates—one crate each, where each hound lived all alone—which were even smaller than the whelping cage that Furgul lived in. For just one hour a day the hounds were released from the crates to feed and exercise. The masters made sure that there was never enough food for all the hounds, and so the hounds had to fight one another, snarling and biting at the filthy troughs of grub to get enough to eat. The older dogs said the masters starved the hounds on purpose to make them compete, so they could find out who was weak and who was strong and who might make a good racer. They did it to teach them that it was stupid to make friends. They did it because they were bullies who thought it was fun to feel so powerful.

When the greyhounds were a year old, the masters trained them to chase mechanical rabbits round a track. If a hound didn't chase the fake rabbit, he or she was punished. If a greyhound was a fast runner—and a clever racer—the masters made what they called money, which they put in their pockets. If a greyhound didn't run fast enough—if she was weak and puny, or if he wasn't clever enough, or when they got old and slow—then the masters got rid of them.

None of the dogs knew exactly how. At least not for sure.

They just disappeared.

And they never came back.

• • •

Keeva was the fastest greyhound—and the most successful racer—any dog at Dedbone's Hole could remember. Because her coat was blue, the masters called her Sapphire Breeze. With each day that passed, as her pups grew bigger and bigger, Furgul felt the fear inside Keeva grow too. One morning, while Keeva was watching his sisters at play, Furgul said, "Mam, why are you frightened?"

Keeva looked at him. Furgul's coat was white. He had a wet black nose and thin black rims beneath his deep brown eyes. "You're my firstborn," she said. This didn't seem important to Furgul, but it seemed to mean a lot to Keeva. Her eyes looked sad. She said, "I'm frightened because you won't be a pup for much longer."

"But I don't want to be a pup," said Furgul. "I want to be a dog."

Keeva said, "You'll be a big dog, but you won't be the biggest. You'll be strong, but you won't be the strongest. You'll be fast, but you won't be the fastest. That's why you'll have to be the bravest."

Furgul nodded. He didn't think this would be too hard. None of the puppies at the feeding troughs scared him. In fact, he had learned to scare them so that his three little sisters from the litter—Nessa and Eena and Brid—could get enough food. If he hadn't fought hard, the other pups would have gobbled up everything, and his sisters would have wasted away.

"Sure, Mam," he said. "Whatever you say."

"And if you're going to escape," said Keeva, "you'll have to be very clever—and very lucky too."

"Escape?" asked Furgul.

He looked at the high wire fence that surrounded the compound. Outside the fence was a junkyard full of trash and the house where the masters lived. Beyond the camp lay sweet green fields. In the distance a mountain rose toward the far blue sky. At the foot of the fence the masters had laid some very hard stuff called concrete so the dogs couldn't dig underneath it. Worst of all, there were two bad dogs who guarded the fence for the masters. For a reward they got lots of meat—fresh, tasty red meat in their own private bowls— and they were never locked in a cage. By breed they were bullmastiffs, so the hounds called them the Bulls. The Bulls were huge and brutal and loved being mean. Even if a hound got over the fence—or so everyone said—the Bulls would tear him apart with their massive jaws.

Furgul had heard other dogs talk about escaping. It was one of their favorite fantasies. Some of them woofled about it in their sleep. But whenever escape was discussed they all agreed: It was impossible.

"But, Mam," said Furgul, "no one's ever escaped from Dedbone's Hole."

"Your father did," said Keeva.

Furgul's throat felt tight. Keeva and his sisters were the only family he had ever known. He'd never imagined there was someone else. He'd never even thought about it. He swallowed. "I have a father?"

Keeva nodded. "His name is Argal."

The name hummed through Furgul's bones and sent a chill down his spine.

"Argal," he said.

The very sound of it made him feel brave, so he said it again.

"Argal."

"Not only did Argal get in here," continued Keeva, "he got out again."

"How?" asked Furgul.

"He hid in the pickup truck that takes us to and from the racetrack in the city."

"Why did he do that?" asked Furgul. "I mean, why did he come here?"

"Argal just appeared one day, like a legend, like a ghost, like a vision. He saw me win a race at the track and he fell in love. He risked his life to spend one night with me." Keeva's eyes grew misty. "He was the fiercest, handsomest, fightingest dog I ever saw. He was crazy and fearless and wild."

Furgul liked the sound of this. "I wish I could play with Argal so that I could learn to be wild and fearless too."

"So do I," said Keeva.

"Where is he?" asked Furgul.

Keeva shrugged. "Your father is like the wind. He goes wherever he chooses and he does whatever he likes."

"Wow," said Furgul, "he must have a really great master."

"Argal doesn't have a master," said Keeva. "He's free."

Furgul frowned. "What does 'free' mean?"

"I don't know," said Keeva. A troubled look came over her face. "Argal tried to explain it to me—something to do with what he called the Doglands."

"The Doglands?" Furgul felt the fur on his back stand up on end. The word sang in his blood. "What did Argal say?"

"I wasn't really listening. I was in love."

"Where are the Doglands?" asked Furgul.

"I don't know that either," said Keeva. Confusion and pain clouded her eyes. She looked out between the bars of the cage in which all five of them had to lie day and night in their own pee. She gazed out beyond the high wire fence, past the rusting heaps of trash in the yard, to the mountain on the far blue horizon. "Maybe the Doglands are somewhere out there."

Furgul looked at the mountain. He felt as if his heart had just grown bigger.

"I'm going to be free," he said. "Like Argal."

Keeva panted and licked her lips, and Furgul could tell she was nervous. She looked about to make sure no other hounds were listening. She lowered her voice.

"Dedbone checked my feet and muscles this morning and gave me the special breakfast. That means the racing season has begun. I'm going to be racing tonight. For Dedbone."

She looked at him. Suddenly Furgul didn't feel quite so brave anymore. Dedbone was the master who did all the shouting and who starved the greyhounds and made them live alone in crates. All the dogs, even the biggest—even the Bulls—were scared of Dedbone. They talked about him all the time. They hated him. But what could they do?

Furgul remembered that the first sight he'd ever seen— when his eyes had just learned to see—was of Dedbone's steel-toed boots. The boots had kicked sparks from the ground as they'd walked past the whelping cage. And they'd smelled of blood. Dog blood.

Furgul said, "You mean you want me to escape tonight?"

Keeva nodded. "When Dedbone comes to the cage to put on my racing muzzle and leash, I'll run away. He'll get angry and chase after me. That's when I want you to sneak past and run to the truck without letting anyone see you. Can you do that?"

Recently Furgul had started to play a game with the brutal, stupid Bulls. During the exercise hour he peed on top of their pee then ran and hid behind the cages, where he could watch them foam with rage when they sniffed his smell. They hunted for him, but he was always too fast and crafty to let them catch him. He was sure he could get to the truck.

He nodded. "I can do that."

Keeva asked, "Do you know what the truck looks like?"

Furgul said, "It's red and has a row of crates on the back."

"Very good. Dedbone always puts me in the last crate, nearest the back. It will have lots of old newspapers on the floor. I want you to jump in the crate, hide beneath the newspapers and wait for me. Can you jump that high?"

Furgul thought about it. The truck was very high indeed, at least for him.

He asked, "Could Argal jump that high when he was only my age?"

"I'm sure he could," said Keeva.

"Then so can I," said Furgul. "But what about the Bulls?"

"The Bulls never come to the races."

"Okay, Mam," said Furgul. "What happens when we get to the track?"

"When Dedbone opens my crate, I'll run away again. While Dedbone's trying to catch me, you must jump out and hide beneath the truck. After a while you'll smell that Dedbone and I have gone. You'll hear lots of roaring and cheering in the distance—"

"From masters like Dedbone?" asked Furgul.

"Yes, except these masters don't have dogs. They just like gambling on them at the track, especially dogs like me who make them lots of money. When you hear the roaring and cheering, you can come out from under the truck. You'll find yourself in a parking lot—you'll be surrounded by lots of empty trucks and cars. There's no fence around the parking lot, so if you run all the way to the edge, you can escape."

Furgul concentrated until he was sure he remembered every detail.

He asked, "What do I do when I'm free?"

"I don't know," replied Keeva. "I've never been free. That's when you'll need to be lucky and clever and brave."

"Why don't you come with me?"

"I've got a number tattooed in my ear. Dedbone would find me."

"Perhaps he wouldn't try," said Furgul.

"Yes, he would," said Keeva. "I'm the most valuable dog he's got. In any case I can't leave Eena and Nessa and Brid."

Furgul suddenly had a terrible feeling.

"Mam, if I go free, does that mean I'll never see you—ever again?"

Keeva turned away, but Furgul could still see the tears in her eyes.

"Yes," she said. "We'll never see each other again."

"Can't I wait a bit longer, then, before I escape?"

"No, Furgul, you have to go tonight."

"But why?"

"Because you were born with a secret," said Keeva. "A dangerous secret."

Furgul was confused. "What secret?"

"You're not a greyhound."

Furgul was stunned.

"What do you mean, I'm not a greyhound?" he said. "All the dogs at Dedbone's Hole are greyhounds, except for the Bulls."

Keeva said, "Your father wasn't a greyhound either."

This made Furgul feel a bit better. "If I'm not a greyhound, what am I?"

"Argal was a mixture of greyhound and wolfhound," said Keeva. "The masters call that a crossbreed—or a mongrel, or a mutt. The masters don't like mutts. I don't know why. They only like pure breeds, with pure bloodlines, which they call pedigrees. That's why they control who we breed with—or at least they try to. The masters love to control things. If they could, they'd control absolutely everything in the world. They would never allow a crossbreed like Argal to come near a dog like me."

"Because you are a pure breed."

"Yes," said Keeva. "But look at it this way. If I wasn't pure, I wouldn't have to live in a crate."

"So I'm a mongrel or a mutt?" said Furgul.

"Argal said he was a lurcher, which means a thief."

Furgul liked the sound of that much better. He cheered up. "A thief?"

"The masters won't feed lurchers," said Keeva, "so Argal became an outlaw. To survive he had to steal his food or kill other animals, like rabbits. That's what you'll have to do when you're free. You see, you're a lurcher too."

This made Furgul remember that he wasn't so sure that he wanted to be free anymore. He didn't want to never see his mother again. He started to feel very sad. He heard a whimper in his throat, and his eyes began to water.

"Don't cry," said Keeva. "This isn't the time. If you cry, you'll be weak. And you won't survive."

"But why can't I stay with you, just a little while longer?"

Keeva said, "When Dedbone finds out you're not a greyhound, he'll get rid of you. He'll take you away and you'll never come back."

Furgul could see that she was serious. He had heard the stories that some greyhounds—the weak, the slow, the old—went away with Dedbone and never came back. He had heard the rumors that greyhounds were drowned in sacks, and shot with guns, and hanged by the neck from ropes, and even buried alive in pits. He had heard that lots and lots of greyhounds, more than any dog here had ever even seen, were "put to sleep"—which really means "killed"—with "injections." But a lot of hounds in the camp didn't believe these rumors. They said the stories were made up just to frighten them and to make them run even faster.

Looking into Keeva's eyes, Furgul could tell that all the stories were true.

"When you're a little pup," said Keeva, "a greyhound and a lurcher look just the same to the masters. But you're growing up fast. Your chest and shoulders are getting too big for a greyhound. I can see it. Soon Dedbone will see it too. And lurchers aren't allowed to race at the track, so you're worthless, at least to him."

Furgul had a horrible thought.

He asked, "Does that mean you'll get in trouble for being in love with Argal?"

Keeva gave him a dog smile and licked his face. The lick felt good.

"Your brain is bigger than a greyhound's too," she said. "But don't worry about me. As long as I'm the fastest, Dedbone won't do me any harm. And I aim to be the fastest for a long time."

Furgul had another thought, even more horrible than the last.

"But what about Nessa and Eena and Brid? They must be lurchers like me. Does that mean Dedbone will think they're worthless too?"

Keeva's eyes darkened. "That's why I want you to escape tonight. You can show them how it's done. If you can do it tonight, maybe they can do it tomorrow."

Furgul loved Nessa and Eena and Brid. He looked at them snoozing together in a heap at the back of the whelping cage. They were beautiful and good. How could they be worthless, just because they weren't pure? Furgul's throat trembled with a growl.

"Will you do this for me and for your sisters?" asked Keeva. "Will you be brave and make me proud?"

"Yes," said Furgul. He swallowed his rage. "I'll make you proud."

The sun began to sink in the gold and crimson sky beyond the mountain. Furgul knew that soon it would be time to make his escape. Keeva had told him not to tell his sisters, in case they became too excited and gave away the plan. That meant Furgul could not say goodbye to them, and this was hard. But he was strong and he obeyed his mother.

He practiced the plan in his mind until it felt perfect. He knew he could get to the truck and jump into the crate and hide beneath the newspapers. At least he would be with Keeva on the journey to the track. He would snuggle right up to her belly all the way. He knew he could hide until he heard the cheers of the gamblers. He knew he could escape from the parking lot. After that—when he was free—he had no plan at all.

Furgul was scared. But he thought of the father he had never seen, the mysterious outlaw—the legend, the ghost, the vision—named Argal. And he thought of his mother, Keeva, the fastest and the most beautiful. And he thought of his sisters, Nessa and Eena and Brid. And even if he did not know what he would do when he was free, he knew that he would make them all proud. Or he would die.

"Furgul," said Keeva. "Get ready."

Through the bars of their cage Furgul saw Dedbone walking toward them.

All masters were bigger than the greyhounds, but Dedbone was a monster. He had a big head with greasy black hair and a neck as thick as a tree trunk. He had strong arms and meaty hands with knuckles like big red walnuts for punching the dogs. His belly spilled from his pants as he swaggered across the yard, kicking up sparks from the soles of his steel-toed boots. His mouth was scarred and twisted. His eyes were small and dead, like pellets of sheep dung. He devoured a leg of fried chicken as he came, and the hungry dogs watched him from their crates and licked their lips.

Behind Dedbone came the two bullmastiffs, slavering from their big fat mouths and flashing their big sharp teeth. Walking next to Dedbone was another master, whom Furgul had never seen before. He had eyes like sheep dung too, but he wasn't half as big as Dedbone. Furgul had the feeling he was one of the masters who gambled on the dogs to make money. They stopped at the cage, and Dedbone pointed at Keeva and puffed out his chest.

"Boast, boast, boast!" droned Dedbone.

Dogs learned a few words of the master tongue, the ones that they heard all the time like "No!" and "Sit!" and "Go!" and "Cage!" and "Bad boy!" But the rest was mainly gibberish. The masters thought they were clever, but the fact was that dogs could learn at least a little of the human tongue, whereas masters were too stupid, or too lazy, to learn any of the dog tongue at all.

Not a single word.

Dogs didn't need to understand all human words because they could read what humans were feeling. Most humans couldn't read dogs at all. In fact, they couldn't even read each other. Furgul couldn't translate what Dedbone was saying, but he knew the sound of boasting when he heard it.

"Brag, brag, brag!" bragged Dedbone.

After being angry and nasty, which he was more often than not, Dedbone liked to brag and boast more than anything in the world. Keeva said he liked to gloat and wave a big fat wad of cash, especially when he beat his friends at the races. Most of all he liked to boast about Keeva. To hear Dedbone talk you'd think that he was the one who ran the races.

Dedbone threw away the chicken leg. The hungry greyhounds watched as the Bulls squabbled for it. Dedbone bent closer to Keeva's cage. His face was blotchy and red. His hairy nostrils flared at the stink from the unwashed concrete floor. Yet his own breath stank of something so vile it made Furgul feel dizzy just to sniff it.

"Gloat, gloat, gloat!" Dedbone went on.

But then the other man—the Gambler—pointed at Furgul.

"Sneer, sneer, sneer!" sneered the Gambler.

Suddenly Furgul felt very bad, though he wasn't sure why.

The Gambler stabbed his crooked finger at Nessa and Eena and Brid.

Though he still didn't know why, Furgul felt even worse.

The Gambler scoffed and laughed. "Scoff, scoff, scoff! Jeer, jeer, jeer!"

Dedbone's face turned even redder than usual. He scratched his head, and greasy white dust tumbled over his shoulders. His eyebrows squirmed and his mouth went all pouty with rage. He bent over and stared at Furgul through the bars of the cage. He stared for a long, long time.

Furgul stared back at Dedbone. He'd never seen a human face at such close range before. Dedbone was ugly, but the pocked skin, the bad teeth, the red nose and the pale dog-bite scars didn't bother Furgul at all. What bothered him was Dedbone's stare. Furgul felt as if the stare were sucking the life from his marrow.

Keeva let out a whimper of alarm.

Furgul had never heard Keeva whimper before.

Dedbone and the Gambler turned around and walked away. The Gambler was still laughing. He seemed to be laughing at Dedbone. Dedbone was so angry he couldn't even shout. The Bulls lingered behind and grinned and slavered at Keeva through the bars. The Bulls didn't have dog names. They answered only to the names that the masters gave them—Tic for the male, and Tac for the female.

"Oh dear, oh dear, oh dear," said Tic.

"Who's been a naughty girl, then?" said Tac.

Tic and Tac barked together—"Rowf, rowf, rowf!"—which was their way of laughing. Then they turned and followed Dedbone across the yard.

Keeva paced around the cage in a state of panic. The girls woke up.

"Mama, what's wrong?" asked Brid.

"You're scared, Mama," said Nessa.

"Yes," said Eena. "What's wrong?"

Keeva stopped pacing so the sisters wouldn't be frightened. "Nothing, my loves," she said. "I'm just nervous about the race."

Furgul didn't believe that this was the reason. A race

could never make her nervous. He tried to catch her eye, but Keeva avoided him. Suddenly Furgul realized what had just happened. And he knew that he wouldn't be escaping after all.

"They know, don't they?" asked Furgul.

Keeva still could not look at him. She didn't answer.

"The Gambler could see what we are," said Furgul. "He told Dedbone that we're not real greyhounds—we're not pure—we're just lurchers—"

"Enough!" said Keeva.

She looked at Furgul. Her brown eyes were filled with a sadness so deep that Furgul wanted to cry. He wanted to lick her face to make her feel better. But Keeva turned away again. Nessa and Eena and Brid huddled together at the back of the cage and said nothing. Keeva hurried over and crooned a song to comfort them. The sisters crowded beneath her legs and licked the teats on her belly to show that they loved her. Furgul wanted to join them. Instead he stood tall and waited by the door of the cage.

"What do you want me to do, Mam?" he asked.

Keeva stopped crooning. For a moment she couldn't speak. She blinked away the tears in her eyes. Then she turned to look at him.

"Stay close to your sisters," said Keeva. "Remember your father, Argal—the fiercest, fightingest dog that ever I saw—and be brave."

Furgul smelled something foul—something evil—and turned his head.

Dedbone and the Gambler were coming back across the yard. Between them they carried a brown cardboard box that was almost as big as a cage. In the crook of Dedbone's arm was a double-barreled shotgun. Furgul had seen him use it to kill crows.

Furgul turned back to his mother.

"Sure, Mam." He swallowed the fear in his throat. "Whatever you say."

CHAPTER TWO

THE BOX

As soon as Dedbone opened the door of the cage with his huge meaty hand, he slapped Furgul aside and grabbed Keeva by her collar, then shoved a muzzle on her snout so she couldn't bite him. Eena and Nessa and Brid whimpered with terror. Furgul, dazed by the blow, watched Keeva howl and struggle as Dedbone dragged her from the whelping cage and locked her in a nearby crate. The sound of her cries broke Furgul's heart. He was small and weak and he didn't know what to do. Then he saw that Dedbone had left the whelping cage open. Furgul slipped out the door, past the fat, slavering Bulls, and ran toward Keeva.

"Mam!" barked Furgul. "Mam!"

"No!" barked Keeva through the bars. "Run away!"

Furgul sank his teeth into Dedbone's ankle. But his teeth

couldn't penetrate the leather. Dedbone laughed and kicked him in the chest with a steel-toed boot. Furgul flew through the air, gasping with the pain. Tic and Tac came after him and laughed as they gouged his ears and face with their big yellow fangs. They could have ripped him apart but they wanted to torment him. Furgul fought back, his own fangs flashing, and ripped open one of Tic's nostrils. Tic backed away with a whimper of shock. Then Dedbone kicked Furgul in the head, and everything went dark.

When Furgul came to his senses, he was inside the big cardboard box that Dedbone and the Gambler had brought with them. Inside the box with him were Eena, Nessa and Brid. The top of the box was closed, and Furgul heard ripping sounds as the flaps were sealed shut. Then the pups tumbled about as the box was lifted from the ground and carried away.

Furgul could hear the masters panting and puffing. Once, the masters dropped the box and the pups were thrown into a squirming tangle in the blackness. Furgul heard Dedbone cursing him and his sisters in his bitter, hateful voice. The Bulls barked with glee. The box rocked over and almost caved in as Dedbone kicked it with his boot, and the pups bounced around inside in a state of panic.

Nessa and Eena and Brid cried out in fear, and one of them—or maybe all three—peed all over the place. Furgul didn't blame them. He kept telling himself: *Be brave. Be brave.* But he no longer knew what being brave meant, or what good it could possibly do them. The masters picked up the box again and on they went.

A moment later the box flew through the air and landed with a dull clang on something metallic. Doors opened and slammed. There came a roar and a tremble and a shudder. A burning, choking smell filled Furgul's nostrils. Then everything moved forward and they swerved first one way and then another. Faster and faster they moved, with more and more roars and shudders. Furgul realized they must be on the pickup truck. He noticed a beam of light coming into the box through a rip in the cardboard on one side. He stood on his hind legs and put his eye to the rip and looked outside.

Green fields and blue skies whizzed by. In the distance he saw that the big wire fence that surrounded Dedbone's Hole was already far behind. Behind the wire he saw the long stacks of greyhound crates and the squalid cage where he and his sisters had been born.

"What's happening?" cried Eena.

"Where are we going?" asked Brid.

"I want to go back to Mama," said Nessa.

Furgul's heart ached. He was filled with despair. He didn't know where they were going. He couldn't tell them what was happening or why. He couldn't tell them they would never see Keeva again. Perhaps he should. But he couldn't. What could he do?

What could he do?

What could he do?

What was the last thing that Keeva had said to him?

Remember your father.

"Argal," whispered Furgul. Once again the very name gave him courage.

Argal would never give up. He was fearless and wild. Argal would escape. Was there a way to escape from the box? The Bulls had been left back at the farm. Their smell had faded away. So there was only Dedbone and the Gambler to worry about. If Furgul could get his sisters out of the box—before they got to wherever Dedbone was taking them—they could jump off the truck and run away.

Into the Doglands.

Furgul tried to widen the rip in the box with his claws, but the cardboard was too thick and too strong. He scrabbled around, searching for a weakness. His nose led him to a patch in the corner that had turned all soggy with pee. He clawed at it as hard as he could. The soft, wet cardboard peeled away in strips. But Nessa and Eena and Brid were so upset they were whimpering and squirming about, and their legs and bodies kept getting in his way.

"Listen," he barked. "Be still. *Be quiet!*"

His bark was so fierce that the girls stopped all at once.

"Okay," said Furgul. "We're going to sing that song that Mam taught us."

Their eyes shone with fright in the gloom. They didn't seem very keen.

"I'll start," said Furgul. "And you can join in."

"Once a jolly greyhound camped by a riverbank
Under the shade of the meaty snack tree
And he sang as he sat and waited for the snacks to fall
Who'll come a-waltzing with Keeva and me?"

Nessa and Eena and Brid were so sad they started crying.
But they joined in the song.

"Waltzing with Keeva, waltzing with Keeva
Who'll come a-waltzing with Keeva and me?
And he sang as he sat and waited for the snacks to fall
Who'll come a-waltzing with Keeva and me?"

While they sang, Furgul returned to the wet patch of
cardboard and scratched and scratched and scratched. His
claws began to hurt, but still he scratched. His claws felt like
they were going to be ripped out of his toes, but he scratched
even harder. A mound of damp peelings grew between his
feet. The cardboard got thinner and thinner. Suddenly his
paw burst through the wall. He could feel the wind on
his pads. He pulled the paw back in and started to make the
hole bigger. The wind rushed into the box. The girls stopped
singing.

"What are you doing?" asked Brid.

"We're going to escape," said Furgul. "Get ready."

"But where will we go?" asked Eena.

"To the Doglands," said Furgul.

"Can't we go back to Mama?" asked Nessa.

Furgul turned on her.

"No!" he said. "Mam doesn't want us to go back. Never ever ever. She wants us to be free."

Furgul twisted his snout into the hole and took a bite of the cardboard in his teeth. He pulled and pulled and chewed and chewed, and a big piece ripped away. Now the hole was big enough to push his whole head through. And he did.

A lurcher is a sight hound. Furgul's eyes were so good he could spot a squirrel in a tree at half a mile. Through the window in the cab of the truck he could see Dedbone and the Gambler. They were drinking amber liquid from a bottle that they passed between them. The truck roared along a desolate road that wound up the side of a craggy, barren mountain. In the side of the mountain Furgul saw a cave. He remembered the stories the old dogs had told. The mouth of the cave was jagged and black and in his gut he knew that the cave was the end of the road.

The hole in the box was still too small for his shoulders. He pulled back inside and took another bite. All the soggy cardboard was gone now, so the work became much harder than before. His face hurt from the bites of the Bulls and Dedbone's steel-toed boot. His jaws hurt from the biting and the ripping. But he didn't give up. The hole got bigger. He pushed his head out to test it. The hole was tight but big enough for him to squeeze through. He turned back into the gloom of the box.

"Nessa," he said. Nessa was his favorite. He knew he shouldn't have a favorite sister, but he did. "You go first."

"I can't," said Nessa. "I'm too scared."

"I'll go first," said Brid.

Furgul didn't have time to argue. Nessa had missed her chance.

"Okay," said Furgul. "When you're out of the box, Brid, jump off the truck and run as fast and as far as you can. Don't let Dedbone see you, no matter what happens."

Brid plunged her head through the hole. Furgul rammed his shoulder under her tail and shoved hard. Brid popped out of the box. She scrambled to her feet on the bed of the pickup truck. She gave Furgul one last look. A love of adventure gleamed in her eyes, and he remembered she was Argal's daughter. Then he watched her leap over the side of the truck. She landed and rolled on a bright green bed of moss. Her legs powered her forward down the glen. She did not look back. And then she was gone.

Brid had done it. She'd escaped. She was free.

In the distance Furgul could see golden hills and forests of green. A wild wind swept out of nowhere and roared down the valley and through the trees, as if to help Brid on her way. For a moment Furgul heard the howl of voices on that wind, ancient voices of hounds long gone, urging him to defiance. Furgul's heart felt like it would burst. His tail was high and wagging. His legs wanted him to jump from the truck and run and run and run forever and ever. But he couldn't leave Eena and Nessa. With alarm he noticed that the mouth of the cave was getting closer and closer. The cave where Dedbone would kill them. The truck had slowed down as they climbed the hill. Once the truck stopped, their chance to escape would be gone.

"Eena, you're next. Hurry."

Eena kissed Nessa and went to the hole. She stood up on her hind legs and pushed her head into the hole. Just as Furgul prepared to give her a push, the truck lurched to a halt in a cloud of dust. Furgul and the two girls fell over and rolled in a heap at one end of the box. Furgul jumped up. He heard doors creak open. Big boots crunched in the dust. The doors slammed shut.

"Hurry, Eena, hurry!" Furgul barked.

Eena put her head through the hole. But then she stopped.

"Go on!" he yelled. "Get moving!"

Furgul pushed her hard. But Eena did not move. He heard her yelp with fright. A second later she was forced back inside, and Furgul saw that a hand was wrapped around her throat.

A wild rage rose inside him and he lunged forward. His teeth clamped around the hand's thumb. He heard another scream—a human scream—much louder than Eena's. It was the Gambler, in terrible pain. The Gambler dropped Eena and tried to jerk his hand back out of the box, but Furgul dug his paws into the floor and wouldn't let go. His mouth filled with blood. The Gambler shook him around inside the box, but still Furgul wouldn't let go. Furgul snarled and crunched with all his might.

The Gambler jerked his arm back so fast that Furgul's head was wrenched out through the hole. The Gambler had laughed and jeered at him, just because he was a lurcher. He wasn't laughing now. He was screaming in agony. For a moment Furgul considered letting go. But then he remembered that the Gambler had revealed his secret to Dedbone. Furgul twisted his head and bit down hard. The Gambler's thumb came off between Furgul's teeth. Furgul dropped back into the box. He rushed back to the hole, but the box was hoisted up into the air. He heard the Gambler gibbering in pain.

"Gibber, gibber, gibber!" bawled the Gambler.

Dedbone's face appeared at the hole. His bloodshot eyes were red with rage. His foul breath spilled into the box as he cursed and swore. Furgul snapped at Dedbone's nose and nipped him between the nostrils. The box crashed into the dust as Dedbone dropped it. The pups fell into a heap, and everything went dark.

Furgul could hear Dedbone coughing and choking and bellowing. But where was the hole in the box? Furgul looked around, but it was gone. He realized that the box had fallen with the hole flat against the ground. They couldn't get out.

The coughing stopped and Dedbone heaved the box up into his arms. The pups fell about higgledy-piggledy. The box started moving. The hole appeared again, but this time at the upper end of the side of the box. It was too high to climb out because the box had turned upside down. Furgul stood on his hind legs and peeped out over the edge. He watched the cave get closer and closer and wrinkled his nostrils as a vile smell drifted out.

Furgul loved most smells, even, perhaps especially, the smell of poop and pee. After all, he was a dog. But this smell filled him with disgust. It was hideous and putrid. It made him feel sick. He wondered what could make a smell so horrible. As Dedbone carried the box inside the cave, the smell got stronger.

Furgul jumped up to the hole in the box and stuck his head out, hanging on to the rim with his claws. For a moment all he could see was blackness. He blinked, and his vision sharpened. The walls of the cave were rugged and dripped with slime. The air was cool and damp. A few yards later, Dedbone stopped, the box clutched to his chest. Furgul peered down from his perch in the hole. He saw that Dedbone's toes had stopped right at a sharp edge of rock.

Beyond the edge of rock was a deep, dark chasm.

Down and down and down it went, until it vanished into nothingness.

The gruesome smell was coming from the black pit below.

This is it, thought Furgul. *Dedbone's going to throw us down into that chasm.*

All Furgul's hopes died in his chest. It was over.

He thought, *At least Brid is free.*

Across the dark abyss he saw a narrow ledge sticking out from the far rock wall. With a long run up to the edge of the chasm, maybe—just maybe—he could have jumped across to the ledge. But from here, inside the box, it was impossible.

Furgul dropped back inside to join Eena and Nessa. He snuggled between them and wagged his tail to cheer them up. They crooned together and waited for the end. But Dedbone didn't drop them into the chasm. Instead he turned around, and they felt him set the box down on the rocky ground. Furgul heard his footsteps walking away. Eena and Nessa were excited.

"Maybe he's going to leave us here," said Eena.

"Then we can climb out and find Brid," Nessa said.

Furgul jumped up again and looked out. The hole, in the vertical face of the box, was now facing the entrance to the cave, where Dedbone and the Gambler were standing. Furgul could see them clearly. The Gambler was swigging from the bottle. Dedbone opened his shotgun and reached in his pocket. He pulled out two red shotgun shells and slotted them into the barrels, just like he did before he blasted a bird from the air. He snapped the shotgun shut and gave it to the Gambler and took the bottle. The Gambler flinched as he almost dropped the gun with his bleeding, thumbless hand.

Dedbone took a swig of the drink. Then he pointed at the box.

The Gambler raised the shotgun and took aim, right at Furgul.

Furgul dropped from the hole.

He yelled at Eena and Nessa, "Get down!"

They squashed flat on their bellies.

BOOM! BOOM!

Their ears popped with pain. Lots of little holes exploded through the cardboard over their heads, with a sound like the buzzing of angry bees. The box tilted backward and teetered for a second in the air. Then it fell back flat.

Furgul spied out through one of the small new holes. Dedbone was reloading the shotgun and squinting at the box. It was his turn to shoot. Dedbone was evil but clever. He would shoot lower than the Gambler. And he had two thumbs.

Then Furgul had an idea. The teetering of the box meant they were sitting on the very edge of the chasm. The chasm and its horrid smell filled Furgul with dread. But maybe there was a chance—even if it was a tiny chance—that the pups could survive the fall. If the blast from Dedbone's shotgun hit them, they would have no chance at all. Furgul saw Dedbone take aim—at the bottom of the box.

"Come on!" barked Furgul. "Help me tip the box over! Like this!"

He crouched down on his hind legs and sprang up at the back of the box as high as he could. The box tilted a little and fell back. Eeena and Nessa crouched beside him.

"Together," said Furgul. "Now!"

The three pups leaped forward as one. The box jumped backward an inch and tilted over the edge. It hovered for a second. Then it started to fall into the chasm of doom.

BOOM! BOOM!

The shotgun blast ripped into the box and Furgul yelped as sharp, hot pellets stung his haunches. His stomach seemed to jump into his throat. A rushing sound roared through the holes. Nessa screamed. Eena didn't make a sound.

They were falling.

Falling.

Falling.

Into oblivion.

The box landed with a great crashing, crunching sound, and all the breath shot out of Furgul's lungs. His vision went black. The box rolled over and over. Furgul and Eena and Nessa tumbled around inside. Then everything was still.

Furgul got his breath and blinked his eyes. It was dark—very dark, even for him—but a dim gray light came from the hole. His shoulder hurt and his legs hurt. Everything hurt. But he plunged toward the hole and struggled outside.

He gasped at the monstrous smell. Something sharp and spiky stabbed between his toes. He looked up toward the light, which spilled from the cave at the top of the chasm. The chasm was like a giant chimney. The air down here was dank and still. He couldn't feel the slightest breath of wind. The stench of evil was overpowering.

As his eyes got used to the gloom, he looked around.

"Oh no," said Furgul. His brain was swamped by horror. "Oh no."

Furgul suddenly realized what he was standing on.

He was standing on bones.

The box had landed on a hill of dead dogs.

Most were skeletons. Racks of ribs and backbones and skulls. Here and there a moldy blanket with a number printed on it was wrapped around a decomposed greyhound. The hill was high and deep. Some of the smells were new; some were very, very old. Dedbone had dumped more dead dogs here than even the worst of the rumors at the camp had suggested. Furgul had never imagined there could be so many.

His head began to swim, and he thought he was going to fall over. He closed his eyes and panted to make himself calm. He wanted to run away. But where were Eena and Nessa? He opened his eyes as Nessa limped toward him over the bones. She used only three legs to walk and held one of her forepaws in the air.

"Where's Eena?" said Furgul.

Nessa shook her head. She couldn't speak. She could hardly even breathe. Furgul clambered back toward the box. No sound came from inside. With dread he poked his head inside.

Eena was dead. Dedbone's shotgun had killed her as they fell.

Furgul was so sad he felt like he would die too. Then

he heard the crunch of boots from the cave high above. He looked up. He heard the masters' voices.

"Joke. Joke. Joke."

"Chuckle. Chuckle. Chuckle."

"Tee. Hee. Hee."

The silhouettes of two men appeared on the edge. He saw Dedbone reloading his shotgun. The Gambler switched on a flashlight and pointed the beam down. A big white circle of light appeared near the box and moved toward Furgul. Furgul realized that Dedbone wanted to make sure they were all dead. Furgul dodged away from the light. He stumbled down the hill of bones. He shouted.

"Nessa, run!"

It was a mistake. The beam of light swung toward him. The masters had heard him. The shotgun boomed. Furgul jumped to one side and felt the zing of the buckshots as they missed him. He reached Nessa as the beam shone right on them. He grabbed her by the scruff of her neck with his teeth and bolted, dragging her along, skittering away down that terrible hill.

BOOM!

Again the buckshot rushed by his ear but didn't hit him. Now Dedbone would have to reload again. Furgul felt his pads leave the bones and land on bare rock. The grotesque hill was behind them. He ran faster. His jaws ached, but he didn't let go of Nessa. The chasm got darker and darker, but his sharp eyes made out the entrance to a tunnel ahead. Furgul aimed for the tunnel. Just as the beam of the flashlight caught up with them, he dashed inside.

BOOM! BOOM!

The buckshots pinged and zinged, but Furgul was inside the tube of rock.

When he was sure that they were safe, he stopped and laid Nessa down. He looked back. The flashlight beam poked around at the tunnel entrance. After a moment it went away. And darkness fell.

CHAPTER THREE

THE CAVERN

In the far distance Furgul heard the faint sound of the truck as it disappeared. Dedbone was gone. He and Nessa were free. But they were stuck in a tunnel, deep underground, with a mountain sitting on top of them.

Furgul was hungry and thirsty. He was hurting from head to toe from the beating and the biting and the shooting and the fall. He twisted his head back and licked the wounds in his thighs. He tasted his own blood, but the buckshot wounds didn't seem deep. He'd been lucky. Now he had to try to be clever.

"Furgul?" said Nessa. "My leg hurts. I can't walk properly."

"Can't you walk on three legs, Nessa?" asked Furgul.

"I want Mama. And Eena and Brid."

Furgul knew exactly how Nessa felt. But his instinct told

him that if they felt sorry for themselves, they would never see daylight again. He had to be tough.

He said, "For the moment all you've got is me."

"You won't leave me, Furgul, will you?"

"No," said Furgul. "But you've got to walk. And you can't cry."

The tunnel was completely dark. Even with his superb eyes he could see nothing. But he wasn't too worried about that. His sense of smell was even better than his sight, and that would guide him. He sniffed about the tunnel.

"Come on, Nessa," he said. "We'll go and find some water. Then we'll find the sunlight. Then we'll find some food and go to sleep."

"Oh I'd love a drink of water," she said.

"Good girl. Just follow me."

They sniffed their way down the tunnel. Even though Nessa had to walk on three legs, she didn't once cry or complain. After a while they reached a fork in the tunnel.

"Rest here for a minute," said Furgul.

He investigated first one tunnel and then the other. In the second he detected a faint smell of water.

"We'll go this way," he said.

On and on they went. Furgul soon realized that this tunnel was going downhill. They were going deeper and deeper underground. That worried him. He wanted to be going uphill, toward the sun. He thought about the great big mountain that must be right above them. The sunlight must be very far away. Should they turn back? He could still smell the water. They needed water more than sunlight. More than anything. Even if they had to go deeper, the water would be worth it.

Deeper and deeper they went.

And deeper still.

His throat became parched and sore. His thirst was terrible. His legs had started to tremble with every step. His nostrils dried up. The water now seemed farther away than ever.

"Furgul?" said Nessa. Her voice was hoarse and feeble. "I'm sorry, I can't go on anymore. Let me go to sleep here. You go on by yourself. I'll be all right."

He found her lying down in the dark. Even though his tongue was dry, he licked her face. Poor Nessa. She was the runt of the litter, and she was even more badly injured than he was. She had been so brave to come this far. Furgul felt like crying, but he had no water left in his eyes for the tears.

"Yes, you have a nap and get your strength," said Furgul. "I'll go and find the water, then I'll come back for you."

He turned away from Nessa and started off down the tunnel. The pain of the buckshot burned in his legs. He felt dizzy. He felt weak. He started to run. In the camp he had only scampered around, too afraid of the masters and the Bulls to stretch his legs and go full-out. But now he did.

For the first time in his life, Furgul really ran.

His heart beat faster, and his lungs sucked in the damp underground air. His muscles flowed into a double gallop. His pads pounded over the rock. His greyhound blood gave him speed and power. His wolfhound blood gave him stamina and grit. Instead of feeling weaker, he felt stronger. And then he realized something amazing. Even though the tunnel was as dark as a starless night, and even though he was running at great speed, he did not collide with the tunnel walls, which were only inches away. Even when the tunnel twisted and turned, he did not crash. Furgul didn't know why. He was just running. It was as if something were guiding his strides. Then a strange wind came from the tunnel behind him. It almost seemed to blow him along. It made Furgul feel as if he could run forever. And from somewhere on that wind—as if a ghost had whispered to his soul—Furgul heard the call of the Doglands.

"You're the dog who runs in darkness," said the wind.

And at that very moment Furgul saw a faint yellow light up ahead.

The light got stronger as the tunnel opened out into a cavern.

Furgul stopped and blinked. The sight that he saw took his breath away.

The cavern was enormous, as high as a bird could fly and bigger than the whole of Dedbone's dog farm. Great pillars of rock, as thick as a giant's thumbs, seemed to grow from the cavern floor. Long spines of rock, as thin as a witch's fingers, reached down toward them from the ceiling. The fingers and thumbs of rock glittered and glowed with pinks and purples and greens. They formed a magical circle. In the center of the circle was a deep lagoon that sparkled turquoise blue.

It was the most awesome place that Furgul had ever seen.

Perhaps it was the most awesome place in the world.

He ran across the crystal cavern to the turquoise lagoon. He padded out into the cool blue water and dipped his snout and drank. The water was delicious and pure. As he lapped it up he felt his strength return. Then he wondered where the light came from and looked up. High in one wall of the cavern there was a hole, and through the hole he could see the sky. But it was impossible to climb up there. On the other side of the lagoon he spotted three new tunnels leading out of the cavern. They would have to take one of those. His head snapped back down as he felt something nibble at his paws.

There were fish in the lagoon, investigating his feet. Before he knew what he was doing, his snout plunged down and he caught a fish in his mouth. He pulled it from the water and chewed it all up—the head, the bones, the tail—and swallowed. The fish tasted almost as good as the water. He grabbed another fish and was just about to eat that one too when he remembered Nessa.

With the fish in his mouth he turned and ran back up the tunnel as fast as he could. Nessa's scent guided him. He found her fast asleep. He dropped the fish by her head and nudged her with his snout.

"Wake up, Nessa," he said. "I've found water and food. We're going to be fine. I brought you a fish to eat."

But no matter how hard he poked her or how loud he barked, Nessa wouldn't wake up. Furgul was afraid. She was too weak to get to the lagoon. He ate the fish himself for strength then picked Nessa up by the scruff of her neck. She was completely limp. He started to drag her down the tunnel.

This time the journey took longer, because he could only walk, not run. He could feel Nessa's heartbeat, but it was as weak as the beat of a butterfly's wing. He grew more and more afraid. When at last he saw the light from the cavern, he trotted the rest of the way to the turquoise lagoon. He laid Nessa down on her side by the water's edge.

Nessa was still asleep. Furgul splashed the cool, sweet water on her face. He splashed and splashed and splashed. Just when Furgul was afraid that she would never wake up again, Nessa opened her eyes. She looked at him and smiled.

"Hello, Furgul."

"Nessa."

Nessa saw the immense columns of rainbow-colored rock. She saw the sparkle of light on the turquoise lagoon. She panted hard to get her breath.

"Where are we?" she said.

Nessa raised her head to get a better view. As she did so she shifted her foreleg, and Furgul saw the buckshot wound that had pierced her through the ribs. It must have caused her tremendous agony. She had lost a lot of blood, which was matted into her fur. But Nessa had been so brave she hadn't even mentioned it. And she didn't mention it now. She gazed about the crystal cavern in wonder.

"Are we in the Doglands?" asked Nessa.

Furgul was so sad he could hardly speak. "Yes," he said. "We must be."

"I wish Mama and Eena and Brid could be here too."

"They'll be here soon," he said, "you'll see."

Nessa said, "I've never been anywhere so beautiful."

"Neither have I."

Nessa laid her head back on the shore of the lagoon. She looked at him.

She said, "I love you, Furgul."

Furgul said, "I love you too."

Nessa smiled and closed her eyes. Her body went limp. Furgul nuzzled her throat to try to wake her again. But the scent of life had vanished from her body.

Furgul choked with emotion. Nessa had never harmed anyone. She wouldn't even fight for her food at the stinking troughs. She was kind and gentle and sweet. And now she was dead. Furgul wanted to cry, but he clenched his jaws and stopped his tears from falling. He promised himself he would never cry again.

Instead, a mighty anger rose inside his chest.

The masters had done all this. So many cruel things they had done. To Keeva and Nessa and Eena and Brid. To all the poor greyhounds they shut away in crates and bullied to race at the track. To all the greyhounds and lurchers they had shot and dumped in the chasm. Furgul decided he wasn't going to die. He was so angry, he was going to live. And he made himself a solemn promise.

One day, when I grow up, I'll set Keeva free.

I'll set all the greyhounds free.

I'll return to Dedbone's Hole, and I'll set the wrong things right.

Furgul craned his neck back and let out a long and terrible howl. The howl was full of mourning and full of anguish and full of rage. It echoed through the belly of the mountain and through the cavern and through the tunnels and through the solid, hard and timeless rock itself. And the mountain's heart was so sad that drops of water fell from the witch's fingers, as if the mountain wanted to cry instead of Furgul.

CHAPTER FOUR

THE RIVER

Three tunnels led out of the crystal cavern on the far side of the lagoon. Furgul chose the one in the middle because somewhere far down inside it he could hear a rushing, roaring sound. He didn't know what was causing it, but the rushing and roaring felt like an echo of the sound inside his head, the sound of the wind, so he followed it.

This tunnel also went down and down and the light behind him grew fainter until it disappeared. The scent of Nessa disappeared too. Now Furgul was alone. He had no one left to lose, except himself.

The rushing sound became so loud it felt like walking down the throat of a roaring lion. Furgul stopped as he almost fell—his front paw had stepped out into thin air. He explored the edge of the rock and found that the tunnel ended in a sheer drop into the blackness. The endless roar came up from directly below. He sniffed the rising vapor. It was a torrent of water. An underground river.

He'd never met a river before, but he knew what it was. His instinct—his inborn dog memory—recognized it. He thought about it. The river must be going somewhere, but where? If it went back into the mountain, the mountain would fill up with water, which was impossible, so the river must be going *out* of the mountain, which was where Furgul wanted to go too.

Furgul had never been in deep water. Did he know how to swim? He knew he didn't look like a fish. His instinct told him to take the risk. His only other choice was to go all the way back to the cavern and follow another tunnel. He didn't like that idea. The crystal cavern was Nessa's tomb. A beautiful tomb, but a tomb just the same. A tomb felt like death; the river felt like life.

Furgul retreated back up the tunnel a few steps and turned. He took a deep breath. He sprinted forward, and when he felt the edge of the tunnel beneath his pads, he whipped his hind legs under him and pushed and jumped as far as he could. He sailed out into the nothingness. Then he plunged down into the dark.

The wind rushed in his ears. He became a part of the roar. He expected to fall forever. Then suddenly he splashed into a deluge of icy-cold water. He wanted to gasp as he went under, but he held his breath. He found himself paddling with his paws. He pushed upward, and his head broke the surface and he panted. Water went in his mouth, and he swallowed. For a second he felt panic flap inside him like a pair of monstrous wings. He made himself think about Argal. He paddled harder to keep his head higher. It worked. If he paddled hard enough and stretched his long neck far enough, he could breathe.

His instinct had been right. He could swim.

The force of the river was incredible. It swept him along at fantastic speed. It was terrifying. But it was exciting. Almost before he knew it, he found that he could see the wavy black surface of the water. White foam splashed against the walls of rock on either side. Total darkness had retreated. He looked up and craned his head above the waves and saw a bright yellow light way up ahead. The river swept him onward, and the light became brighter and brighter till it almost dazzled him.

He blinked until the light didn't hurt anymore. He was rushing toward a hole in the side of the mountain where the river escaped. Just beyond the hole he saw something he could hardly believe. It was the curve of a rainbow. What was a rainbow doing in a river? Then the river swept him out of the hole in the mountain's side—right into the rainbow itself—and Furgul found out why.

When the river left the mountain, it became a waterfall.

He fell through the air—through the colors of the rainbow—with the wild cataract roaring under his paws. He looked down. Far below was a bubbling white vortex. He plummeted straight toward it. He took the biggest breath he could take and—WHOOSH—he splashed through the foam and went down and down.

He struggled underwater in a turbulence of bubbles and swirling green whorls. Just as he thought his lungs would burst, the current thrust him back to the surface and carried him onward. By the time he caught his breath, Furgul had left the waterfall and its rainbow far behind.

He looked back at the mountain. The sun was going down behind it, and the sky was all red and gold. The mountain had a double peak, and to Furgul it looked like a greyhound's snout, with its jaws wide open and howling up at the sky. Furgul decided he would call it Dogsnout Mountain.

As Dogsnout Mountain got farther and farther away, Furgul felt sad. He had almost died in the mountain, but it wasn't the mountain's fault. He felt as if the mountain had helped him escape. He believed that Nessa's spirit would find peace there, inside the crystal cavern, which she had loved. He hoped that Nessa would find Eena and show her the rocky witch's fingers and the beautiful turquoise lagoon. He hoped that Nessa would guide the spirits of all the murdered dogs to rest in the cavern. They deserved peace too. Then the river swept Furgul around a bend, and he saw Dogsnout Mountain no more.

The river carried Furgul for miles and miles. He paddled and paddled to keep his head above the water. He tried to get to the bank but the current was too strong. Bit by bit he used up the energy and strength he had gained from the fish. First he became tired. Then he became exhausted. His head felt too heavy to hold above the waves. His forelegs and hind legs could hardly move at all. He started to think how nice it would be just to go to sleep and sink under. His eyes began to droop, and he felt all dreamy.

Yes, he would let the river cradle him to sleep, just for a while.

Something stung him in the scruff of his neck, and he woke up. He thought it was a hornet or a wasp. But then something started to pull him, and the stinging got worse. He tried to raise his hind leg to scratch it with his claws, but he was too weak. The pulling got even stronger. It yanked him in violent tugs toward the riverbank. The more he tried to swim away, the harder he was jerked and tugged.

Furgul turned toward the bank. A man stood there in high rubber boots, holding a long, thin, bendy pole in his hands. From the end of the pole a thin, shiny wire stretched all the way to Furgul's neck. The man cranked the handle of a little machine on the pole, and the more he cranked the more the wire pulled. Was he a friend of Dedbone who'd been sent out to recapture him? Furgul tried to reach up for the wire and chew it with his teeth, but it was just too high and he was just too tired. Little by little Furgul felt himself reeled in to the shore.

By the time he got there he was too worn out to fight. The man waded over in his high rubber boots and looked at

Furgul with amazement. He pulled a hook out of Furgul's neck and picked him up by the scruff. He carried him dripping to the shore and laid him down on the sand beside a small heap of dead fish. Furgul stood up, but his legs were as weak as grass and he fell down again. He curled up by the fish, feeling as cold and lifeless as they were, and started to shiver. There was nothing he could do.

The Fisherman knelt beside him and Furgul waited for something horrible to happen. But the Fisherman looked concerned. His eyes seemed kind. Furgul was confused. He'd never seen a master with kind eyes before. The Fisherman patted him softly on the head.

"Soothe, soothe, soothe," said the Fisherman.

Furgul panted and shivered. He shivered and quivered and chattered so hard he thought his teeth would fall out. The Fisherman saw the wounds from the buckshot in his haunches. He became even more concerned.

"Mutter, mutter, mutter," said the Fisherman.

The Fisherman stood up and disappeared. Furgul closed his eyes and shivered. One moment he felt burning hot, the next freezing cold. The Fisherman returned with a blanket, which he spread out on the ground. He picked Furgul up and put him on the blanket and wrapped him up snug and warm.

"Murmur, murmur, murmur," said the Fisherman.

The Fisherman picked up Furgul in his arms and carried him toward a shiny green truck. It looked quite different from Dedbone's. The Fisherman put him inside, on a seat that smelled of leather. It was the softest thing that Furgul had ever laid on. The Fisherman loaded his gear into the back. Then he sat in the front next to Furgul, behind a wheel. He took out a little machine that made beeping sounds when he touched it. He put the machine to his ear and started talking.

Among all the talking, Furgul heard the human word "vet."

Keeva had told Furgul about vets. Sometimes Dedbone took Keeva to the vet, when she was sick or injured. Dedbone had to give the vet money, so he didn't like going there. He took Keeva because, as his best racer, she was worth it. Sometimes the vet put dogs to sleep with "the needle," she said. Furgul wondered if the Fisherman was going to put him to sleep. At that moment sleep was all Furgul wanted.

The green truck started to rumble and move. Furgul fell into a snooze on the soft leather seat. He had a horrid dream and woke up and it had gone dark. The green truck was speeding along. Patches of artificial light flashed by outside the windows. Furgul wanted to look out the windows and see more, but he was too weak and the blanket was too tight. After a while the truck slowed down and stopped, and the Fisherman switched off the rumbling. He picked Furgul up in his blanket and carried him out.

They walked across a small black field that had no grass and which smelled of bitter smoke. There were lots of other cars, and Furgul realized that this was a parking lot, like the one Keeva had described at the racetrack. The Fisherman carried him through a door into a room full of harsh bright lights. Furgul had never been inside a room before, and it frightened him. He felt better when he saw that there were other dogs here, of different breeds, each with a master or a mistress. The Fisherman talked to a man in a white coat behind a counter. Furgul couldn't tell what they were saying, but he could hear the talk of the other dogs.

"That poor little mutt's in bad shape," said one dog.

"I wonder what happened," said another.

"Must have been up to some mischief," said a third. "He's been shot."

"If you ask me," growled the second, "it doesn't look like he'll make it."

The man in the white coat took Furgul from the Fisherman and carried him into a second room where the lights were even brighter. Furgul guessed that this man was the Vet. The Vet unwrapped the blanket and laid him on a shiny metal table. Then he poked and squeezed Furgul all over. It hurt, badly, but Furgul was too exhausted even to yelp.

"Tut, tut, tut," said the Vet. "Worry, worry, worry."

The Vet went away. Furgul started to shiver again. Then the Vet came back. In his hand he held a little plastic cylinder. In the end of the cylinder was a sharp, thin, gleaming thread of steel. Furgul felt a sharp jab, like the hook that had gone into his neck. He tried to get up from the table, but he couldn't move. Then his eyes closed, even though he didn't want them to, and everything went black.

• • •

Furgul came around to find himself standing in the first bright room again. He couldn't remember how he had gotten there. His brain was all fuzzy and foggy and blurred, and so was his eyesight. He could hear the other dogs woofling, but he couldn't make out what they were saying. His legs felt weak. His haunches ached. Yet he could feel that the buckshots had gone. All he really wanted to do was lie down and go back to sleep.

The Fisherman bent down and smiled at him. He didn't seem so concerned anymore. He picked Furgul up and carried him back to the green truck. Furgul was happy to curl up on the soft leather seat, where he went to the land in his head where dogs made dreams.

After that everything seemed like he had made it in a dream. There was more rumbling and more driving through the night. The Fisherman took him inside a house that was full of strange smells, many of them wonderful. There was a woman there. When she saw Furgul, she glared at the Fisherman and started ranting.

"Rant, rant, rant!" she said.

The Fisherman waved his hands as he tried to explain himself. Furgul thought he seemed a bit scared of the woman. Eventually the woman patted Furgul on his head. She cooed with pity when she saw his wounds. Then she put something in his mouth. Furgul crunched it up and swallowed. Whatever it was, it was delicious.

Perhaps it really was all a dream.

Finally a dog wandered into the room. He was a bulldog, and his belly was so big it almost scraped along the ground. He sniffed around Furgul, and the woman wagged her finger. The bulldog shrugged and lay down next to Furgul. Then he looked at him.

"Hello, mate," he said. "My name's Kinnear."

To Furgul that didn't sound much like a dog name. It must be the name the masters had given him. He said, "I'm Furgul."

Kinnear chuckled. "They'll soon change that," he said. "You've had a rough time, from the looks of you, but your luck's just changed for the better. In fact, you've hit the jackpot."

"Where am I?" asked Furgul.

"In the Household."

"What do they want?"

"They want you to be a pet."

"I'm not a pet," said Furgul. "I'm a free dog."

Kinnear chuckled again, in a way that made Furgul feel stupid.

"You'll learn," he said. "Now, if it's all right with you, I'm the dominant dog in the Household. At least, in theory, I should be. After all, you are only a puppy, whereas I'm a fully grown dog. And I have been here a lot longer than you, so you could say, in theory, that this is my territory.

Although, of course, it's the master's house—or, I should say, the mistress's—not ours."

Furgul stared at him. Compared to the dogs he had known at Dedbone's Hole, Kinnear was about as dominant as a pigeon. Furgul's stare seemed to make Kinnear feel uncomfortable.

"However," said Kinnear, "that's always something we can reconsider, from time to time, especially if it causes conflict in the Household. In the Household only the Grown-Ups are allowed to have conflict."

Furgul had no idea what he was on about.

"Let me go to sleep," said Furgul.

"Righty-ho," said Kinnear. He all but bowed. "I'll show you to your bed."

PART TWO

THE DOG WHO RUNS IN DARKNESS

CHAPTER FIVE

THE HOUSEHOLD

Nine months later Furgul was fully grown. He was healthy, strong, solid with muscles, and could jump a four-foot fence from a standing start (though he kept this ability a secret). He was still living in the Household with the bulldog, Kinnear, and the two Grown-Ups—the kindly Fisherman and his wife, whose names, he had learned, were Gerry and Harriet. He had a soft, warm place to sleep and two large bowls of chicken-flavored food pellets per day. He got his share of patting and stroking, which he had to admit was rather nice. And from time to time he got crunchy treats and spectacularly tasty leftovers from Gerry and Harriet's meals.

In short he had everything that any pet dog could wish for. Yet bit by bit Furgul realized that if you want a share of the treats from the Grown-Ups' table, your soul has to pay the price. And day by day he felt as if his spirit was dying inside him.

In his first few days in the Household—after he'd recovered from the sleepy drugs the Vet had given him—Furgul had found that he had a lot to learn. He found himself living in a world of rules. Rules that either didn't make much sense or, even worse, were completely unfair. These rules were as follows.

Don't do this and don't do that.

Don't go here and don't go there.

If you have an impulse, restrain it.

If you want something, you can't have it.

Keep quiet.

Don't disturb the Grown-Ups when they're staring at the noise-screen.

Don't lick your sack in front of the mistress.

And even if Grown-Ups do something, it doesn't mean that you can.

As Kinnear put it: "If you have the natural urge to do something fun—anything fun at all—then it's a safe bet that you've broken another rule, even if no one has told you what it is."

First of all came the rules of peeing. Furgul learned—after much yelling, shock and horror from the Grown-Ups—that he couldn't pee on tables or chairs, on Harriet's bike, on the piano, or on Gerry's leg. Indeed, he couldn't pee anywhere inside the house at all. The Grown-Ups could, but they had special peeing rooms, called bathrooms, which the dogs weren't allowed to use. He couldn't even pee on the grass in the garden, or on the gardens of any of the neighbors, even though it was clear to Furgul that plenty of other dogs were doing it when Harriet wasn't looking.

Kinnear, who was an expert on every aspect of life in the Household, explained that the Grown-Ups—that is, Gerry (who was often called "You Idiot") and Harriet (who was often called "Yes, Darling")—were "responsible" dog owners. So Furgul and Kinnear had to be "responsible" dogs. They could pee on lampposts, parking meters, car tires and fire hydrants, and sometimes, if they were lucky, even on trees, but not on grass because their pee was "acidic" and would kill it. Since there was so little grass around—pathetic little squares of it called lawns—Furgul could understand why it had to be protected, so he learned to hold his pee in for hours and hours.

Taking a dump was even more complicated.

Taking a dump in a wardrobe, which Furgul tried just once—when he was desperate, and because it seemed like the least offensive spot—caused more uproar and panic when it was discovered than anything he'd ever seen, even in the Household. Kinnear pointed out that Grown-Ups didn't like the smell of dog poop, which Furgul thought was strange because he liked to sniff it. Yet even though they hated the smell, the Grown-Ups carried plastic bags and picked up the poop outside whenever Furgul or Kinnear got the chance to dump some. Furgul had never seen anything like it in his life. If the Grown-Ups couldn't find a plastic bag, they looked all around as if terrified that someone had seen them with the pooping dogs. Then they scurried away from the poop as fast as they could. Grown-Ups were weird.

Furgul decided there was no point trying to figure them out.

During this time, Furgul had to come to terms with a great humiliation.

Gerry and Harriet started saying the word "Rupert."

To Furgul it seemed like they said it all the time, at least when he was around. They said it, they murmured it, they muttered it, they shouted it, and most of all they repeated it. At first he had no idea what they were talking about.

They yelled "Rupert!" a lot when he peed on the piano and when he took that dump in the wardrobe, so he thought it was all about peeing and dumping.

Then there was the time he jumped onto a chair in the kitchen and found two enormous raw steaks on the counter. Strangely, the room was lit with candles and filled with flowers, while next door Gerry and Harriet laughed and drank fizzy liquid from a bottle that went "POP!" Furgul had wolfed down one steak—very tasty it was too—and was halfway through the second when the yelling started, louder than ever.

"RUPERT! RUPERT! RUPERT!"

They wagged their fingers and got red in the face. Harriet

burst into tears and ranted at poor Gerry for the rest of the night. Furgul was sorry for upsetting them. But those steaks were the most delicious food he'd ever tasted.

Gradually Furgul realized that they both said "Rupert" every time they spoke to him, even when he hadn't done anything wrong. Even when they petted him.

"Rupert and Kinnear," they'd say. Or "Kinnear and Rupert."

Finally, Kinnear—who had watched these disasters with amusement—explained it to him. "Don't you get it?" he said. "Rupert is your new name. Your pet name."

"Rupert?" said Furgul, horrified. "That's even worse than Kinnear. Or Tic and Tac. It sounds like a bear's name. A bear who wears checkered pants."

"They can call you whatever they want," said Kinnear. "They own you."

"I don't want to be owned. And I don't want to be called Rupert."

"Well, you better get used to it—Rupert." Kinnear chuckled.

Furgul showed Kinnear his teeth. "I can't stop the Grown-Ups' calling me that," he snarled, "but if you ever call me Rupert again, I'll bite your ears off."

"Okay, Furgul," cringed Kinnear. "Righty-ho!"

Then there was walking.

You would think that walking was the easiest thing in the world. But no. Walking was a whole new dimension of yelling and rules. First of all Furgul had to wear a collar all the time, which he hated. Then, whenever the dogs went outside, a leash was attached to the collar, so that Furgul had to walk in step alongside a Grown-Up. Whenever he stopped to examine an interesting, unusual or delightful smell—like another dog's pee—the Grown-Ups would tut and mutter and pull him away.

Kinnear's golden rule was correct: "If something is fun, it's wrong."

Grown-Ups walked very slowly, though not quite as slowly as Kinnear. Whenever Furgul pulled on the leash to walk a little faster, the Grown-Ups would pull him back until he was choking, while shouting another word he grew to hate.

"Heel!" they'd yell. "Heel! Heel! Heel!"

Kinnear explained that the "heel" was the back of a Grown-Up's shoe and that this was where a good dog learned to walk. A Grown-Up's shoe was the most boring place in the world—especially as they wouldn't let you chew on them—but for some reason, if Furgul shuffled along at their heels, it made them happy.

Other dogs—stranger dogs, also trudging along at the heels of their masters—were another problem.

What could be more natural, when two dogs met, than to have a good old sniff of each other's butts, get to know who was who, have a little chat and maybe even have a playful scrap to see who was the boss? But no, this broke numerous rules because the masters got all flustered and afraid, and they quickly pulled the dogs away from each other and hurried on. The masters with dogs didn't even talk to each other much, except to mutter, "Sorry." Furgul heard them say it so often, it was one of the new words he learned the fastest.

"Sorry, sorry, sorry," they said. "Ever so sorry."

The walks always took them past rows and rows of houses, just like the Household. They reminded Furgul of the rows of greyhound crates at Dedbone's Hole. Often they went to a "park," which was an area of grass and trees many times bigger than a lawn. In the park the Grown-Ups took Kinnear off his leash, and Kinnear would waddle around and sniff and snuffle in the undergrowth. But for a long time they kept Furgul on his leash. He was dying to get off the leash and run and feel his untamed blood pump in his heart. But the Grown-Ups wouldn't let him.

This wasn't fair, of course, but as Kinnear explained, "The Grown-Ups don't trust you yet. You've got to prove that you're a good dog, just like me."

"Does that mean they think I'm a bad dog?" asked Furgul.

"Well, you are a bit too wild," said Kinnear.

"But I *am* wild," said Furgul. "And I like it. Being wild is great."

"You've got to stop thinking like that," said Kinnear. "You've got to start thinking correctly. Pets aren't wild. That's the whole point of being a pet. You have to toe the line and play it by the book. You have to fit in and stick to the routine. You have to keep your tail down and mind your pees and poos. In short, you have to know your place and not rock the boat. Otherwise, well—who knows? They might not feed us! And then where would we be?"

"So I've got to stop being wild in return for a bowl of little brown pellets?"

"There you go!" said Kinnear. "You're smarter than you look."

"What you're saying is that we've got to live with our tails between our legs."

"Well, of course," said Kinnear, wiggling the pathetic docked stump that was all he had left of his tail. "Doesn't everyone?"

So Furgul tried not to be wild. He obeyed the masters. He plodded along at heel, even though his legs ached to run. He peed where he was supposed to. He avoided making friends with strange dogs. For weeks and weeks and months and months he gritted his teeth and did everything he could to be a good, responsible dog and to think correctly. If he wanted some exercise, he carried his leash to Gerry in his mouth. If he wasn't in his basket, he was nibbling little brown pellets from his bowl. He lived as though he were afraid—even though he wasn't—of the world, of other dogs, of going out alone, of getting lost, of numberless invisible dangers that he couldn't even name. He learned to live the way the Grown-Ups wanted him to live, which was the way they lived themselves. One winter night he was locked outside by mistake and stood whining at the kitchen door, tired, hungry and cold, until Harriet let him back inside. And Furgul realized that, despite himself, their fear had seeped into his bones. The fear of losing the comfort and the safety that was his reward for betraying his own true nature.

Then one day in the park Gerry bent down and took Furgul off the leash.

For a moment Furgul couldn't believe it. A great joy surged through his heart. His muscles felt like they would burst into roaring flames. His head went dizzy with excitement. His tail flapped so hard he felt like he might fly. He took a big breath and coiled back on his hind legs.

"Steady on! Steady on!" warned Kinnear. "Just follow me and do what I do."

With the biggest effort of self-control that Furgul had ever made, he uncoiled his legs and lowered his tail and panted with the strain of standing still. Then he pottered around after the bulldog. He found some good smells in the bushes. He ate some tasty grass. He even dared to take a few small bounds, and had a very satisfying dump—in private, behind a shrub, where the Grown-Ups couldn't put it in a bag. It was better than being on the leash, true, but he still felt like he had chains on his ankles. His legs were five times longer than Kinnear's, and soon, without even knowing it, he had left the bulldog behind. He pushed his snout through the bushes and looked across the park. Suddenly his heart started pounding in his chest like thunder.

In the distance he spotted a little white poodley dog. It was prancing around with his master and yapping in a little yappy voice. Something exploded in Furgul's brain, and he took off out of the bushes at astounding speed. The wild joy of running pumped through his blood. His jaws gaped wide as he filled his lungs with air. He didn't know what he would do when he got there, but he wanted to hunt the little yapping poodley to the ends of the earth. He didn't want to hurt the little poodley, not for a second. He just wanted to see how fast the little feller could run.

Far behind he heard Gerry and Harriet screaming in terror. "RUUU-PERRRT!!!"

But Furgul just couldn't stop. He knew he should. He just couldn't.

As he got closer the poodley's master snatched the little dog off the ground and held him tight in his arms and trembled with fright. The master's face went almost as white as the poodley's snowy fur. Furgul was puzzled. What was the problem? What was there to be frightened of? Why were all the Grown-Ups losing it? Furgul wasn't.

Just before he reached the poodley, he saw in the distance—another dog. A big, fierce dog—a German shepherd female, with a coat as black as the sky on a moonless night. She'd seen Furgul. And unlike everyone else in the park, she wasn't scared.

Great! thought Furgul. *I bet she's up for a scrap.*

He swerved toward the shepherd, circling around the

poodley's master, who fell over flat on his back with a cry of fear. The distant shrieks of "RUUU-PERRRT!!!" grew hysterical. But to Furgul's delight—as a dark shiver of excitement ran down his spine—the German shepherd broke away from her mistress and charged across the park toward him like a bolt of black lightning.

Faster and faster she came.

Closer and closer.

Furgul had never seen such a magnificent dog. Except maybe Keeva. But Keeva was his mother, so that didn't really count. And the shepherd was a lot bigger and a lot more dangerous, which tickled Furgul's fancy.

The two charging dogs came head to head. The shepherd coiled her haunches to spring and Furgul whizzed around her in a tight circle. The shepherd wasn't quite fast enough to catch him, and Furgul charged her in the haunches with his shoulder. The shepherd rolled over and growled—with amazing white teeth—and reared up on her hind legs, eager to fight. Furgul could have run more circles round her, but he realized he was faster so he decided to give her a chance. He reared and barked too, and they met in midair and boxed and nipped and tumbled. They parted and bowed to each other— their heads dipping deep between their forelegs, their eyes meeting across the arena—to show that it was just a game.

"No blood?" barked the shepherd.

"No blood," Furgul agreed.

Then they fell on each other, wrestling and pawing and

growling and snapping like fury. But it was clear to each of them that they weren't angry growls or killer bites. They didn't go for the throat, and they drew no blood. Furgul dodged away and let the shepherd chase him, then he circled about and chased her, then they fell to wrestling again, rolling around, one on top of the other on the grass, snorting and growling with pleasure.

Then the Grown-Ups arrived in a puffing, sweating, fearful gang.

Harriet and Gerry were out of breath, and the man with the little poodley was red in the face. The woman who was the mistress of the German shepherd was in tears. There was a very great deal of shrieking and hullabaloo.

"Rupert!"

"Samantha!"

"Rupert!"

"Samantha!"

Furgul and the German shepherd broke apart and grinned at each other.

"I suppose we should give it a rest," said the shepherd, "before they all burst into tears."

Furgul laughed. He thought the German shepherd was outstanding. He definitely wanted to hang out with her more often. Every day, if he could. Maybe even every hour.

"Samantha isn't your real name, is it?" he asked.

"No way," said the shepherd. "You can call me Dervla."

"Wow!" said Furgul.

"I'm hoping you're not really called Rupert," said Dervla.

"Make it Furgul."

"Well, it's an improvement," said Dervla.

"Can we do this again?" asked Furgul. "Like, tomorrow? Or maybe this afternoon? I could even jump the fence this evening, after dark."

"I'd love to," said Dervla, "but it might not be as easy as you think."

Furgul choked as his leash was clipped back on and his collar tightened round his throat. He struggled until his tongue went blue as Gerry hauled him backward. But it was no use. Dervla's mistress clipped her leash on her too. The two new friends reared up on their hind legs as the masters dragged them apart.

"Rupert!"

"Samantha!"

"Rupert!"

"Samantha!"

The worst of it was that Furgul knew that the masters thought they were doing the right thing. They thought they were stopping a fight. They couldn't see beyond their own fear—their own fear of not being perfect dog owners, with perfect dogs. They couldn't see what was obvious—that Furgul and Dervla were soul mates.

The Grown-Ups stopped shrieking and settled down to a lot of "Moan, moan, moan!" and "Tut, tut, tut!" and "Heel, heel, heel." The poodley man put his little dog down. He was much more shaken and upset than his poodley dog was.

"Whine, whine, whine!" bleated the poodley man.

"Sorry, sorry, sorry!" groveled Gerry. "Terribly sorry."

Harriet glared at Gerry. Furgul knew that, later, there would be ranting.

The little poodley dog yapped, "That looked great, can I join in?"

"Grow about two feet taller and we'll think about it," said Dervla.

Dervla and Furgul laughed at the poor yapping poodley. Perhaps it was unkind, but it was funny. Furgul realized that he and Dervla were friends.

He had never made a real friend before.

It was the best feeling in the world.

"Hey, Dervla," said Furgul, "have you ever been to the Doglands?"

"No," said Dervla. "Where are they?"

"I don't know," said Furgul. "But dogs like us could find them—if we tried."

"Let's do it," said Dervla. "Next time we meet."

"There are no Doglands," said Kinnear. "And there won't be a next time either. You mark my words."

Dervla gave Kinnear a real growl. The growl was so threatening that even Furgul's blood ran cold. Kinnear fled to hide behind Harriet's legs. He stood there shaking.

"Who's the bag of marrowbone jelly?" asked Dervla.

"That's Kinnear," said Furgul. "He's all right, really."

"Thanks," said Kinnear. "But that girl is what you call a bad influence."

"Hey, fatty," growled Dervla. "If you want to know what 'bad influence' looks like, just come over here."

But, as usual, Kinnear knew exactly what he was talking about.

There was no next time.

Harriet and Gerry went straight from the park to their favorite pet store and bought Furgul the most hated of all contraptions—a plastic muzzle.

They strapped it over his snout and then looked pleased with themselves. After that Furgul had to wear the muzzle every time they took him out. They never let him off the leash again. And whenever Furgul saw Dervla across the park and barked her name—and heard her bark back—Gerry and Harriet turned around and walked him the other way.

One day Furgul and Kinnear snoozed in their baskets while the Grown-Ups were out at work. In his best dreams Furgul dreamed about Dervla. In the bad ones—like the one he had today—he dreamed about Dedbone's Hole. He dreamed about his mother, Keeva, who was still there, living in a crate. Furgul saw her, huddled all alone, crying in the night as she thought about her pups. The pups that had been torn from her and sent away to die.

When Furgul woke up, he felt sick inside. He was ashamed of himself.

In the cavern under Dogsnout Mountain he had sworn that when he was grown up, he'd set Keeva free. Well, now he was grown up—and what had he done about it? Nothing. He just lay here in this basket feeling sorry for himself, getting more and more like Kinnear—more and more tame, and more and more afraid—and less and less like Argal, his father. Keeva had named him "the brave," but Furgul wasn't brave at all.

"I'm a coward," he muttered to himself.

"What's that?" said Kinnear, waking from his nap.

"Nothing."

"Cheer up, mate," said Kinnear. "Look on the bright side. Everything you have to put up with—even the muzzle—is worth it in the end because you get this warm bed to sleep in, lots of love and affection—well, more than you probably deserve—and a bowl of fine food twice a day."

"Those little brown pellets that look like stale cat dung and taste even worse?"

"No, no, no," said Kinnear. "Chuck Chumley's Extra Meaty Dog Feed is designed by scientists. It's the perfectly balanced diet—all the protein, nutrition and vitamins we need for a shiny coat, a waggy tail, sweet breath—"

"And a belly that scrapes on the ground."

Kinnear ignored this insult. "It's over four percent real chicken, you know. Plus another ten percent meat and animal derivatives!"

"Yes," said Furgul. "Beaks, feathers and butt holes. I need something I can get my teeth into. The taste of blood. The crunch of bone. Something to make me feel like a dog. Living like this makes me feel like—"

He stopped. It made him feel like he should have stayed in the river and drowned. But he didn't say so. He felt bad. He felt confused. He didn't know what to do.

Kinnear stuck his pug nose in the air. "I've never tasted blood in my life and I'm proud of it."

Furgul wondered what Kinnear's blood would taste like. He licked his lips.

"I know what you're thinking," said Kinnear, "but I won't fight you. I don't believe in fighting. It's antisocial. It isn't safe. And it's against the rules."

"Even in play?"

"Accidents do happen," said Kinnear. "Better to be safe than sorry. And as you know, fighting upsets our masters."

"Then why don't they get a parrot?"

"I'm a pure pedigree bulldog," said Kinnear, puffing out his chest with pride. "The masters have got the certificate to prove it. We bulldogs used to kill bulls. Imagine that. Real bulls, with horns, the kind who hate red rags. We used to be fast and feisty and bold. But those days are gone. Over the generations the breeders have bred all our aggression out of us. We don't need to fight anymore to prove that we're dogs. We get along with all other dog breeds—and even with parrots and cats and rabbits and sheep. And we certainly wouldn't mess with a bull. We're not wild, we're tame. We're docile. We're obedient. We're correct. We're the perfect family pet."

Furgul scratched himself. He felt more miserable than ever. "I try to be docile, I try to be obedient, I try to be not wild. I even try to be correct. And I'm still not a good pet. I'm just a failure."

"Don't say that," said Kinnear. "You didn't have my advantages in life. You haven't got the right—erm—background. You haven't got my breeding."

"I know," said Furgul. "I'm not pure."

"But even the likes of you can learn the rules of a good pet—if you work hard at it."

"The problem is," said Furgul, "I don't want to be a pet at all, not even a good one."

"Then what do you want?"

"I want to be free. I want to find the Doglands. I want to go back to Dedbone's Hole and set my mother free."

Kinnear didn't say anything. He just looked at Furgul with pity.

Furgul said, "And I've failed at all that too."

After this conversation Furgul kept hearing the Grown-Ups use the word "vet" at the same time they used his human name, "Rupert."

"VET, blah, blah, RUPERT," they muttered. "RUPERT, blah, blah, VET."

This made Furgul nervous. He became even more nervous when Harriet—wearing rubber gloves and a paper mask that covered her mouth and nostrils—trapped Furgul in the kitchen and ran her fingers over his balls. Furgul didn't like it and snapped at her hand. When Harriet had gone away, Furgul asked Kinnear what was going on.

"Ah, you've reached that time of life," Kinnear explained. "In fact you've got away with it longer than most. All pet dogs have to face it sooner or later, but it's not as bad as it sounds. And once it's done you'll appreciate the benefits."

"The benefits of what?" asked Furgul.

"Well," said Kinnear, "it stops you from torturing yourself about girls, which, believe me, is a greater blessing than you can imagine. It results in less aggression, which—if I may say so—is just what you need, my boy. And—listen to this—it produces a ninety percent reduction in the tendency of dogs to roam. All your restlessness—all these feelings of failure that you've been having—will just disappear. In short, it will make you happy."

Kinnear was never more pleased with himself than when he was showing off the breadth of his general knowledge. His cheeks wobbled with pride.

"It *can* cause an unfortunate gain in weight—which is why your rude comments about my belly are so unfair. But, on the whole, the effects are positive for everyone concerned."

"They don't sound positive to me," said Furgul. "For a start, I like roaming. I haven't even started to roam. I haven't had the chance to. I haven't had a chance to torture myself about girls either. But you still haven't told me what *it* is."

"Neutering, of course," replied Kinnear.

"Neutering?"

"They're going to pay the Vet to cut your nuts off."

Furgul stared at him for long enough to realize that Kinnear wasn't joking.

The smirk on Kinnear's face told him it was true.

"Cut my nuts off?" gasped Furgul. He looked down at them. He licked them twice a day to keep them clean. He was very fond of his nuts. And they were his.

"What if I don't want all these benefits?" he said.

"Well, it's not just for your benefit," answered Kinnear.

"Surprise, surprise," said Furgul.

"It's for the greater good of society."

"You mean it's for the good of the masters."

"I saw how you looked at that unladylike German shepherd, Samantha."

"Her name is Dervla," warned Furgul, his hackles rising.

"Don't take it out on me, Furgul. The Grown-Ups saw it too. You fancied her, didn't you? And they don't want even more mutts and mongrels running around. There's far too many already. Humans don't want them, you see. So the vets have to 'put them down' with the needle."

"I'm not a mongrel, I'm a lurcher," said Furgul, restraining the urge to go for Kinnear's fat throat.

"Lurchers, mongrels, half-breeds—it's all the same. There's just too many."

"But it's different for the pedigrees."

"Well, there's always a healthy demand for pure pedigrees,

at least among the better sort of masters," sniffed Kinnear. "But pedigrees don't just breed with anything that moves. We don't just fancy another dog and go charging across the park."

"Dervla did."

"Don't take offense," said Kinnear, "but Dervla should have known better. It's for our masters to decide who we breed with. The masters know best. Quality must be crossed with quality. The results speak for themselves—" Kinnear saw his own reflection in the glass kitchen door. He sucked his belly in. The difference it made was invisible. "That's why we pedigrees are worth so much money. It's not that we're bigger, stronger, faster, more useful or more clever. We're just better. We're valued. And that's why the masters can't get rid of mongrels fast enough—because you're not."

If the situation hadn't been so serious, Furgul would have told him what he thought of pedigrees and their masters, but he had bigger things to worry about. Like his nuts.

"So what can I do?"

"Stop worrying," said Kinnear. "Believe me—you won't feel a thing."

CHAPTER SIX

THE VET

Next morning the Grown-Ups didn't give Furgul any breakfast. He watched Kinnear guzzle down his pellets of Chuck Chumley's Extra Meaty Dog Feed, but before Furgul could steal a mouthful, Gerry put on his muzzle so he couldn't eat. Furgul didn't know why—for once he couldn't think of anything he had done wrong. Kinnear filled his belly, then cheerfully confirmed that the day had come when Furgul would lose his nuts.

Kinnear said, "You can't have food before an anesthetic—that's the injection that puts you to sleep—in case you throw up."

When the breakfast bowl was empty, Gerry came back and took the muzzle off. He gave Furgul an unusual amount of petting, along with guilty smiles, unconvincing chuckles and so much sympathy that you'd think that Gerry himself had been neutered. Furgul felt sick. It was just as well he hadn't eaten. He felt like throwing up already. Gerry disappeared.

Furgul tried to think clearly.

What would Argal do?

He thought back to his first visit to the Vet. It wasn't easy to remember because he'd been wounded with buckshot and was shivering to death with exhaustion, but he tried. Yes. There was a parking lot outside. Then a door into a bright room where other dogs were waiting. Then there was a counter. Somewhere behind the counter—in a second bright room—was the shiny steel table where they had given him the sleeping injection.

"Kinnear," asked Furgul, "will I have to wear the leash when the Vet cuts my—" He couldn't bring himself to say what the Vet was going to do. "You know."

Kinnear shook his big jowly head. "The shiny table has to be super-clean—that's why it's shiny! The leash has dirty germs on it, so once you get in there, the Vet will take it off."

Furgul frowned. "So I'll be on the leash until I'm in the shiny table room."

Kinnear nodded. "I know what you're thinking, mate, but you'll never make it. Accept your fate. When it's all over, you'll be much happier here, I promise. You won't feel so restless. You won't want to roam. You'll forget these foolish fantasies about freedom and the Doglands. Gerry and Harriet are good masters—it's hard to find any better. In their way they love us dogs. And in our way we love them back."

"You're right," said Furgul. "Gerry saved my life. And Harriet, erm—" He tried to think of something nice to say. "Harriet did let Gerry go fishing that day."

"That's the spirit. And tonight we'll have a slap-up supper. Why, I'll even give you half my Extra Meaty Dog Feed. Or maybe a quarter."

Furgul smiled. "You've been good to me, Kinnear. You've taught me a lot about this world—and about humans. I'm sorry I made fun of your belly."

"You've threatened to kill me a few times too."

"I didn't mean it," said Furgul. "I'm sorry for that too."

"I forgive you. Life's been a lot more interesting since you've been around. But you're not serious, are you? No one gets away from the Vet. It can't be done. In any case, where would you go?"

"To the Doglands."

"How many times do I have to tell you? The Doglands are a fairy tale. A myth."

"No, they're not," said Furgul. "I felt the wind. I heard a voice."

"A wind? A voice?"

"It told me I was the dog who runs in darkness. I don't know what it means, but I'm going to find out."

He saw a gleam in Kinnear's clever black eyes—as if, just for a moment, Kinnear believed him. Beneath all his breeding and knowledge Kinnear was still a bulldog. Somewhere deep inside he still wondered what it would be like to be wild. And in the soul of every dog Furgul imagined there lingered the forgotten legend—the lost dream, the long-abandoned memory—of the Doglands.

"Then take my advice," said Kinnear. "Whatever it is you've got in mind, don't give the Vet any warning. Be meek, be docile, be obedient. Then they won't hold on to you so tight. Sometimes cunning works better than brute strength."

Furgul heard the jingle of the leash. He sniffed the air. Harriet was coming to take him for the chop. Furgul gave Kinnear a friendly shove.

"Wish me luck, you big fat dog."

Kinnear did something he'd never done before.

He licked Furgul's face with his big fat slobbery tongue.

"Good luck, old son," said Kinnear.

Harriet arrived, twittering in a way she obviously thought was comforting, but she only made Furgul feel worse. She clipped the leash to his collar. Furgul rubbed his neck against Harriet's leg. Harriet was surprised at such affection. She smiled and twittered and patted Furgul's head.

Kinnear gave Furgul a wink. "That's the way. Keep her sweet."

"Tell me, Kinnear," said Furgul. "What's your real name?"

"My real name?" Kinnear's eyes grew distant. He smiled. "My mother called me Crennig. It means 'head like a rock.'"

"Goodbye, Crennig," said Furgul.

"If I don't see you at supper," said Kinnear, "I'll remember you in my dreams."

Then Furgul walked at Harriet's heel to the garage.

Harriet's truck pulled into the parking lot. Furgul saw the Vet's through the rear window. He'd panted with worry the whole way there. Now the worry became fear. The fact was, he didn't have a real plan of escape. The leash hung from his neck like a hangman's rope. If he couldn't get rid of the leash before they took him to the room with the shiny table, he could say goodbye to his nuts and he'd have to spend the rest of his life with Harriet and Gerry. What frightened him the most was the thought that he wouldn't even want to roam anymore—that he wouldn't even want to be wild. And he'd never have the will to go and find Keeva and rescue her.

What would Argal do?

The truck door opened and Harriet gave him a stiff, fake smile. There was a second when Furgul might have dashed past her. But he knew he wouldn't get far before someone grabbed the leash and read the disk on his collar with his name—RUPERT—and address. Getting rid of the leash was the key. He jumped from the back of the truck and waited at Harriet's heel to make her think he was obedient. Harriet took the leash and led him toward the Vet's.

Time was running out, second by second and yard by yard.

The door of the Vet's was just a few steps away.

Then Furgul saw a heap of fresh dog poop on the ground.

It was a beautiful sight.

He remembered what Kinnear had said about the super-clean shiny table and the dirty germs. And a whole new plan exploded in his mind.

Furgul let out a pitiful yelp, the most painful and heartrending sound he'd ever made. He jerked his front paw from the ground and hobbled forward on three legs. Harriet looked down in alarm—just as Furgul wanted her to, she thought that he had injured his paw or stepped on some broken glass. As Harriet bent forward to check the paw, Furgul pretended to lose his balance. He fell over. He landed on the ground so that the collar round his neck went right in the dog poop.

The trick worked. Harriet pulled a face but didn't yell at him. She just helped Furgul to his feet. Still pretending he had a sore paw, Furgul hobbled on three legs to the door of the Vet's. Harriet pushed it open, and they went inside.

There were two other dogs in the waiting room, who got excited when they smelled him. Furgul ignored them. The Vet came out from behind the counter in his long white coat. The Vet and Harriet exchanged some "Blah, blah, blah," while Furgul balanced on three legs, as meek and obedient as could be.

Then the Vet frowned and wrinkled his nose and pointed at Furgul's collar and shook his head. Furgul waited. Harriet muttered, "Sorry, ever so sorry." Then she bent down with a look of disgust and *unbuckled* Furgul's collar.

For the first time in months his neck felt free. And good old Kinnear had been right. The room with the shiny table was super-clean—and the Vet wouldn't let the dirty germs on the poopy collar go inside.

Furgul felt the urge to run rise up inside him—but he didn't move. He could see nowhere to run to yet—the front door behind him was shut. The Vet took Furgul gently by the scruff of his neck and guided him toward the open gate in the counter. Again Furgul forced himself to be docile and obedient. He didn't struggle, and he didn't give the Vet any reason to hold too tight. The Vet closed the gate in the counter behind them. Furgul could see a door, and through this door he saw the shiny table.

Suddenly he was afraid that his plan wouldn't work.

But the Vet wrinkled his nose again and said something to Harriet and pointed to the front door. Furgul craned his neck and peered over the counter. Yes! Harriet walked to the front door, holding the smelly collar and leash at arm's length. She was going to take it outside. Furgul waited. He had to time this perfectly. Harriet reached for the handle of the door. She pulled it open.

Now!

Furgul sat back on his hind legs and jumped right over the counter in a single bound. The Vet was so surprised he couldn't stop him. A greyhound can go from standing still to running at forty miles an hour in just two seconds. Furgul wasn't that fast—but he was fast enough. He shot across the waiting room and past Harriet's legs and in a trice he was racing across the parking lot.

He'd done it.

He'd escaped from the Vet.

At the other side of the parking lot Furgul found a road. He'd learned a lot about roads from Kinnear—who, of course, was an expert—but he didn't like them. He could run faster than the cars driving past, but they were dangerous. You couldn't predict what they would do. So Furgul turned and sprinted down the sidewalk. He saw a narrow alley and turned there. At the end of the alley was a Dumpster full of trash, and he hid behind it and stopped to think about what to do next.

If he ran too fast, people would take notice. They might try to stop him. He decided to walk like a good, responsible dog. He was in a town, he knew that much. He'd driven through it with Gerry and Harriet, but he'd never walked around there. Kinnear said that these days there were hardly any buildings that allowed dogs to go inside, so there was no point. Besides, Furgul didn't want to go in a building. He wanted to get out of town, away from the masters and Grown-Ups and Vets and people. He sniffed the air to find some scent of the Doglands. He was sure that he would know it if he smelled it, and surely they couldn't be too far away. But all he could smell was car smoke and garbage and filth.

He left the Dumpster and trotted down the nearest street.

Where should he go from here? He needed some advice, some directions, some help. He moved smoothly between the legs of the people walking by, so slick that most of them didn't even notice him. Some looked at him, but he didn't look at them. He trotted on before anyone could stop him. Hundreds of smells flooded into his nose. Human smells. Cat smells. Rat smells. Car smells. Smells of cooking. Fried chicken. Fried potatoes. Fried meat. Grease. Grease. Grease. Smelly armpits. Smelly feet. But not a whiff of dog to be found.

Then he found more dogs than he could handle.

A man with a funny mustache and wearing tight black shiny shorts was pulling eight dogs along by their leashes. Furgul counted again. Yes. Eight! The man must have been one of the "dog walkers" Kinnear had told him about. Furgul had found it hard to believe, but lots of people paid *other* people to walk their dogs for them. Kinnear said that this was because these people spent so much time sitting at their screens, or sitting in the hairdressers, or sitting in their cars, that their legs had just stopped working.

Furgul decided to blend in with the dogs so he wouldn't stand out so much.

At the time it seemed like a clever idea.

Furgul slipped into the middle of the pack and slunk along as close to the ground as he could. He blended in like Kinnear at a squirrel's birthday party. There was a Pomeranian, a cockapoo, a mini schnauzer, a Jack Russell, a Cavalier King Charles, a Yorkie, a dachshund and a chow. One had a bright pink collar with golden studs and another a leopard-print leash. Some wore ribbons and jewels in their hair. The dachshund wore a little red dress.

The tallest of them was twelve inches shorter than Furgul.

Worst of all, every one of the eight "dogs" was a girl.

They all gaped at Furgul with their tongues hanging out.

"I'm traveling in disguise," whispered Furgul. "So just act natural, girls. Don't attract attention—and, please, keep your voices down."

He was instantly deafened by a clamor of giggles, squeals and chatter.

"Who's this tall drink of water?"

"Don't look now, ladies, but he's a dog. A real one."

"You know what they say about a long snout."

"Look at those scars!"

"And those thighs!"

"I bet he goes like a train."

"The cheeky devil isn't even wearing a collar!"

"He's stark naked!"

Furgul started panting with embarrassment and panic. He couldn't think of anything to say. His only experience of girls was of fighting tooth and claw with Dervla in the park. This pack of tiny females terrified him more than a gang of wolves. He scanned the street above their heads in search of help. He felt a small sharp snout exploring the gap between his hind legs. It was the dachshund.

"He's got a full set!" squeaked the dachshund.

"What, both of them?" yelped the mini schnauzer.

"Trust me," replied the dachshund. "There aren't any scars down here."

"Think about it, girls," said the Cavalier. "They'll only ever let you breed with a dog who looks exactly like you."

"And how much fun is that if you look like me?" wailed the cockapoo.

"How much fun is it for any of us?" grumbled the chow. "We're all size zeroes."

"And this hound is ripped!" gasped the Jack Russell.

"Those haunches are making me dizzy," swooned the Yorkie.

"This might be our last chance!" sobbed the Cavalier.

"He looks a bit rough," sniffed the Pomeranian.

"That's the way I like 'em," growled the mini schnauzer. "Get out of my way."

There was a desperate scuffle between the girls, and Furgul almost tripped. The bright designer leashes twisted around and around in a terrible tangle.

The Dog Walker sensed the upheaval. He stopped and turned.

"Milly! Molly! Mandy!" snapped the Dog Walker. His eyes bulged out as he spotted Furgul, entangled in a mob of yapping fans.

"Whimper! Shout! Bleat!" said the Dog Walker, looking alarmed.

Furgul jumped clear of the web of leashes. The pack

strained at his heels, snagging the Dog Walker's ankles and almost dragging him off his feet.

"Come back, handsome!"

"You can give me fleas anytime!"

"My address is on my collar!"

"At my place there's some gourmet beefy dog treats!"

"I'll be here tomorrow at the same time!"

Furgul plunged away into the crowd of people who had stopped to stare at the canine uproar. With his long-range eyesight he spied another dog across the street.

Furgul checked out the traffic, left and right and left again, then galloped across the road. Horns blared, and hairs on the back of his neck stood on end. But he made it. Furgul ran up to the dog, who was a chocolate-brown Labrador with chocolate-brown eyes. Instead of a leash the Labrador wore a complicated harness around his chest and shoulders with a handle attached. Next to him stood his master, who wore dark glasses and held one hand to his cheek, which appeared swollen. He seemed to be in great pain.

The two dogs sniffed each other up and down.

"I'm on the run," panted Furgul.

"I'd never have guessed," said the Lab.

"I'm Furgul," said Furgul.

"Pace," said Pace.

"Why are you wearing that harness?" asked Furgul.

"I wear it so stray dogs can ask me stupid questions."

"You're a comedian, then," said Furgul.

"I don't mean to be patronizing—that means 'talking down to someone,' by the way—but I'm a Seeing Eye dog. My master here can't see—blind as a can of sardines—so I'm his eyes. It means I can go places where other dogs are banned."

"Can I ask another stupid question?"

"Make my day," said Pace.

"Any idea how a fugitive might get out of here?"

"What are you wanted for?" asked Pace. "If you don't mind my asking."

"They don't want me, they want my balls."

"They'll be after all three of you by now," laughed Pace. "And I don't mean those rich dames yapping across the street. No collar? No leash? You won't last long in this town, I can tell you that much."

"Why not?"

"This town is too small to be a stray in. No place to run. No place to hide. The Traps will have that noose around your throat before lunch."

"The Traps?"

"Dog catchers," growled Pace. "They've got their own van and they're tight with the cops. Cameras, radios, tranquilizer guns—you name it, they've got it. Informers and spies too." He nodded at the people walking by. "Any one of this lot could turn you in. Even as we speak. Look at him. That's a squealer if ever I saw one."

A man was muttering into a cell phone. He was staring directly at Furgul.

"They're all against you, brother," said Pace. "Every last one of them. I wouldn't like to be in your paws. You'll be eating your dinner in the pokey."

Before Furgul could ask what the pokey was, Pace said, "The dog pound, the big house, the slammer, the pen—the Needles. In other words, behind iron bars."

"Anything else I should know?"

"If you're going to get out of town, you'll need some wheels."

"I can't drive."

"I'd never have guessed that either," said Pace.

"Dentist! Dentist! Dentist!" moaned Pace's master.

Pace ignored his master. He considered Furgul for a moment.

"But you're in luck," said Pace. "See that shopping mall, there? The street without any cars? Just lots of people, milling around, spending money they haven't really got on stuff they don't really need?"

Furgul turned and saw the mall. He nodded. "I see it."

"There're two cops in there—well, security guards—and they hate dogs," said Pace. "They hate them because all dogs are banned from the mall—all except for me, of course. Dogs interfere with the shopping, see. They distract the consumer's attention from spending money, which is a crime. And brother—with no leash and no collar?—the cops will hate you most of all."

"So I'd better stay out of the mall," said Furgul.

"On the contrary," said Pace. "The cops in there are floaters—they patrol around looking for trouble. They could be anywhere—up on the mezzanine, down by the fountain, watching the plasma screen noise-boxes in the windows. They wear funny blue suits, a shiny badge, and caps that make their heads look big and flat and—if you ask me— pretty stupid too. Which in fact they are. Stupid as a bottle of carrots."

Furgul was totally confused but thought he should be polite. "Wow. That's really stupid," he said.

"They don't call them vegetables for nothing."

"They call the cops vegetables?" asked Furgul.

"No, the carrots, in the bottle. But you know what? Vegetables. Veggies. Veggies." He rolled the word around as if tasting it. "Mmm. Better than 'cops,' don't you think? Veggies. Yes. That's the best *bon mot* I've coined in quite some time."

"It's the best I've ever seen coined," agreed Furgul.

Pace looked Furgul up and down, as if his opinion of him had just gone up.

"Bit of a greyhound, are you?"

"A lurcher," said Furgul.

"Unlike most, I've got a soft spot for lurchers," said Pace. "If you're as quick on your feet as you look, you might just make it through. Through the mall, I mean. As long as you don't stop and let the veggies grab you."

Furgul began to wonder if he'd picked the right dog to ask for help.

"Why would I want to make it through the mall?"

"Now that's a very good question," said Pace. "But I've got a very good answer. In the street on the other side of the mall—about a hundred strides to the right—you'll see a furniture van. You won't mistake the scent—I cocked a leg on the rear wheel on my way here."

"What's a furniture van?"

"It's a van with furniture inside. Sofas, tables, chairs, beds, *objets d'art*—"

"I get it."

"The point is, they're loading the van—even as we speak. And that means that very shortly they're going to drive it somewhere else." Pace raised one eyebrow. "Somewhere far away from here."

"Pace," said Furgul. "You're a genius."

"Anything to help a brother in need."

"Dentist! Dentist! Dentist!" pleaded Pace's master.

"I'd come with you," Pace said to Furgul, "but the master here would never find his way. Helpless as a bag of dead frogs. And anyway, I've got diabetes."

"Not enough red meat?" guessed Furgul.

"Tell me about it," said Pace. "Four percent real chicken with ten percent meat and animal derivatives. They must think we're as stupid as they are."

A truck screeched to a halt by the roadside. Harriet's face glared from behind the steering wheel. She started to rant from the window at the top of her voice.

"Who's Rupert?" asked Pace.

"Gotta go," said Furgul. "Thanks a lot, Pace."

"Watch out for the weirdos! And the veggies!"

As Harriet jumped from the truck, Furgul sprinted toward the mall.

CHAPTER SEVEN

THE MALL

As Furgul approached the mall his eyes caught a sign with a drawing of a dog inside a circle. The dog in the circle had a big red X stamped across it. A wide open archway led into the mall. When he sprinted inside the first thing Furgul saw was a security guard. Or, as Pace would now call them, a veggie.

The veggie was licking an ice cream cone and at the same time picking his nose with his little finger. He was so busy picking and licking that he didn't see Furgul shoot past. Furgul should have just kept on going as fast as he could, but he was stunned by the dazzling interior of the mall.

It was full of bright lights and bright colors and a fantastic amount of glass. There were more people there than he'd ever seen in one place, rushing and chattering and carrying lots of bags. There were plants and trees and a fountain. He could see the heads of even more people moving around high above. Some people floated up to join them, without moving their legs or flapping their arms, while others floated back down again, as if in shopping malls human beings could fly.

All the walls on every side were made of sheets of glass. Behind the glass were thousands and thousands of "things." He knew people loved "things"—Gerry and Harriet were always bringing home "things"—but Furgul had never imagined there could be so many. Behind one window alone there were hundreds and hundreds of shoes. In another there were strange pink plastic shapes dressed up like people. There were windows with lots of glittery things and windows with the flashing noise-screens that people loved to stare at. From one window came a mixture of the horrid smells that Harriet put on her hair and her face and her armpits and in her knickers. After a minute all the windows started to look the same— glaring, blaring, dreary, loud and ugly.

What stopped him in his tracks was the smell of food.

Every smell he had ever detected in Gerry and Harriet's kitchen was there—all at the same time. There were also other food smells he'd never come across before. He followed his nose and found a whole part of the mall that was full of little kitchens, hidden behind metal counters. In the kitchens people wearing little paper hats cooked heaps and heaps of food. Fried chicken and fried fish, noodles, pizzas and tacos, barbecued ribs and hot dogs, cheeseburgers, bacon burgers and jumbo burgers. His stomach was rumbling with hunger. It had been so long since he'd had some food, he would have eaten just about anything. In front of the kitchens were lots of tables, where dozens of customers munched and guzzled and gulped down fizzy drinks.

To Furgul's amazement some of the people carried a lot of their food from the tables on little trays—and dumped it into the mouth of a tall gray plastic bin.

The thought of these bins full of wasted food was too much for Furgul. He forgot about the veggies. He decided to help himself to a quick snack. He stalked his way into the food court without attracting attention. He stood up on his hind legs to peer into the mouth of a bin. The bin toppled over. The lid burst off. A flood of fizzy brown liquid, soggy paper, empty cups and half-eaten food spilled across the floor.

He heard an uproar of yells.

People rose from their seats in alarm.

The Paper Hatties shouted from behind their counters.

Furgul wolfed down some bits of burger and a hot dog. A little fat man lumbered toward him with his hands outstretched like claws. Furgul dodged this way and that as the fat man grabbed for his neck. Furgul circled around him in a flash, and the fat man slipped in the muck. He fell flat on his back in the spreading pool of filth. Ketchup and mustard and grease and fizz splashed up in every direction, splattering the clothes of the customers. The shouting got even louder.

Now everyone was furious.

Furgul dashed away.

To his left he saw a second veggie running toward him. Furgul swerved right. A man wearing one of the little paper hats staggered by, his arms carrying a huge cardboard box. Furgul charged his shoulder into the back of his knees. The man threw the box in the air and toppled onto his face. The big box burst open, and hundreds of raw beef ribs scattered over the floor. The second veggie skidded on the ribs. He waved his arms and knocked his big flat cap from his shiny, bald head as he nosedived to the ground.

Furgul jumped over him and ran toward the exit.

He was so confused—by the hordes of people, the bright lights and the glaring, ugly windows—that it wasn't until he saw the first veggie again—his ice cream finished but still picking his nose—that he realized he had gone the wrong way. He was back at the very same arch where he had come in. Then Harriet stormed through the archway, red-faced with rage and ready to rant. She stopped with her fists on her hips and scanned the mall.

Furgul sneaked behind a brightly colored machine with stubby little wings. A little boy sat inside the machine and laughed as he bobbed up and down.

Harriet stared at the first veggie and fired off a rant of disgust.

"Rant-rant-rant-rant-rant!"

The veggie pulled his finger from his nostril and sucked it clean. He and Harriet both scanned the mall with their angry eyes. Furgul peeped around the up-and-down machine. The second veggie slithered around on his hands and knees in a greasy sea of beef ribs. He looked even angrier than Harriet.

Furgul realized his escape through the mall was a disaster.

The up-and-down machine stopped going up and down. The little boy climbed out. He saw Furgul and smiled with delight. He stroked Furgul on the neck. Furgul liked the little boy and would have been happy to play with him. But Harriet and both of the veggies all spotted him at the same time.

Three angry fingers pointed at Furgul.

He was trapped.

But then, just outside the open archway, Furgul saw the gang of girl dogs with their Dog Walker. The Dog Walker was talking to another—taller—Dog Walker, who had *twelve* new dogs, of all different shapes and sizes. The two packs of dogs were yapping and chatting away to each other. Furgul gave the little boy a lick on the hand to say goodbye. Then he wagged his tail and barked toward the street.

"Hey, ladies! Come on down here! Free beefy treats!"

Mandy, the mini schnauzer, turned and saw Furgul. Her eyes went wide.

"THERE HE IS!" she yelped. "WHAT ARE WE WAITING FOR?"

All at once *both* gangs of dogs charged through the archway. The two Dog Walkers were so surprised, they were dragged clean off their feet. Their heads crashed together as they fell down on their knees. They lost their grip on the leashes.

Twenty howling dogs roared into the mall.

Their invasion caused pandemonium among the shoppers.

Milly, Molly, Mandy and the five other girl dogs swarmed around Harriet, sniffing and yapping and snapping at her heels in a frenzy. Furgul realized that they could smell his scent on Harriet's clothes. Harriet hopped from one foot to another, flapping her hands and squawking.

"Down! Down! Down!" squawked Harriet.

The first veggie was so shocked, he just put his finger up his nose again.

The second veggie—still on his hands and knees and covered with rib grease—opened his mouth with horror as the twelve new dogs bounded toward him. Their tongues lolled out of their panting mouths, and their sharp teeth were bared with greed. Furgul closed his eyes as the veggie disappeared beneath a yowling pack of hungry canines.

"HELP MEEEEE!" cried the veggie.

The veggie's voice was drowned out by ferocious barks and the crunching of beefy ribs. Then Furgul heard another voice, close by his ear.

"I thought I told you not to stop."

Furgul opened his eyes. It was Pace. His master was clutching the handle on Pace's harness. The master seemed bewildered by all the commotion. He still held his jaw.

"Pace!" said Furgul. "What are you doing here?"

"I assumed that you lacked the intelligence to do what I

told you," said Pace. "So I thought I'd better come along and help you out."

"But how?" said Furgul. "Everybody's going mad."

"It's just as well that one of us is sane, then, isn't it?"

"But how can you run with your master holding on?"

"We're not going to run," replied Pace. "Just walk along right beside me, nice and easy, and no one will take any notice. And even if they do, they'll think you're a Seeing Eye dog too."

"Pace," said Furgul, "you're a genius."

There was a high-pitched shriek, and Furgul looked back over his shoulder.

Harriet was running from the mall with the pack of girl dogs in pursuit.

Pace started off, and Furgul walked beside him, shoulder to shoulder. They walked past the second veggie, who was curled in a ball with his bald head covered in claw marks. The dogs who surrounded him were snarling with pleasure as they wolfed down the tasty beefy ribs. Furgul and Pace walked past mobs of shoppers, who were shouting into their cell phones and milling around in panic. And Pace was absolutely right. As they calmly strolled toward the far end of the mall, nobody even gave them a second glance.

"Dentist! Dentist! Dentist!" groaned Pace's master.

"Why does he keep saying 'dentist'?" asked Furgul.

"Because that's where he wants me to take him," answered Pace.

"What is a dentist?"

"A dentist is like a vet who takes care of human teeth. Gums too. But not tongues or lips. Never been able to work out the logic of that one. But then that's humans for you. Nutty as a dachshund in a little red dress."

"Why does he want to go to the dentist?" asked Furgul.

"Because he's got a toothache, of course," sighed Pace. "Must be hurting him something cruel by the sound of it. I reckon it's a major drilling job, myself. Root canal work. That's as agonizing as it sounds, by the way. And guess who'll have to stand there by the chair and listen to the screams?"

"Doesn't seem fair," agreed Furgul. "It's not even your tooth."

"Never expect fairness from a human and you won't go too far wrong."

Furgul was still a little confused by who was going where. He said, "So, the dentist is over on this side of the mall— where we're heading right now."

"Actually," said Pace, "it's in the opposite direction. But the master here can't tell the difference. Clueless as a box of corn flakes." The three of them reached the street on the far side of the mall with no problem.

Pace pointed down the street. "There's your furniture van. Good luck."

"I don't know how to thank you," said Furgul.

"Just jump in that van before it leaves," said Pace. "That's all the thanks I need. And please don't get emotional. It's bad for my diabetes."

"DENTIST!!!" Pace's master now sounded quite desperate.

"I'd better get Moaning Minnie to his appointment," said Pace. "Have you noticed that human beings don't have any patience? It's always about them."

Pace turned around with his groaning master and walked back into the mall.

Furgul jogged down the road toward the van. It was huge and painted yellow. The two big doors at the back stood wide open. A thin man in blue overalls stood by the driver's door. The driver leaned out the window while they talked. Just as Furgul reached the van, the thin blue man turned and walked toward him.

Quick as he could, Furgul dodged out of the thin man's sight—behind the van—and sprang up into the back. Just as Pace had predicted, it was full of all kinds of furniture. Furgul squeezed his way between some armchairs, then jumped onto a table and scrambled over a tall stack of boxes. Behind the boxes was a long leather couch. Furgul lay down on the couch. His heart was racing.

Wow! thought Furgul. *That was exciting.*

The two big doors clanked shut. Everything went dark. The engine rumbled.

Then Furgul felt the couch start to shake as the van drove away.

CHAPTER EIGHT

THE TRAPS

The leather couch was comfortable, and Furgul stretched out and had a snooze. When he woke up to take a pee, the van was still trundling along toward its unknown destination. He didn't want to pee near the couch where he was snoozing, so he climbed over the boxes to find the most distant spot.

A bit of light came in from a crack in the doors, and to his surprise he thought he saw a tree. He went closer. It wasn't a real tree. It was a painting of a tree in a big gold frame. But it was better than nothing. Furgul cocked his leg. When he'd peed on the tree in the picture to his satisfaction, he went back to his couch for another snooze.

When he woke up again the van had stopped. He knew that vehicles sometimes stopped only for a moment before moving again. But the rumbling engine was silent, which usually meant that the vehicle had gotten to where it was going. He stretched out the sleep from his legs and muscles. He had to be ready to move fast. He climbed over the boxes again and hid underneath the table. He figured that the men would carry something out of the van, starting near the doors. While their hands were busy holding a box or a chair, he'd jump from the back and run away.

There was a clanking noise and the two big doors swung open. Furgul peeped out and saw the driver and the thin man in the blue overalls. There was a third man with them that Furgul hadn't seen before. He wore a very clean suit with very thin stripes and a fat gold watch on his wrist. He had eyes like the snake that Furgul had once seen in the grass at Dedbone's Hole. Although he reeked of almost as many perfumes as Harriet, underneath he smelled as nasty as Dedbone himself. The first thing the thin blue man pulled out of the van was the painting of the tree. The man in the thin-striped suit took one look at it and exploded in a torrent of bad words.

"XXXX! XXXX! XXXX!" he swore.

Furgul poked his head around an armchair so he could see the painting. The tree had disappeared. All that was left was a streaky brown stump. The leaves had melted and dribbled all down the picture like green rain. Furgul wondered how that could have happened. The man in the thin-striped suit shook his fist at the two furniture-van men, who shrugged and said something that Furgul had heard Gerry say to Harriet.

"Wasn't me! Wasn't me! Wasn't me!" said the van men.

Furgul ducked his head back, but too late. The man in the thin-striped suit saw him. More bad words echoed around the van. Furgul decided to make a run for it. But just as he jumped out from behind the armchair, the van men slammed the two big doors tight shut.

Furgul waited in the dark near the doors. Next time they opened, he would jump right away. He was faster than the three men, and without a collar he was much more difficult to catch.

Time passed. It seemed like a long time, even though it wasn't. Then he heard some mumbling outside. There was a clank, and he knew the doors were about to open. He sat back on his hind legs, ready to leap. Light flooded in. The doors slowly opened six inches. He couldn't see the men. Just a few more inches. Still no men. It was now or never.

Furgul jumped out.

For a second he saw a kind of hoop flash through the air in front of him, but he didn't take much notice. He hit the ground running. Then Furgul was yanked to a sudden halt. His feet left the ground as something tightened around his throat and strangled him. He twisted and ducked backward, but the strangling got worse. He clawed at his throat with his right hind paw and realized there was a plastic noose around his neck. From the corner of his eye he saw a long steel pole. He lunged forward again. His eyes bulged out as the noose drew even tighter. The noose was attached to the end of the long steel pole.

Then Furgul heard the man in the thin-striped suit laughing.

Furgul stopped struggling and got his breath back. There was a man in an orange uniform holding the pole. He was one of the Traps—the dog catchers that Pace had warned him about. The man in the thin-striped suit handed the Trap some folded money. The Trap shook his head, but the man shoved the money into the Trap's pocket. The Trap pulled on the long pole, and Furgul followed him toward an orange and white truck. The back door of the truck was open.

Furgul's heart sank as he saw that the truck was full of cages.

Furgul was locked in one of the two cages nearest the door. The cage facing him was empty. The Trap gave Furgul a smile as he closed the door of the truck. It was meant to be a comforting smile. The Trap seemed like a nice man. But it was still the smile of someone who had nearly strangled him and locked him up behind bars.

The Trap truck rumbled off.

Furgul curled up on the cold, hard floor of the cage and wrapped his tail over his eyes. He could smell other dogs in the truck and didn't want them to see how dismayed he felt. He'd woken up that morning in his basket next to good old Kinnear, in a warm home with kind masters. Now he was in a strange cage in a strange place miles and miles and miles away.

He'd only wanted to hang on to his nuts. He didn't even know what his nuts were for. He'd wanted to find his mother, Keeva, too, so she wouldn't have to live in a crate, so she could have a little bit of freedom. Now he was prisoner himself. Perhaps he was a bad dog after all.

He couldn't help letting out a sigh of despair.

"Cheer up," said a small female voice. "It isn't over till it's over."

"That's true," added a sly male voice. "But it might be over sooner than you think."

Furgul stood up and looked around. "I'm Furgul."

In one of the cages opposite was a tiny bundle of silky white fur. She was a papillon by breed. "My dog name is Zinni," she said. She indicated a shy white and tan female beagle in the next cage. "This is Tess." Then, with some misgivings, Zinni pointed through the bars of the cage next to Furgul's. "And that's Skyver."

For a moment Furgul wasn't sure that Skyver was a dog at all. All he could see was a mound of dirty fur. The fur was a mixture of so many lengths and shades—here the hair was long and red, there it was short and black, and there it was white and tufty—that Furgul wondered if there was more than one animal in there. Then the fur jumped up onto four lanky legs, and a head appeared with two bright, crafty eyes—one blue and one brown—and one ear sticking up and the other hanging down. Skyver grinned at him with a set of huge, yellow, broken fangs.

"That's my 'pile of dead cats' trick," said Skyver. "Not bad, eh?"

"Amazing," said Furgul.

"I've been fooling the Traps with that one for years. Dead cats is garbage, you see—waste disposal, not animal control. Different van, different uniform—different jurisdiction, as they say. Many a time those garbage boys have shoveled me into their truck and driven me right to the dump, where the eating can't be bettered. You wouldn't believe the grub that people throw away these days. But tonight the dead-cat scam worked too well—one of the Traps trod right on my—" Skyver glanced at Zinni and Tess. "Well, let's just say I barked so loud I set off half a dozen car alarms. Anyway, it's nice to meet a fellow mutt."

"I'm a lurcher," said Furgul.

"Oh, I see, putting on airs and graces, are we?" said Skyver. "Well, I've been told I'm the scruffiest dog in the world, but you don't hear me bragging about it, do you? Everyone's equal in the Needles. Five days to live, or five days to die, whether you're a purebred pedigree, the son of the son of the son of a mongrel's son—like me—or a lurcher."

"What do you mean?" asked Zinni.

"Once you're in the Needles, you've got only two ways out," said Skyver. "Either you get lucky and some dog lover rescues you because she thinks you're cute—which in your case, Furgul, is a long shot because most people think that greyhounds are vicious and insane killing machines that will run down anything that moves."

"Or?" asked Furgul.

"Or what?"

"What's the second way out of the Needles?"

"Oh," said Skyver. "Or you leave in the back of the truck for the incinerator."

"The incinerator?"

"It's the machine that they burn dead dogs in."

"Why would I be dead?" asked Furgul.

Skyver gave a sour laugh. "If no one rescues you within five days, they give you the lethal injection. The needle—the Needles—get it?"

"They'll just kill us?" asked Furgul.

"Some animal shelters have a no-kill policy," Skyver explained. "They feed you and look after you until you get lucky—for as long as it takes. They don't kill dogs—unless you've got rabies or you're a total psycho. But there aren't very many no-kill shelters around, and where we're going isn't one of them. For every ten dogs they take to the Needles, only four get out alive."

Furgul could hardly believe what he was hearing. It sounded even worse than Dedbone's Hole. Dedbone wasn't killing six in ten of his dogs.

"But why," said Furgul.

"Why what?"

"Why would they kill us?"

"The pound has got a fixed number of cages, see," said Skyver. "For every dog that goes in, another dog has to go out—one way or the other. The masters kill millions of us dogs every year. Millions and millions, didn't you know? Cats too, though, of course, that's no great loss."

"I quite like cats," said Zinni.

"I live with one," said Tess. "They're not so bad, once you get used to the rituals."

Furgul didn't know what a million was. But it sounded like an awful lot. He asked, "So because I'm going in there, some other dog has to die?"

"That's the way it works." Skyver shrugged. "Five days to get lucky. Then it's our turn. You and I will take that last long walk to the death house side by side."

"There is a third way out," said Tess. "Your owner can come and claim you. That's what mine will do. I've been in there four times. I'll be home tomorrow in time for lunch."

"You've got a name tag and collar, Tess," said Skyver. "Furgul here hasn't."

"I haven't got a collar either," piped Zinni. "Some sneaky guy stole me, then he took my collar and abandoned me in the street."

"What kind of weirdo would steal a dog collar?" wondered Skyver aloud.

"My collar had diamonds on it," said Zinni.

"Then don't worry," said Tess. "Your owner will call the dog pound and find out if you're there."

"Perhaps your owners will call the dog pound too, Furgul," said Zinni.

"Furgul didn't have any diamonds round his neck," laughed Skyver.

"My masters are far away," said Furgul. "But maybe there's a fourth way out. Maybe we can escape."

"Dream on," said Skyver. "The Needles is a maximum-security pound. They're not going to take their eye off a bad boy like you."

"I don't think he looks so bad," said Zinni.

"You can't see the buckshot scars," said Skyver. "A dog doesn't get himself shot for nothing."

Furgul felt his tail hanging down. He didn't see any point in explaining why he'd been shot. Had he escaped from Dedbone's Hole just to die in some stinking dog pound? He remembered the promise he had made, to go back and set Keeva free, and set the wrong things right.

"I won't give up hope," he said.

"Good for you," said Skyver. "As my long-suffering mother used to say: 'Skyver, life is like a bowl of dog food. Most of the time it's like eating your own poop. But every now and again somebody leaves a raw steak lying on the table.'"

A sudden buzzing and squawking exploded from the radio inside the driver's cab. The driver squawked back. A siren wailed. Then the dogs were thrown against the bars of their cages as the truck made a sharp turn and picked up speed.

"Blue lights!" said Skyver. "Some big bad dog is causing havoc somewhere!"

• • •

The truck hurtled along and took several more violent turns. The other dogs became quite frightened, even Skyver, but Furgul had a funny feeling in his stomach. He didn't know why, but he was exhilarated. The truck screeched to a halt. The Traps jumped out of the cab and they weren't smiling anymore.

Outside, beyond the doors, Furgul heard the sound of a roaring dog.

It was a roaring such as he had never heard before—proud and defiant and enraged. It made all the hairs on his shoulders stand on end, but not with fear. It made his heart pound faster in his chest and his tail wag high in the air. The roar was savage, yet it thrilled him. It was a sound such as the last free dog in the world might make.

Tess cowered in her cage. Zinni was full of curiosity. Skyver slunk down as close to the floor as he could get, like a pile of cowardly dead cats.

As well as the savage roars, Furgul heard the terrified shouts of the Traps. He heard the wailing of sirens. Flashes of dim blue light winked around the inside of the truck. It sounded like a battle was being fought. Then the snarling roars were choked off and replaced by a low, monstrous growl. Something slammed into the doors of the truck, and a Trap cried out in agony. There was scuffling and shouting and groaning. And then even more shouting and more yells of pain.

Furgul could smell the great dog that stood beyond the doors. He had never picked up this scent before—and yet he felt as if he had. There was something in the scent that he recognized, something he could not describe—as if he'd known that scent from the very first day he was born. Or even before that. Though he did not know why, the tiny flame of hope in Furgul's chest burned brighter.

The other dogs seemed to sense something too.

"I don't believe it," said Skyver.

"It can't be," whimpered Tess.

"What do you mean?" piped Zinni.

The doors of the truck were flung open, and Furgul blinked.

Night had fallen outside, but the headlamps of several vehicles lit up the darkness. In the background a man lay moaning on a little bed on wheels. Two other men pushed the bed into the back of a white van with a flashing blue light on the top. Another man sat in the road, holding his head with both hands. Several other men—cops and Traps—were standing around with clubs and guns.

In the middle of the chaos stood the biggest dog that Furgul had ever seen.

He had the rough red coat of an Irish wolfhound, but his huge head was shaped more like a lurcher's. Keeva had told Furgul something of the history of the wolfhounds. They had roamed the wild Doglands for thousands of years, in the old times long before masters—before fire, before the wheel, before collars and leashes and muzzles. They had fought for the ancient Celts as dogs of war. They had struck fear into the ancient Romans. They'd even fought and killed lions in the arena. They had fought against the English and dragged the knights in armor from their horses. They'd killed wolves and wild boars. In those long-gone days the wolfhound had no equal on the earth.

The great hound outside the truck fought against three of the nooses on poles that were looped around his neck. Each pole was held by two Traps, and the dog was so strong he almost pulled all six of them off their feet. He rolled his huge shoulders and strained the muscles in his neck. His jaws gaped open, panting for air. Blood gleamed on his fangs. Behind him another man locked a chain around his ankles. Then all seven of them tried to manhandle the mighty hound into the truck. Even though he was choking, the hound dug his paws into the ground and would not move.

"It *is* him," gasped Skyver, with awe.

"Who?" squeaked Zinni.

"Is it true he's escaped from prison a dozen times?" asked Tess.

"More," said Skyver. "Stone and chain cannot hold him. They say he's cheated every executioner that ever tried to kill him. Some places down south they use a gas chamber, not the needle. One time they dragged twenty-five dogs in there and gassed them for thirty minutes. At the end of it he was the only one still standing. They were so amazed they let him go."

"I thought he was just a legend," said Tess. "I didn't think he really existed."

"There he stands," said Skyver. "But they've got the old outlaw cold this time."

"But who is he?" cried Zinni. "I'm dying to know!"

Furgul wanted to hear the answer too, though he already knew it in his bones. Outside the outlaw hound had still not budged an inch, and the Traps were sweating and cursing. The Trap at the back opened a long gun—a bit like Dedbone's shotgun—and slotted a plastic cylinder with a bright shiny needle into the barrel. He snapped the long gun shut.

Furgul clawed the bars of his cage.

"Don't shoot him!" he barked at the top of his lungs.

Furgul's bark was so fierce that all the Traps stopped and looked at him.

The great hound looked at him too. His gaze met Furgul's, and Furgul felt the world shift beneath his paws. The hound's eyes were like tunnels bored back into the long-gone days when wolfhounds and greyhounds roamed the vast wild Doglands in absolute freedom.

As the wild hound stared at Furgul, his rage seemed to melt away. He reared up on his enormous hind legs, and the Trap raised his gun. But the hound didn't fight anymore. He put his forepaws on the floor of the truck. He looked at the Traps as if to say, "It's over. Let's go." The Trap lowered his gun.

Again the hound looked Furgul right in the eye.

The hound said, "You're the dog who runs in darkness."

Furgul remembered the whisper on the wind that he had heard inside Dogsnout Mountain. It had said the same thing. Furgul swallowed a lump in his throat.

"Yes," he said. "That's me."

"Strange winds," said the hound. "Strange winds blow us here tonight."

He climbed into the truck. The Traps released their nooses, and he backed into the cage facing Furgul. The Traps locked the door and closed the back of the truck.

Furgul couldn't take his eyes off the wild fighting hound.

"Please," hissed Zinni, "just tell me who he is!"

A whisper came from the heap of fur, as if Skyver hardly dared to speak the name.

"It's Argal."

CHAPTER NINE

THE NEEDLES

The Trap truck rumbled through the night toward the Needles.

Argal was squeezed into the cage facing Furgul's. Skyver, Tess and Zinni lay in silence, in awe of the renegade hound. There wasn't much light in the truck, but Furgul could see Argal's face and the gleam of his eyes in the gloom. Furgul himself felt intimidated. He dropped his gaze in respect.

"Don't turn away," said Argal. "Look at me."

Furgul looked at him. Argal didn't say anything. He just stared back at him—for ages and ages and ages. Furgul wanted to look away again. He didn't know why. Argal's deep wild eyes were overpowering. They were frightening. Furgul ground his teeth together. He just knew he would have to turn away soon. Then Argal spoke again.

"You look like Keeva more than you look like me," said Argal. "That's good."

"So I am your son?" Furgul still couldn't quite believe it.

"You're asking me for reassurance," said Argal. "That weakens you. Don't ask me, ask yourself. What does your nose tell you? What does your instinct tell you? What does your heart tell you? If you can't trust those, you won't survive."

"You're my dad."

"Yes. I'm your father. Wildness flows in your veins where blood should run. And that will make your road in life tougher than you can imagine. It already has, otherwise you wouldn't be locked in that cage with only five days left to live."

Argal's face came closer to the bars. If pieces of flint could have burned like coals, such would his eyes have looked like. They were cold yet full of fire.

"Think hard, son," he said. "Are you ready for such a life? For the hungry days and the lonely nights? For the killing, the fighting, the scavenging? Living on the run, hiding in the dark, waiting for the Traps to come? If you try to live without a collar, every man will turn his hand against you. Are you sure that's the way you want it to be?"

Furgul thought hard, though he already knew the answer.

"If you're smart," said Argal, "you'll turn away from the wild and rambling road. You'll take my advice. Learn how to please the masters. Flatter their vanity. Learn how to live with their whims and their rules. Love them if you can—and if you can't, pretend to. Quench the fire that burns inside and live a long, comfortable, well-fed life. Be a pet."

"I've already been a pet."

Argal nodded slowly, as if he were sad for Furgul but also proud of him.

"You should listen to Mister Argal," said Skyver. "He knows what he's talking about—and so do I."

Argal gave Skyver a look. Skyver groveled on his belly in fear.

"You might not remember me, Mister Argal," whimpered Skyver.

"No. I don't," said Argal.

"Oh," said Skyver. His lopsided ears drooped with disappointment. "Well, I once saw you take down three angry malamutes. Perhaps it was four. Or even five!" He chuckled, obviously hoping that Argal would like him. "I bet they wish they'd never left Alaska."

"I'm talking to my son," said Argal, without smiling.

"Yes, sir. I was taking good care of young Furgul myself, even before you turned up. Wasn't I, Furgul?" Skyver licked the sweat off his nose. "Boy, wait till my old mother hears about this."

"Shut your yap or you won't live to tell anyone," said Argal.

Skyver crawled to the back of his cage and hid his head beneath his paws.

Argal turned back to Furgul. For the first time Furgul saw some warmth in Argal's face, the love of a father for his son. But with the love came a shadow of fear.

"We haven't got long," said Argal, "so listen. Whether you decide to be a pet or you decide to let the winds of the Doglands take you where they will, your next step is the same. If you can't be smart, at least you can learn some cunning."

"Whatever you say, Dad."

"Think of your mother, Keeva. Don't close your eyes. Picture how beautiful she is. Remember how much she loves you."

Furgul did as he was told. He pictured Keeva. He started to feel sad.

"Perfect," said Argal. "We'll call that your Keeva face. Now think of a time when you were happy. Think of the happiest day in your life."

"When I played at fighting with Dervla in the park?" said Furgul.

"Good," said Argal. "Picture that day."

Furgul pictured it without closing his eyes. He felt his ears prick up. He held his head high. He wagged his tail without even thinking about it.

"Good," said Argal. "We'll call that your Dervla face. Do you know how to sit and heel? And those other silly commands that make the masters feel as if they're in control?"

Furgul nodded. "I learned them when I was a pet."

"Even better. Now, you have to get out of the dog pound within five days. Do you know why?"

"I explained all that, Mister Argal. Didn't I, Furgul?" said Skyver.

Argal gave Skyver another look. Skyver bowed and scraped, as if even a scowl were an honor. Argal turned back to Furgul.

"That means that within five days you have to persuade a dog lover to pick you out from all the other dogs. You have to make them want to take you home with them. And you have to persuade the workers at the Needles to recommend you. Do you understand?"

"I think so," nodded Furgul.

"Show the workers that you're obedient, even if you don't feel like it. Act like a good, responsible dog—all the time. Avoid fighting, even if your blood is boiling. And no play-fighting either—most humans can't tell the difference. Don't bark. Don't whine. Keep your cage clean. Make their lives easy. And give them your Dervla face—your happy face—every time you see them. The strange thing is, the humans who work in the dog pound really love dogs, more than most of all the other humans in the world. Win the pound workers over and they might even give you more than five days. Do you understand?"

"I understand."

"Sooner or later you'll find strangers—maybe with children—looking at you through the bars," said Argal. "Show them your Keeva face, with your big brown eyes. Lift one paw toward them, but slowly and gently—and don't look too desperate."

Furgul nodded again. "I can do that."

"The strangers might make those 'aawwwh' noises they make when they see something cute. If they do, you put on your happy Dervla face and wag your tail. Stick your tongue out and pant—they like that—but don't bare your teeth. If they bend down and start waffling at you, you're nearly there. Keep on your happy face and croon at them, as if they're already your best friends. Don't bark or snarl, even if they pat you in places you don't like—such as on the head. Pretend you love it. Keep looking right at them. There's a good chance they'll want to take you home right there and then. If they start to walk away, give them your Keeva face again. And don't worry—humans love to shop around. It makes them feel powerful and clever. If they come back to see you a second time, you can close the deal. Just give them a super-happy Dervla face, with lots of tail wagging, and they'll have you outside on a leash within fifteen minutes. Can you remember all that?"

"Yes," said Furgul. "What do I do next?"

"They'll take you to their home," said Argal. "And then, in time, you make your choice—to be a pet, or to escape and run with the winds."

Skyver had crept back to the front of his cage. "Excuse me, Mister Argal, sir, but was that 'stick your tongue out and pant' or 'don't pant'?" he asked.

Argal gave Skyver a dark look. "Listen, fleabag, if you try any of this before Furgul is free, I'll have your skin peeled off. Understand?"

"Yes, sir," whimpered Skyver. "Perfectly."

The truck came to a halt. The rumble of the engine stopped.

"We're here." Argal lowered his voice to a whisper so that Skyver couldn't overhear. "Stick close to me. I haven't much time left—and I want to spend it with you."

"What do you mean, not much time?" whispered Furgul. "We'll have five days."

The back doors of the truck swung open. Six nervous Traps peered in.

"I won't get five days," said Argal.

"Why not?"

"I've already been sentenced to death. First thing in the morning they'll kill me."

The Needles was a long gray concrete building with harsh lights outside. Beside it was an exercise yard surrounded by a high wire fence. As the dogs got out of the van, Argal was quiet and obedient. The Traps mopped sweat from their faces, relieved that they didn't have to use their nooses. They smiled again, though Furgul could see that the smiles were false, and said "Good boy!" Furgul hated being called a boy. He wasn't a boy. He was a dog. He was sure that Argal hated it even more. But Argal stayed cool. He let them put a collar and leash on him and didn't fight them. They leashed Furgul and the others too, and Furgul stayed close to Argal. The Traps took them into the Needles side by side.

Inside were more harsh lights and lots of corridors. The Traps met with the shelter workers. They were both women, one with blond hair and one with red, and both with very kind faces. They gave the dogs treats and lots of smiles. The Traps talked to the women while looking at Argal, and the women looked concerned and sad.

"Watch," said Argal. "They're going to blunt my teeth."

The blond woman brought a muzzle and strapped it round Argal's snout. Argal didn't struggle. He gave her a mournful look and shook one hind leg. The chains on his ankles rattled. The blonde unlocked the chains and took them away. She took the leashes of Argal and Furgul from the Traps, and the redhead took the leashes of Skyver, Zinni and Tess. Then the two shelter women took the dogs to the cellblock.

"They'll put me in a cage first," said Argal. "Try to get in there ahead of me."

When they reached the cellblock the redheaded woman switched on a light to reveal a huge room filled with long rows of cages. In front of each row was a concrete gutter and a series of metal grates in the floor. In nearly every cage lay a sleeping dog. The smell of so many dogs was tremendous, and Furgul could tell that most of them didn't keep their cages clean. The light woke them up and a chorus of woofing and whimpering and whining arose. Argal barked just once.

"Quiet!" commanded Argal.

It wasn't an angry bark or even a loud bark. It didn't frighten the two shelter women. But its effect was amazing.

Silence fell over the cellblock in an instant as every dog obeyed Argal. The two women looked at each other. They realized that Argal was a dog among dogs. The blonde said something sad to the redhead, and the redhead nodded. Furgul sensed that they were sorry that such a dog as Argal would have to die.

Near the entrance to the cellblock stood a series of extra-large cages for extra-large dogs. In one of them lay an old, starved Saint Bernard. His ribs poked out like knife blades through his loose, saggy skin. He was covered with weeping sores and scabby patches where his hair had fallen out. One eye was swollen shut with some monstrous infection. His right ear had been cut off—so recently that the wound was still bloody. Furgul had never seen a dog in such terrible condition, even at Dedbone's Hole. It was a wonder the Saint Bernard was still breathing.

While the redhead took Skyver, Tess and Zinni down the walkway between the cages, the blonde opened the extra-large cage next to the Saint Bernard. As she bent down to release Argal's leash, Furgul dashed into the cage, plucking his own leash from the blonde's hand. Argal lunged in after him and turned to guard the door. The blonde wasn't angry, but she put her hands on her hips with a look of concern, as if she were worried for Furgul.

"Show her your Keeva face," said Argal, "and rub your shoulder against mine."

Furgul did so and looked up at the blonde. As she

considered whether or not she should separate the dogs—which she knew would not be easy—Furgul crooned to her to let her know he'd be fine. The blonde seemed to understand. She nodded and closed the door of the cage, leaving them together. She walked away.

"Get this thing off me," said Argal.

Furgul bit through the strap behind Argal's ears, and the muzzle fell off.

Argal looked at the Saint Bernard and the wretched state he was in. Furgul tried to imagine how a huge Saint Bernard could be starved into a tottering bag of bones. The Saint Bernard clambered painfully to his feet. He nodded to Argal, as if they were old friends.

"Hello, Brennus," said Argal. "Hard times."

"I've known better," said Brennus. "And I've known worse too."

Argal looked at the dreadful wounds on Brennus's body. "So I see."

"My master locked me in a dark cellar, for months. He never said why."

Argal's face darkened with rage and sorrow at seeing such a noble dog brought low. "Some of them don't need a 'why,'" he said. "They just like being mean."

"Why did they cut your ear off?" asked Furgul.

"I had a tattoo in my ear—a number," said Brennus. "My master didn't want the Traps to be able to trace me back to him, or he'd be in trouble. I pretended to be nearly dead, which was easy enough. He threw me on a garbage dump to die."

Furgul didn't know what to say. Brennus gave him a wink with his one good eye.

"At least in here they feed me well and let me see the sunshine in the exercise yard." Brennus looked at Argal. "But you look fighting fit, as always."

Argal nodded. "For what good it'll do me. This is my last shout."

"That's hard to believe," said Brennus.

"Believe it," said Argal. "The wild and rambling road ends here."

"You ran with the winds for longer than most," said Brennus. There was something haunted in his huge green eye. "And at least they never broke your spirit."

"Chin up, Brennus. There's nothing wrong with you that a few raw steaks won't cure."

"Right. They serve me T-bones three times a day," said Brennus. "Speaking of red meat, how's your brother, Sloann?"

"Haven't seen Sloann in years," said Argal. "Don't even know if he's alive."

"Sloann?" Damaged though he was, Brennus almost laughed. "Sloann's not like the rest of us. He's not even like you. Of course he'll be alive."

"If he is, he'll be up to no good."

"Sloann was always one to bite first and ask questions later."

"Sloann never asks questions," said Argal.

Furgul's mind reeled at the thought that Argal had a brother just as scary as he was. Before he could ask about him, Brennus looked at him and said, "Who's the kid?"

"My son, Furgul," said Argal. "We'll be talking for a while."

"Talk away," said Brennus. "You won't keep my old bones awake." He studied the fresh swellings and bruises on Argal's face. "Resisted arrest, huh? You'll be leaving at first light, then."

"I reckon so," said Argal.

"At least you'll be remembered," said Brennus.

Brennus turned away and tried to curl up on the floor. The painful sores on his flanks made it hard, but he put his head on his paws and closed his eye.

Furgul felt a great anger and a great sorrow swelling through his chest. How could such lordly dogs as Brennus and Argal be treated with such disrespect and brutality? He found himself baring his teeth, but he didn't growl in case he disturbed the Saint Bernard. He found Argal looking at him. Argal didn't speak.

"Why are humans so cruel to us?" asked Furgul. "What have we done to hurt them?"

"We've done nothing to hurt them," growled Argal. "All we've done is to be their most faithful companions for thousands of years. We protected their children, their homes, their farms. We herded their cattle and sheep. We showed them how to hunt. We fought in their wars. When they were lost, we guided them home. We put food in their mouths when they were hungry, and we saved their lives when they were dying. We even wiped out our brothers—the wolves—for the benefit of men and to our shame because men asked us to do it. Now we capture their criminals and sniff for their dangerous explosives and poisonous drugs. The rich use us to make them look even richer, and beggars use us to help them pay for their booze. In their darkest nights we bring them comfort. In their brightest days we bring them joy. We've given the human race more love than any other creature on this earth. They even have the nerve to call us man's best friend." He looked about the death house. He looked at Furgul. "And this is our reward."

Tears welled in Furgul's eyes, but he fought them back down. He looked at Brennus's ravaged body through the bars of the cage. And he realized that Brennus was awake. And not only Brennus but all the other jailhouse dogs too, their ears pricked forward to catch the words of truth.

Every dog in the Needles was listening to Argal.

Furgul turned back to him. "But why? I don't understand it."

"What you must understand is that it's not just us dogs. Humans exploit all animals. We've all got something that they want. They exploit all of nature's bounty. They believe that the earth was created just for them. They take and use the things they want, and when those things are worn out—or when they just get bored—they throw them away. Of all living things, humans are the most greedy, the most ruthless, the most selfish, the most deceitful. That's why they rule the world. And the most terrible truth of all is that they treat each other with even more cruelty, dishonesty and stupidity than they treat us dogs. They shackle us with muzzles and collars and chains, yes. But the chains men hang upon each other—and upon themselves—are stronger than the bars of this prison."

Furgul stared into Argal's eyes, and in them he saw all the suffering that Argal had endured. He saw the genius that enabled him to understand so much. He saw the defiance that had kept him alive for so long in a world that was out to break him. He saw why Argal was a king among dogs—a king among all living things. A king who had never been crowned but who had made himself a king through his life and his deeds and the courage that burned in his heart. Then Furgul realized he was the son of a king and he was scared.

"Be brave," said Argal.

"That's what Keeva told me. But I'm often afraid."

"So am I," said Argal.

"You?"

"I've spent half my life being afraid. That's the only time you really need to be brave. I'm scared right now. In the morning they're going to walk through that door with their nooses and their needles and their guns, and they're going to kill me."

"Why won't they give you even one day?" asked Furgul.

"They've classed me as a dangerous dog." Argal gave a shake of his head, as if he could not begin to express his contempt for humanity. "You saw me fighting the Traps. If I'd wanted to be dangerous, they'd all be dead."

"Did they attack you first?"

"Of course they did," said Argal.

"Then it's not right," said Furgul.

"Humans aren't right. Didn't Dedbone's Hole teach you that?"

Furgul nodded. "I bit a man there. I was trying to save my sisters." He hung his head and felt ashamed. "I failed. Only Brid got away."

"Furgul, I'm proud that you're my son."

Furgul lifted his head. "Really?"

"I've never been so proud of anything," said Argal.

Argal turned away, as if to hide some feeling that he didn't want Furgul to see. The cellblock suddenly went dark as the lights were switched out. But enough light came through the windows from outside to see by. Argal turned back to him.

"Sleep beside me for a while," he said. "I'd like that."

"I'd like that too," said Furgul.

"Except for that one night with Keeva," said Argal, "I've never felt the warmth of my family before."

Argal lay down on the cold concrete floor and Furgul curled up between his huge paws, with his back nestled into Argal's belly. It felt good. Almost as good as when he had slept with Keeva, and with Nessa and Eena and Brid. In some ways it felt even better. Even though he was in prison and his dad was going to die in the morning, he felt safer and more free than he'd ever felt in his life. After a while Furgul heard Argal breathe in sleep. And then he let fall the tears that he'd held inside.

Furgul slept deep and dreamed of the Doglands. Or perhaps the Doglands dreamed of him. He felt happy and strong. He felt neither fear nor sorrow. He felt Argal dreaming with him. He felt their two hearts beating as one.

When he woke up, it was still dark. Argal had woken before him, and they talked in low voices in the prison's dank gloom. Furgul told Argal what had happened at Dedbone's Hole and in Dogsnout Mountain. He told him he was going to go back and rescue Keeva, but about that Argal said nothing.

Instead he told Furgul how to fight. He told him the strengths and weaknesses of different breeds, including his own. He told him how to live off the land, how to survive in the wilderness far from the gaze of men. He told him to beware of the towns and, even worse, the cities, where the dangers were greatest of all. The light of day came up, and the other dogs began to stir.

Argal said, "But despite all I've told you, my advice hasn't changed. Be a pet."

"After everything you've told me? Why?"

"There's no dishonor in being a pet," said Argal. "Most of the happiest dogs alive are pets. I'd even say that most masters, in their hearts, are decent and kind. If they don't know how to treat us right, it's because they don't understand us. The shame of it is, they don't try. But I don't want you to end up like me. If you take the wild and rambling road, then sooner or later it will bring you right back here—to a filthy cell, in a prison, waiting to die."

"I want to run with the winds," said Furgul.

"Do you know what the winds are?" asked Argal.

Furgul shook his head.

Argal closed his eyes and raised his snout. A low, rhythmic growl arose from his throat, an ancient chant. The fur on Furgul's back stood on end, and he sensed the other prisoners stirring in their cages, roused by the dog song that none had ever heard but which all of them had known all their lives.

Argal sang:

> *"When leaves die they turn into earth.*
> *When mountains die they fall into the sea.*
> *When stars die they turn into darkness.*
> *When dogs die they join the winds."*

Furgul felt his throat go tight, and from the sniffles he heard from the other cages he was not alone. The song pierced his heart. Argal fell silent and looked at him.

"Furgul, have you ever felt that wind in your hair—that special wind—that makes you feel like you could fly? That makes you feel as if you've been alive for ten thousand years? And that you'll live for ten thousand more?"

Furgul remembered the eerie wind in the tunnels of Dogsnout Mountain.

"Yes!" said Furgul. "Yes!"

"That wind is the spirit of a free dog passing by. If you run with the winds when you're alive, then when you die, as the dog song tells us, you join the winds. You become the winds. You *are* the winds."

"So a free dog doesn't die forever?"

"A free dog never dies. He only moves on."

For a moment Furgul's thoughts were deep. The wind he had felt in the mountain—that had told him *"You're the dog who runs in darkness"*—must have been Eena's. She died fighting to be free—and so she was free. So had Nessa. In death they'd given Furgul the seed of life. They'd set him on the wild and rambling road that led to the Doglands.

"Dad?" asked Furgul. "Where are the Doglands?"

Argal studied him. "Who told you about the Doglands?"

"Keeva did. She didn't really tell me about them. She just said that that was where you came from, and that no one knew the Doglands as well as you did. I want to find them again—but I don't know where they are."

"The Doglands are everywhere—and nowhere."

"I don't understand," said Furgul.

"The Doglands are right here, in this prison."

Furgul was stunned. He looked around at the squalid

cages, the stained walls, the filthy gutters. He heard the sighs and groans of the captive dogs.

"In here? I thought the Doglands were wild and free, with mountains and rivers and trees and wide-open spaces."

"Those are the Doglands too," said Argal.

"But I've seen them," said Furgul. "I smelled them. I felt them."

"I know you did. Because the Doglands are here"—Argal raised a massive paw and put it on Furgul's chest—"in your heart. Every dog whose heart is free knows the Doglands. Whether we're pets or strays or prisoners. We carry the Doglands inside us, wherever we go."

Furgul started to understand. "Even in death?"

"Especially in death," said Argal. "That's why death will never hold me."

Furgul had a terrible thought. He said, "When Keeva talked about the Doglands, she sounded as if she'd never been there."

He looked at Argal. Argal looked grave.

"No," he said. "I don't think she ever has." He saw the expression on Furgul's face. "It's hard for greyhounds. From the moment they're born, the masters work hard to crush their spirits. You escaped before they could crush yours."

"Then it's even more important that I go back," said Furgul. "I've got to tell Keeva. I've got to show her where to find the Doglands."

"You know what?" said Argal. "Maybe you should."

The doors of the cellblock clanged open, and four Traps entered carrying stun guns, steel poles and nooses. Behind them came a Vet in a white coat. The blond woman came too. They approached Argal's cage, and the blond woman opened the door. Furgul thought she looked upset.

Argal turned to Furgul. "We've said our long goodbyes, so let's make this one short. Keep your tail up."

"I'll help you fight them," said Furgul, his blood rising. "Let's do them all!"

"No," said Argal. "It's time to be strong inside."

He licked Furgul's face. Furgul struggled to be strong inside, for Argal.

"And remember," said Argal, "we two shall meet again. On the winds."

Furgul's throat was so tight he couldn't speak.

He licked Argal's face.

Argal walked to the door. He looked at the Traps and their nooses and their guns. Then he looked at the Vet who had come to kill him as if to say: *Do you want to do this the easy way? Or do you want me to paint this cellblock red with blood?*

The Vet knew dogs very well. Well enough to understand Argal's grim expression. He murmured to the Traps, and they lowered their nooses and guns. The blond woman looked at Furgul, and something in his face must have got to her. She clasped her hands over her mouth, and her eyes filled with tears. She turned away and walked from the cellblock.

Argal stepped out of the cage. The Traps closed the door behind him.

Argal looked down the long gray walkway to the Death House.

Then he turned his head to look at Furgul.

"Tell Keeva that I always loved her."

Furgul rose on his hind legs and leaned on the bars. His eyes met Argal's.

"I'll tell her. I promise."

Argal turned and walked away down the cellblock, tail held high.

The Traps and the Vet trudged along in dishonor behind him.

Though all the dogs were awake, and stood with their snouts pressed through the bars, an enormous, heavy silence had fallen across the cages. The pads of Argal's huge paws slapped on the concrete and echoed from the walls.

Then Brennus reared on his hind legs and let out a furious growl.

"For shame!" roared Brennus. "FOR SHAME!"

"You show 'em how it's done, Mr. Argal!" barked Skyver. "We're with you!" He started chanting. "AR-GAL! AR-GAL! AR-GAL!"

Cage by cage, bark after bark, all the other jailhouse dogs joined in the chant.

"AR-GAL!"

"AR-GAL!"

"AR-GAL!"

It got louder—louder—until their outrage shook the prison to its foundation stones.

The Traps and the Vet hunched their shoulders in fear. Or perhaps it was shame.

Furgul was the only dog who couldn't speak. He poked his head through the bars and watched as Argal strode toward his end. Argal looked neither left nor right. He held his head high, as calm and strong and fearless as any dog that ever growled.

"AR-GAL! AR-GAL!"

At the end of the walkway stood a big black door. As Argal approached, the big black door swung open. Some of the dogs started yowling with horror. When Argal reached the threshold of the Death House, he stopped and turned.

The dogs stopped chanting and yowling.

Argal looked about the cellblock, at the faces of the dogs who would live and the faces of the dogs who would die. He wagged his tail in salute. Then, down the length of the walkway, he looked at his son, Furgul, for the last time.

Their eyes met. Furgul felt Argal's heart reach out across the gray and grimy flagstones. He felt his courage and defiance. He felt his power to understand. He felt the living essence of the wild and rambling road.

"Farewell to the king," whispered Furgul.

Brennus heard him, and took up the cry.

"FAREWELL TO THE KING!"

The captive dogs howled in unison.

"FAREWELL TO THE KING!"

Then Argal turned away.

Furgul watched Argal walk into the Death House with his killers.

The black door clanged shut.

Furgul couldn't take his eyes off it.

And silence fell once again across the Needles.

CHAPTER TEN

THE REVOLT

Furgul had no appetite for breakfast. He wasn't alone. Though dogs would normally keep eating even in an earthquake, many of the prisoners left their bowls of dry biscuits untouched. The two morning shelter workers seemed unsettled too. When they let the dogs out into the exercise yard for their morning hour, they heard a lot more growls than they were used to. Among the dogs who milled about the yard, dashing from one gang to another, all the talk was of Argal.

Furgul wandered round in a daze. He didn't want to talk to anyone. He saw Tess sobbing and Zinni trying to comfort her. He overheard Skyver telling tall tales to a group of seething pit bulls.

"So there we were," said Skyver, "trapped in the headlights with the cops on one side and the Traps on the other. 'What shall we do, Skyver?' says Argal. So I say, 'There's only eight of 'em, Argal. I'll take the two on the right, and you take the six on the left. . . .'"

Furgul wandered around the perimeter, glancing at the wasted land beyond the wire. The warm sunshine didn't feel warm. The blue sky didn't seem blue. There wasn't a breath of wind. He felt empty. Skyver trotted up and walked along beside him.

"I'm sorry, Furgul," he said. "We're all sorry. A lot of us are angry too."

Furgul didn't answer him.

"But you and me can get out of here—if we do like Argal told us, when the animal lovers come." He smiled to cheer Furgul up. "I'll let you go first, of course. I wouldn't break a promise to Argal, even though he's . . . Well, I won't break my promise. Mutts like you and me don't have many friends out there. We should stick together."

Furgul didn't bother to say he was a lurcher. After all, he was a mutt. A mixed breed, a half-caste, a mongrel. That's why Dedbone had tried to kill him.

Skyver grinned. "We can both be pets and wear diamond collars like Zinni."

Still, Furgul didn't answer. They stopped near the edge of the main prison building. They watched a truck pull up near the back, and two men in yellow jumpsuits got out. The men went inside the prison.

"Anyhow," said Skyver, "who knows what happened to

Argal? Maybe the needle couldn't kill him. Maybe he escaped from behind that big black door."

"You think so?"

"That's what I've been telling the crew. And remember what you said yourself—and you were right—*never give up hope.*"

"I suppose it isn't impossible," admitted Furgul.

"Nothing was impossible for Argal. Nothing is." Skyver pointed through the wire with a paw. "He's probably out there right now, eating fresh deer meat and drinking cool water from a river."

"I guess being a pet again won't be so bad," said Furgul. "At least for a while."

"That's the spirit," said Skyver. "The mild and grumbling toad! Funny, when you think about it, that Argal should follow a toad. But who are we to argue with the king?"

Furgul didn't bother to correct him about "the wild and rambling road," but he smiled. The thought of Argal by the river eating meat made him feel a bit better. As he started to walk away from the fence, Skyver's raggedy ears drooped, and his tail fell between his legs.

"What's wrong?" asked Furgul.

Skyver turned quickly and trotted toward the center of the yard.

"Nothing," he said. "Nothing at all. Come on, let's go make fun of the pit bulls."

Skyver was a good liar, but this time Furgul didn't believe

him. He looked back through the fence to see what had bothered Skyver.

The men in yellow jumpsuits had come back out of the prison. They staggered under the weight of the enormous dog they carried between them. It was Argal. His big red-haired body was all floppy. His head hung down and his jaws sagged wide and flecks of dirty foam dripped from his mouth. His eyes were open, but Furgul knew they couldn't see. Argal was dead.

He watched the men heave the body in the back of the truck like a sack of garbage. Then they got into the cab and drove away.

Furgul felt his heart breaking inside him. He felt even worse than when Eena and Nessa had died. Then he'd only been a puppy. He hadn't understood the true nature of the world. Now he did. Argal had told him. And Argal was gone.

Furgul turned away and wandered after Skyver. He didn't believe his own words anymore. He had given up hope. He didn't even know if he believed in Argal's words. He no longer felt the Doglands inside him.

Then the wind came.

At first it was just a soft, gentle breeze, and Furgul didn't pay it much mind.

Then it grew stronger. And a fiery chill tingled through his blood. His heart had been on the edge of breaking, but now it pounded harder than it had ever pounded before. He raised his snout and took in a deep breath. Furgul howled with joy.

All the dogs in the yard stopped what they were doing and turned to look.

Skyver ran over, worried. Then he saw Furgul's face and stopped.

"Can you feel it?" asked Furgul.

"What?" asked Skyver.

"The wind."

The wind was getting stronger and stronger.

"That's Argal's spirit passing by," said Furgul.

"Yes," said Skyver, his ears flapping in the wind. "I feel it. It *is* him!"

As Furgul felt Argal's spirit fill his chest—and his bones and his muscles and his skull—the urge to run flowed through him. He sprang forward into a gallop and took off across the yard.

"Let's tell the others!" shouted Skyver.

But Furgul couldn't stop and didn't want to. He ran through the other dogs, who jumped aside and stared at him as if he'd gone mad. Perhaps he had. But he didn't care. He ran and ran and ran, faster and faster and faster, and as he ran, the wind blew even stronger. He ran in a great circle round the yard, then started round again—as if he'd run for ten thousand years. He heard Skyver yelling to the others. Then Skyver started running too, shambling after Furgul in his shaggy patchwork fur and yowling through his broken yellow teeth. And in ones and twos, then threes and fours, then in one great roaring, panting, galloping pack, the jailhouse dogs followed Furgul around the yard.

The wind got even stronger still.

It whirled around and around above their mad and circling charge, and in that circle every jailhouse dog felt free. The wind howled, and they howled back.

It was Argal's last shout.

And Furgul knew that it would blow around the Doglands forever.

With a final halloo the wind gathered force and roared away across the sky. Somewhere out there, there were other dogs in peril—lost or abandoned, frightened or doomed—who needed to feel that wind roar through their souls.

Argal's reign was not finished. It had only just begun.

As the last breath of wind spiraled off into the wild blue yonder, the pack of running dogs slowed down and finally stopped. All except for Furgul. He ran on and on and on. Until, at last, he heard the whistling.

Two different shelter workers stood at the entrance to the cellblock. They were both men. One was fat and one was bald and both were red in the face from blowing on their whistles. As Furgul stopped among the pack, the men lowered their whistles and gaped. They'd watched the dogs galloping round and round with Furgul in the lead—and they'd never seen anything like it in their lives.

Furgul panted hard to cool himself down. In fact, all the dogs were panting. Terriers and spaniels, basset hounds and coonhounds, Dobermans and retrievers, rottweilers and poodles, hunting dogs and toy dogs, tall dogs and small dogs, and mongrels and mutts and crossbreeds of every stripe. Furgul felt good. They all felt good. It was the biggest, happiest crowd of dogs that had ever gathered together inside the wire. They were imprisoned in the Needles. More than half of them would be put to death for the crime of being alive. And this morning they didn't care.

The shelter workers waved and whistled for the dogs to come back inside.

The pack didn't move.

Skyver came and stood by Furgul. He looked at him and raised one eyebrow.

"I feel about a hundred feet tall," said Skyver. "What about you?"

Furgul felt even taller. He didn't speak.

All the dogs turned to look at him. He was Argal's son.

Furgul shouldered his way to the front of the pack. He looked at the bewildered workers. Then he turned to face the horde of dogs.

"They want us to crawl back to our cages," said Furgul. "But I don't feel like answering to a dog whistle today. I think I'm going to stay out here."

"Right on, brother!" shouted Skyver. "Follow the grumbling toad!"

"Argal showed us how to run with the wind—together," said Furgul. "That's why he chose to take the long walk. He did it for me. For you. For all of us."

A murmur arose among the pack. An angry murmur.

"You think Argal was beaten?" asked Furgul. "You think the Traps won? You think Argal was scared of their nooses and their needles and their guns?"

"NO!" roared the pack.

"They don't just want us to *live* with our tails between our legs," said Furgul, "they want us to *die* with our tails between our legs too. I say—no more."

"NO MORE!" barked the pack.

"We're not going to let them muzzle us no more. We're not going to let them starve us no more. We're not going to die behind black doors no more."

"NO MORE!"

Skyver shouted, "I've heard they sing a song about us! 'How much is that doggy in the window?' You know, 'The one with the waggly tail.'" Skyver wagged his own tail and broke wind toward the guards.

Furgul laughed. The other dogs all laughed too. The two shelter workers whistled again. They were walking nervously toward the pack, rattling metal bowls of cheap dry biscuits.

Skyver said, "Fatso and Baldy think they can buy us doggies with chicken beaks and butt holes."

"Let's show them how much a dog really costs!" said Furgul. The pack howled.

"Let's make them pay!" roared Furgul.

With one deafening snarl the pack rushed at Fatso and Baldy.

"No blood!" called Furgul.

The two men dropped their whistles and bowls and sprinted for the prison. They waved their arms and yelled in panic as terriers and pit bulls tore their pants to ribbons. They reached the door and stumbled inside and slammed it shut. A number of dogs cocked their legs and peed on it. The rest yapped and laughed and barked with excitement.

"That was fun," said Skyver. "What happens next?"

"I don't know," said Furgul. "The next move's up to them."

An hour later, half a dozen Traps emerged from the prison, brandishing their long poles and nooses. If they thought they could take the dogs back inside one by one, they were wrong. On Furgul's command, the pack charged again and sent five of the Traps crawling back inside, half-naked, covered in poop and bleeding from the ankles. The sixth Trap scrambled up on top of the roof. A gang of mutts and coonhounds followed him. They surrounded him and barked at him until he was almost crying with terror.

"Now he knows what it feels like," said Skyver.

A fire engine arrived with a siren and flashing blue lights. They raised a ladder to the roof, and the dogs let the sixth Trap escape, but they gave him a good soaking as he climbed down.

Furgul noticed that the riot had drawn a crowd of curious humans to the fence. To Furgul's surprise they seemed quite friendly. They waved at the dogs and threw treats over the wire. At first Furgul was suspicious. Perhaps this was a trick and the treats were poisoned. But the dogs who ate them seemed fine, and as time passed the crowd grew even bigger.

Sometime around noon a flying machine appeared and fluttered in a circle overhead. A man leaned out of it with a strange tube held up against his eye.

"This is great!" said Skyver.

"What is it?" asked Furgul.

"It's TV!"

"What's TV?"

"You know those flashing screens that humans love to stare at day and night?"

Furgul nodded.

"That's TV," said Skyver. "When something big happens, they send a helicopter—that's the flying machine—and when that man points the tube at what's happening, it all appears on TV."

"So we're on TV?"

"You can learn a lot about humans from watching TV," said Skyver. "We've hit the big time."

"But what's so great about being on TV?" asked Furgul.

"I don't know," admitted Skyver. "But every human in the world wants to be on TV."

As far as Furgul could see, all that being on TV meant was that the crowd of spectators got bigger still. In fact, it became huge. Every inch of the fence was crammed with people. Some of them had the strange tubes like the man in the helicopter, and others had little silver boxes, and they pointed them at the dogs and went "click, click, click." Most of the dogs were friendly to the crowd—and Skyver showed them he could walk on his hind legs—but some, like Furgul, didn't go near the fence. The crowd seemed to love them.

Tess saw her owners and ran over to them. They gave her treats and seemed overjoyed to see her. After a moment she came running over to Furgul.

"My master and mistress want to take me home," said Tess.

"That's great," said Furgul. "Next time the Traps open the door, you can go."

"I do want to go home," said Tess, "but not until this is over. I don't want to let you down. It will be over, won't it?"

"It can't go on forever."

"How will it end?"

"I don't know, Tess," said Furgul. He felt a bit guilty. "I don't really know what we've got ourselves into."

"You'll think of something," said Tess.

Furgul wasn't so sure. The fence was too high to climb. The Traps could keep them here until they starved. How could this revolt end? Except in defeat?

A little later Brennus came padding over to Furgul. Furgul was in awe of the big Saint Bernard, even though he was weak and sick. He bowed to show his respect.

"This is quite a rumpus you've started," said Brennus.

Furgul didn't know if Brennus approved or not. He didn't reply.

"Argal would have been impressed," Brennus said.

"What should we do next?" asked Furgul.

"It's a question of what the Traps will do next," said Brennus. "This riot of ours has made them look bad. Very bad. Especially since it's on TV. They'll want to get us back in our cages as soon as they can. Chances are, they'll hit us in the dark—after midnight. And it won't be Fatso and Baldy. The Traps'll hit us hard. More Traps and more guns than we've ever seen."

"What can we do, Brennus?"

"Do you see that lady behind the fence—green T-shirt, long hair?"

Furgul scanned the crowd and saw the lady. She was looking right at him.

"She told me she wants to talk to you," said Brennus.

"She *told* you?"

"She's what we call a Dog Talker," said Brennus. "It's only the second time I've ever met one. There aren't many around. She speaks dog tongue—a kind of dog tongue anyway. It's odd, but it works. You'll see."

"What does she want to talk about?"

"I don't know. You'll have to go and find out."

"But why me?"

"You're our leader," said Brennus. "You're Argal's son."

"I'm not sure I want to be the leader."

"Heavy is the head that wears the crown." Brennus saw that Furgul didn't understand. "It's hard to carry all that responsibility," he explained. "But if you don't, all this will fall apart. It will all be for nothing. And they'll make every one of us pay."

Brennus's eyes gave Furgul courage.

"Stand tall," said Brennus.

Furgul trotted over to the lady at the fence, feeling suspicious.

"Hello, Furgul," she said. "I'm Jodi. I believe you are the leader of this pack."

Furgul was shocked. He could understand her. She wasn't speaking human words, and neither did she have a dog voice. She just made a kind of murmur. Yet her meaning was clear, as if it were going straight from her brain into his.

Jodi asked, "Is that true?"

"Yes." He remembered Brennus and raised his tail. "I'm their leader."

"If you like, I can get you out of here. I can take you to my farm, Appletree Dog Sanctuary. There are no cages, no muzzles, just fields and trees. You can run with the winds."

"You know about the winds?"

"I've heard about them, from other free dogs," said Jodi. "You can live at Appletree for the rest of your life, if you want. Unless you meet a new owner you'd like to live with. But that would be your choice. There are other free dogs to run and play with."

"Are you saying I'd be completely free?"

"No one's completely free, Furgul. Not even humans.

Especially not humans. Including me. But it's as free as you can be without getting into trouble."

"Why me?" asked Furgul.

"Because I like you." Jodi had deep blue eyes, and they bored into Furgul's heart. "And because I want to save you from the needle."

"How do you know I'll get the needle? I might persuade an animal lover to take me home as a pet."

"They won't let that happen," said Jodi. "Not now. You're the leader of this revolt. You've caused them a lot of trouble and made them look bad. They won't let you go."

Furgul hadn't thought about that. But, of course, she was right. As soon as this protest was over, he'd have to take the long walk to the black door, just like Argal. His tail drooped. He pulled it back up. He had an idea.

"Why don't you take all of us with you?"

Jodi shook her head. "I haven't got enough room."

"There's never enough room, is there?" said Furgul. "That's why they kill us."

"I agree with you, Furgul. It's a tragedy. It's a crime." He saw the sorrow in her eyes. "But I can't change the whole world by myself. I can only change it a little. Will you come with me?"

"They'd let you take me away? Even though I'm the leader?"

"Yes. They know me well. They know I have experience with rebel dogs."

"But we're all rebel dogs now. Brennus says they'll make us all pay. And even if they don't, they'll kill any dog that isn't rescued within five days."

"I don't control the pound. The politicians do."

Furgul didn't know what a politician was, but he didn't like them. He searched inside his soul. He liked Jodi. He liked her a lot. He would love to run at Appletree Dog Sanctuary. But he felt sick inside. He felt confused.

What would Argal do?

"I can't," he said. "I can't betray my friends. I won't. We're going to fight to the death. And I'm going to fight with them."

"I've already spoken to the manager of the pound. If you don't surrender, you'll all be classed as dangerous dogs. And you know what that means."

"They have no idea how dangerous we are."

"What can I do to make you change your mind?" asked Jodi. "If you end this quickly—and peacefully—I can persuade them that you're not really dangerous."

"What then? Back to business as usual at the Needles? Five days to live?"

"At least some of you would survive. Talk to the rest of the pack," said Jodi. "You're their leader, but you can't make this decision on your own. It's their lives too."

Furgul thought about this. "Jodi? Did they tell you how Argal died?"

Jodi hesitated. Then she said, "It took four lethal injections to kill him. And even though they caused him terrible pain, he didn't make a sound. The Vet said Argal was the strongest dog he'd ever seen."

Furgul swallowed the emotions in his throat. The sadness. The wild rage. He felt Argal's spirit rise inside him. *If you can't be smart, at least you can be cunning.*

He said, "I'll go and talk to the pack."

As Furgul trotted back to Brennus, Zinni ran up to him in a fury.

"How could she?" snapped Zinni. Her tail wagged slowly with anger.

"Jodi's only trying to help," said Furgul.

"I don't mean her. I mean my mistress. Look."

Zinni pointed out a very thin woman in a very pink dress with a very pink, very large, hat. The woman was cuddling a Chihuahua with a diamond collar.

"She's got a new dog already, the pink bitch. And that little brown bitch dares to tell me I'm not wanted anymore. Chihuahuas have become more fashionable than papillons. I'm going to be abandoned."

"I'm sorry to hear that, Zinni, but we've got bigger steaks to fry. And I need your help. We're going to hold a council of war. I want you to get all the small dogs together."

Zinni's tail stopped wagging. "You want me to be leader of the small dogs?"

"Who else?"

Furgul sent Brennus to talk to the big dogs, Zinni to talk to the small, and Skyver to talk to the mutts. The pit bulls wanted to be included with the big dogs, but Zinni wouldn't let them go. Then the three leaders met with Furgul and they made a plan.

At first the discussion was gloomy. None of the different groups wanted to surrender, even though Skyver had tried quite hard to persuade the mutts. Like Furgul, they all said they'd rather fight to the end than go back to the way things were. Then Furgul suggested some cunning ideas, and Brennus gave his wisdom. Zinni had some demands of her own, and Skyver—who had more experience than any of them in surviving on the streets—had the most cunning suggestions of all. When they had agreed on what they should do, Zinni, Brennus and Skyver went back to tell their gangs, and Furgul went back to the fence to speak to Jodi.

"They won't surrender," said Furgul. He saw a flicker of fear in Jodi's face. He added, "Not unless the politicians meet all our demands."

"What do you want?" asked Jodi.

"We want food and water in the yard," said Furgul.

"I'm sure I can arrange that."

"We want the two nice women to bring it, the redhead and the blonde, not Fatso and Baldy. And no Traps."

"Okay. What else?"

"We want the best Vet in the world to take care of Brennus."

"I used to be a Vet," said Jodi. "Maybe not the best in the world, but—"

"Great. We want you. But why did you stop being a Vet?"

"Being a Vet's very hard. It's hard because Vets love animals very deeply. They devote their whole lives to helping animals—and yet being a Vet means you have to kill animals too. With the needle. Especially dogs and cats."

"You killed dogs?"

"Yes," said Jodi. "It's part of the job."

Furgul took a step backward. He started to turn away.

"I know what you're thinking," said Jodi, "and it's difficult for you to understand. Perhaps it's impossible. But the people who love animals the most—like Vets, and like the people who work in shelters and dog pounds, and even the Traps too—are the people who have to do all the dirty work for everybody else."

"You mean the politicians?"

"No, I mean the masters who abandon their pets and the masters who are so cruel that their dogs run away. I mean the pedigree breeders who breed too many dogs—like the greyhound farmers. And the people who buy 'birthday dogs' and 'Christmas dogs' for children who think they're toys. It's their fault that there are too many dogs and not enough people to take care of them. But it's the Vets and shelter workers who have to do the killing. Some can only do it for a few years because it breaks their hearts. After a while I burned out too. I couldn't take it anymore."

Furgul tried to take all this in. "Is it true they kill millions and millions?"

"Yes. All over the world. And I won't lie. I killed some of them myself. Do you still trust me?"

Furgul studied her. He remembered all that Argal had said about humans. They were a very strange breed indeed. But one thing was for sure: They weren't going to go away. Furgul had to learn how to tell the good from the bad.

"I trust you," he said.

"What else do you want?" asked Jodi.

"We want the Needles to become a no-kill shelter. Even for dangerous dogs."

Jodi frowned. "I don't think the politicians will pay for it."

"You see all those cameras?" said Furgul, who now had much more knowledge of these matters. "You see that helicopter in the sky?"

Jodi nodded.

"Tell your politicians to turn on their TVs," said Furgul, "and instead of watching dogs sell beer, they can watch us being slaughtered."

He looked at Jodi. She could see that he was deadly serious. She saw the other dogs. They stood behind Furgul in a silent pack, the tall, the small and the scruffy. They were all deadly serious too.

She said, "I'll see what I can do." She was scared.

"No one else can save us, Jodi," said Furgul. "It's up to you."

CHAPTER ELEVEN

THE SHOWDOWN

The blonde and redhead hauled out sacks of food and buckets of water. They slashed the sacks open, and the hungry dogs had a feast. Brennus made sure that each dog got a fair share and prevented any squabbling. It had been a long day, and Furgul was famished too. As he was about to tuck into his grub, Skyver trotted up, licking crumbs from his whiskers with his yellow-coated, foul-smelling tongue. He grinned with his horrible teeth, which were stained and decayed from years of eating garbage, and Furgul believed that he really was the scruffiest dog in the world.

"Listen, boss," said Skyver.

"Don't call me boss," said Furgul.

"Okay, I understand. The 'proud but humble' routine—that's exactly the way I'd play it too," said Skyver. "It's always a winner with the masses. But, since you *are* the boss—and since everyone knows I was Argal's best friend—I figure it's only fair that you and me should get a double ration of food."

Skyver seemed very pleased with himself for coming up with this idea. He scratched himself under his mangy chin with the claws of a mangy hind leg. Furgul retreated a step to avoid the fleas.

"I'll tell you what," said Furgul. "Since I'm the boss I want this yard kept as neat and clean as possible. So I'm putting you in charge of policing all the poop."

Skyver wriggled his flea-bitten brows. "In charge of policing *what?*"

"If a dog wants to take a dump, they do it over there—in the corner by the back of the cellblock. I don't want it scattered all over the yard."

Skyver was aghast. "But why me?"

"Because everyone knows you were Argal's best friend."

Furgul picked up a biscuit and crunched it. When you were this hungry, anything tasted good. As Skyver skulked away, he developed a pronounced limp that Furgul had not noticed before. A none-too-bright pit bull called Cyril asked Skyver what was wrong.

"Don't you worry, Cyril," said Skyver, with a pained but heroic smile. "It's nothing. Just some injuries I got when me and Argal were fighting off the Traps—you know, when we tried to help Furgul escape from the back of the truck."

"Gee," said Cyril, "it looks pretty bad to me."

"Naw," said Skyver. "Can't be more than a broken femur. And a couple of cracked ribs. Those Traps came on pretty heavy with their clubs. And their steel-toed boots."

Cyril looked horrified. "That's terrible, Skyver."

"I'd love to stop and chat, old pal, but I've got too much work to do."

"With a broken leg and two cracked ribs?" gasped Cyril. "How can I help?"

"It's a very important job," said Skyver. "That's why I wanted to do it myself."

Cyril's ears drooped. "No one's ever given me an important job."

"That's because no one's spotted your true potential, Cyril."

"You think I've got true potential?" panted Cyril.

"Are you kidding? I haven't spotted so much potential since I first saw myself in the mirror as a pup." Skyver frowned. "But it really is essential that this job get done with one hundred percent commitment and dedication."

"Oh please, Skyver," begged Cyril. "Just give me a chance, that's all I'm asking."

"Well," said Skyver, "as I was just telling Furgul, I think we should keep this exercise yard as neat and clean as possible. . . ."

Furgul grinned and finished crunching up his biscuits. Then he had a good drink of water and picked a nice spot in the sun to have a snooze.

He woke up feeling chilly and saw that the sun had gone down.

As the evening wore on, the people at the fence drifted away with their cameras and their treats. The helicopter flew off into the distance. The dogs were left alone in the yard. The shelter workers did not reappear. Nor did the Traps. And neither did Jodi. The stars came out. A full moon rose. The night was cold and still, without a breath of wind or breeze. The pack lay down in one great pile to keep each other warm, like in the old days before dogs were pets. And as they waited longer and longer for something to happen, the hopes of the rebel dogs started to fade.

At some time after midnight, as Brennus had predicted, harsh white electric lights suddenly flooded the yard and the door of the prison opened and the Traps marched out.

"Here they come!" barked Zinni.

The pack woke up and stretched their limbs. They watched as five Traps lined up to the left of the cellblock door. Five more lined up to the right. Some carried clubs and some carried nooses and some carried guns that fired the knock-out needles. Then another five Traps came out. And another five. And another and another and another—until more Traps stood out there in the night than any dog in the pack had ever seen before.

"They must have called in every Trap for a hundred miles around," said Skyver. "We don't stand a chance."

"At least we've got the full moon on our side," said Brennus.

"Yeah," said Zinni. "Let's remind them we're related to werewolves."

"Each gang behind their leader," ordered Furgul.

From the corner of his eye he saw a long black limousine drive by the fence. The door handles shone gold and were shaped like dog bones. Then the limo disappeared and Furgul gave it no more thought.

The big dogs gathered behind Brennus, the little dogs behind Zinni, including the pit bulls, and the mutts milled about behind Skyver, whose limp had been miraculously cured. Furgul walked toward the long line of grim, silent Traps, his tail held high, then he turned to face the pack. There wasn't even a faint breath of wind. Argal was far away. Furgul was on his own.

"Someone just said we don't stand a chance," said Furgul.

Skyver glanced around with a fierce, bold face as if to say, *Who was that?*

"In one way he's right," Furgul continued. "Humans have the power to crush us. They always will. In that sense we never had a chance. And maybe the world will never know what we do here tonight. The TV cameras have gone. In the morning they'll shovel our bodies into trucks and burn us in the incinerator."

Furgul looked at the faces of the dogs before him. All the different breeds and crossbreeds. They were all great dogs.

And some of them had become real friends. For a moment he wondered if he was doing the right thing.

"We're with you, Furgul," said Brennus, his voice steady. "Tell us what to do."

Furgul took a breath and carried on. "But even if we don't have a chance, we still have a choice. We can go to the slaughter like sheep, listening to their lies and letting them pat us on the head as they stick the needle in—"

"Never!" cried Skyver.

"Or we can go down fighting," said Furgul, "and show them why our ancestors were the freest creatures on the earth."

The whole pack howled at the moon.

"We're still free—even here in the Needles," said Furgul. "Argal showed us that. You're all free dogs. So each of you can make the choice for yourself."

With one hind leg Furgul scraped a line in the dirt.

"You've already put up a brave fight. If any dogs want to leave and go back to the cages, they only have to walk across this line. They can go with all honor and with my respect."

Without a moment's hesitation Skyver trotted toward the line.

When he was nearly there, he realized that he was the only dog in the whole pack who had moved. And they were all looking at him. He slowed down. With a flash of inspiration, he changed course to stand at Furgul's right shoulder.

"Live free or die like a gerbil!" barked Skyver.

To his disappointment no one took up this battle cry or even cheered. Their attention was on something behind him. As Skyver turned to look, Furgul turned too.

Behind the line of Traps, some workmen had erected two ladders against the cellblock wall. They climbed up the ladders holding a long roll of cloth between them. They nailed the cloth to the wall and let it unfurl downward. It was a giant yellow banner with big red letters. In the middle was a huge painting of a dog. It was a really stupid-looking dog. In fact, it didn't look much like a dog at all. Its eyes were too large, its ears were too big, and its tongue hung down to its knees. In one hand it held a spoon—and in the other a bowl of biscuits.

"They're taunting us!" said Zinni.

"What does that mean?" asked Cyril, the pit bull.

"They're making fun of us," Zinni explained.

The pack growled with anger. Furgul turned back to face them.

"Take your positions," he ordered. "Brennus, you and I and the big dogs charge in the front line. The Traps will shoot at us first. Zinni, your gang will charge right behind us. While the Traps are reloading their guns, go for their ankles. Skyver—Skyver?"

Furgul looked about. Skyver suddenly seemed six inches shorter. He was crawling on his belly toward the rear of the gang of mutts. He stopped.

"I'm going undercover!" said Skyver. "I'm planning a sneak attack!"

"When Zinni's gang brings the Traps down, you charge with the mutts to finish them off."

Barking fiercely, the dogs drew themselves up in three battle lines.

Furgul joined Brennus at the front. The big dogs were eager to attack.

The Traps stood motionless, their clubs and nooses and guns at the ready.

"This is it!" said Furgul. "Charge on my command!"

Then a strange new commotion boiled up around the cellblock door.

"Wait!" ordered Furgul.

A whole bunch of cameramen spilled from the cellblock. They pointed their cameras at the dogs and clicked. There were a lot of blinding flashes, and Furgul wondered if this was some strange new weapon. Even more bizarrely, two women appeared—a redhead and a blonde—but they looked nothing like the two shelter workers. They were wearing scanty clothes and tottered on pointy shoes with very high heels. They shivered in the cold, which wasn't surprising, but when the cameras pointed toward them, they smiled with very white teeth and contorted their bodies.

"Can we attack them as well?" asked Zinni.

"No," said Furgul, "they don't have any weapons."

The women in the pointy shoes stepped aside, and the cameras clicked even faster as a big man emerged. He wore a big suit and a big watch and had the biggest, whitest teeth that Furgul had ever seen. With the women on either arm, he went to stand beneath the banner with the picture of the stupid dog. The cameras followed like a herd of geese. But all of them were careful to stay behind the line of armed Traps.

Furgul and the pack watched it all with amazement.

The big man smiled at the cameras a lot. Someone pointed a stick with a fuzzy ball on the top at his face. Then the big man started to talk and wave his arms. He pointed at the banner. He pointed at the dogs. His face became very sad, though Furgul could tell at once that he was just pretending. Then the big man started to drone.

"Drone, drone, drone!" he droned.

"Furgul?"

Furgul turned. His heart leaped when he saw Jodi walking over.

"It looks like you were serious about fighting," she said.

"We're still serious," said Furgul. "But who's the guy?"

"He calls himself the Greatest Dog Lover in the World," said Jodi, "and right now he's the best friend you've got. That's Chuck Chumley, the dog-food tycoon."

"What's a tycoon?" asked Furgul.

Jodi smiled. "A man with lots and lots and lots and lots of money."

Furgul almost gave Zinni permission to attack him. Then he got it.

"You mean he's going to pay for the Needles to become a no-kill shelter?"

"That's right," said Jodi. "You'll all be taken care of. And so will all the dogs who come here in the future. Chumley's agreed to hire good Vets. He'll build a new shelter. No more 'five days to live.' No dog will ever be killed at this pound again, even if he or she is dangerous. You did it, Furgul."

"Why is Chuck Chumley being so kind?" asked Furgul.

"He's not really being kind, just clever," said Jodi. "I explained to him that if he saved you rebel dogs, the publicity would make him famous all over the world."

"You mean the TV?"

"The TV, the newspapers, and every sack and tin of Chumley's Extra Meaty Dog Feed that he sells. In fact, he'll sell so much extra dog food that he'll make a huge profit from funding the new pound. But at least you'll be alive."

Furgul turned to look at Chuck Chumley. He was posing in front of the banner for the cameras, both fists raised above his head in a gesture of triumph. "Boast! Brag! Preen!" cried Chumley. While Chumley showed off and peddled his products, Furgul trotted back to the waiting army of dogs. Most of them still had no idea what was going on.

"We told them we wanted food, and we got it," said Furgul.

The pack pricked up their ears.

"We asked for the best Vets, and we've got them too."

The pack started wagging their tails.

"We told them we wanted a no-kill shelter—and that's what we're going to get."

The pack let out a huge rebel yell.

"That's right!" said Furgul. "No more dogs will die at the Needles!"

Skyver jumped up in front of him and yelped, "In other words: WE WON! PRAISE BE TO ME!"

Skyver jerked his head at Cyril the pit bull, who, as if remembering instructions, barked: "THREE CHEERS FOR SKYVER!"

The dogs cheered and barked. Skyver stood on his hind legs while the pit bulls scampered around him.

Furgul looked at Jodi. She was the first human being he had ever trusted. And she hadn't let him down.

"For the humans," said Jodi, "the hero of the riot will be Chuck Chumley."

"That's fine by me," said Furgul. "I just want to get out of here."

"I'd still love to take you back to Appletree."

"On one condition."

"What's that?"

"I want you to take Brennus and Zinni." Furgul hesitated. "And Skyver too."

"Which one is Skyver?"

"He's the tattiest, mangiest, dirtiest, scruffiest, craftiest, greediest dog you ever saw."

CHAPTER TWELVE

THE SANCTUARY

Jodi drove them away from the Needles and into the night. The dogs were exhausted and fell asleep at once—Furgul in the passenger seat, Brennus filling up the rear, Skyver and Zinni curled on a blanket in the trunk space of Jodi's truck. When Furgul woke up, it was dawn. Jodi had stopped the car outside a big old ramshackle house, and the four dogs climbed out. They blinked and stretched and shook themselves awake. They looked about the landscape in the rise of the sun, and their jaws opened wide with amazement.

The house was surrounded by rolling meadows and lots of splendid trees. Oak and ash, maple and birch, yew and rowan, holly and hawthorn and elm. In an orchard the apple trees were covered with blossoms. A stream tumbled through the orchard, and as the dogs took it all in, birds of every kind began to sing.

"How do you like your new home?" asked Jodi.

"It's beautiful," said Zinni.

"Magnificent," said Brennus.

"Do we have cable TV?" asked Skyver.

Jodi looked at Furgul. "What do you think?"

Furgul said, "I'm going for a run."

Life at Appletree Dog Sanctuary was everything Jodi had promised. Brennus gradually recovered his health and strength. Zinni was happy not to live inside a rich woman's purse; in fact, she proved to be unusually agile and athletic, weaving, scrambling and leaping through the woods, and sometimes even outmaneuvering Furgul on her short, nimble legs. Skyver was appalled to discover that Jodi didn't own a TV, but he passed his time spinning ever taller tales to the other dogs who already lived there.

Furgul loved the freedom of Appletree, but as time passed he found it hard to settle down. His soul was restless. The wild and rambling road, for all its dangers, was where he felt he belonged. And Keeva preyed more and more on his mind. While the other dogs slept and ate in an old barn near Jodi's house, Furgul trained himself to live in the open countryside. He found the spots in the woods where leaves were thickest to shelter from the rain. He made a nest of pine needles and bracken. He learned to eat berries, roots and rotting fruit. He ate beetles, insects and worms. He learned to kill rabbits, hares and rats, snakes and voles, stoats and ducks. Sometimes he went hungry. He became hard and lean and tough. The other dogs thought he was crazy, and perhaps he was. Sometimes he missed the comfort of living with the pack, but he knew it would weaken his resolve. Furgul was always preparing for the day when he'd return to Dedbone's Hole and free Keeva.

Brennus became a great mentor. The wise old Saint Bernard taught him many things about the human world and schooled him in the lore of the Doglands. He showed Furgul how to find his way at night by looking at the Dog Star—the brightest in all the sky. He explained how the phases of the moon might affect a dog's moods, which meant that certain days were better than others for getting certain things done—or for exploring certain thoughts and feelings. He talked about the theory of the Doglines—*"the paw prints of the ancestors"*—which form a web of invisible pathways that wander all over the earth. These days most modern dogs had never even heard of the Doglines, but Brennus told him all he knew. He also told him legendary tales about the life and times of Argal. Argal had been a king, but Brennus was a shaman, and he instructed Furgul in secrets that even Argal hadn't known.

When Furgul struggled with the urge to search for Keeva, Brennus would say, "Be patient and wait for your moment. For your moment will come. And remember that you have to see it, for it's easily missed."

Various other dogs lived at the sanctuary, and from time

to time one of them would leave to live with a nice new owner. The new owners offered good homes, and if Jodi trusted them, and if the chosen dog liked them, they would take the dog away. That gave Jodi the space to rescue another poor dog. Brennus was a little too old to move on, and Jodi never offered him up for adoption. Lots of people wanted to take Zinni, but in Zinni's opinion they were never quite good enough, and she always chose to stay.

Because Furgul wasn't around so much, Skyver appointed himself the ambassador of the pack. He was good at judging people and always took part in deciding which dog should go with which new owner. Because he enjoyed the power and the sense of importance—and, as Brennus once pointed out, because no new owner would be fool enough to take him—Skyver also stayed with Jodi.

Furgul never offered himself for adoption. He didn't intend to stay at Appletree forever, but he didn't want to deceive a new owner into taking him just so he could run away. His thoughts of Keeva troubled him more and more. The problem was that Dedbone's Hole was likely very far away—and he had no idea where it was.

He told Jodi the story of Dedbone's Hole, of how he and his sisters had been trapped in the box and how he had managed to escape. Jodi was very angry to hear about the greyhound farm, but she didn't know where it was either. She tried to find it, but 'Dedbone' wasn't a real human name; it was the name the dogs had called him. Then Jodi had an idea.

"Keeva's a successful racer, isn't she?"

"One of the best," said Furgul. "That's why Dedbone wouldn't harm her."

"What's Keeva's racing name?"

Furgul racked his brains. He couldn't remember. To him, Keeva was always Keeva. He vaguely remembered that Keeva had once told him her racing name. But it was long ago, when he was just a puppy, and he hadn't really listened. It was a silly name, a money name, so why should he remember?

"I don't know," he said. "Why do you ask?"

"If I knew Keeva's racing name, I could trace her owner. You see, in order to race at the track, she has to be registered."

"What does that mean?"

"When the tracks schedule a race, they put the names of the runners in the newspaper. That way, the gamblers can decide which dog to bet on."

Furgul thought about this. "So, whenever there's a race, the names of the greyhounds are written in the newspaper."

"Yes."

"Okay," said Furgul. "Every time there's a race somewhere, I want you to read all the names to me. If I hear Keeva's racing name, I think I'll recognize it."

Weeks passed by, and each time there was a race Jodi read out the names of the racers. Furgul listened carefully to endless lists that made little sense to him—"Dust Devil," "Late Arrival," "Regency Stuart," "White Lightning," "Monkey

Business"—but he never heard a name that reminded him of Keeva.

"Don't give up," said Jodi. "If Keeva is still racing, we'll find her."

One day two men came to the sanctuary to adopt a dog. Furgul didn't usually take much interest in these matters, but he smelled them from the field. They smelled of engine grease, hot dogs and cotton candy. They hadn't washed for weeks. He knew at once that they were not real dog lovers. They smelled like men whose only real love was money. He ran over to the house to investigate. A battered pickup truck stood outside with one door open. Various strange dog smells drifted out, but none of them dogs that Furgul would care to meet. He found the two men having an argument with Jodi. Brennus and Zinni stood at Jodi's sides to protect her. They were glad to see Furgul.

Jodi was being very cold toward the men. She could see for herself that they weren't dog lovers. She shook her head and spoke sternly in human tongue.

"No. No. No," said Jodi. She folded her arms across her chest.

One man was young and skinny and had crusty red spots all over his face. The older man had blue-black tattoos on his neck. He waved a rolled-up newspaper in his fist.

"Argue! Argue! Argue!" said Tattoo.

Spotty pointed at the barn, where the other dogs were. Evidently, he wanted one.

"Gripe! Gripe! Gripe!" griped Spotty.

Tattoo noticed Furgul, and his eyes lit up. He pointed at Furgul.

"Perfect!" said Tattoo. "Perfect! Perfect! Perfect!"

"Give! Give! Give!" demanded Spotty.

Furgul bared his teeth and gave them a low, menacing growl that meant: *You'd better get back in your truck while you can still walk.*

Brennus backed him up with a savage bark, which meant: *We'll eat your shins to start with, then work upward till you beg us to tear out your throats.*

And I'll claw your eyes out too! snarled Zinni.

Both men turned white and stepped backward. Jodi smiled.

Furgul caught a sniff of something intense, a rich, over-ripe aroma, with a hint, perhaps, of turmeric and ginger. It was coming from the pickup truck. He turned as Skyver trotted over, looking pleased with himself. Skyver rose up on his hind legs and panted up at Tattoo. The men scowled and shooed Skyver away.

"Goodbye!" said Jodi.

She gave the men a wave. Tattoo spat on the ground at Jodi's feet.

As one, the four dogs snarled into action and went for one ankle each. The two men danced away in panic. Tattoo swiped at Zinni with his rolled-up paper, and Brennus gave his arm a light crunching with his giant teeth. The newspaper fell to the ground. Both men turned and sprinted away for their truck.

"Let them go," said Skyver. "The best is yet to come."

The two terrified men jumped back in their truck. Skyver wagged his tail with joy as Tattoo sat down behind the steering wheel and slammed the door. Both men started bellowing and groaning with horror.

"What did you do?" said Jodi to Skyver.

"The driver's seat was lovely and warm," said Skyver. "And after the tin of Chumley's Curry Supreme I ate last night, I needed a poop real bad."

Tattoo and Spotty jumped out of the truck holding their noses. The four dogs growled with maximum ferocity and charged at the two men. Tattoo and Spotty jumped back into the truck even faster than they'd jumped out. The dogs barked with laughter as the truck drove away, Tattoo's head sticking out of the window as he gasped for air.

Zinni said, "It's going to be a long drive home."

When the dogs turned around, Jodi was reading the newspaper that Tattoo had dropped on the ground. As the dogs trotted toward her, Jodi looked at Furgul. "Does 'Sapphire Breeze' ring any bells?"

That night Furgul couldn't sleep. He wandered around the fields thinking about Sapphire Breeze. As soon as Jodi had read out the name, he had remembered: Sapphire Breeze was Keeva. And she was racing tomorrow evening at a track that wasn't too far away. Jodi had promised to take Furgul to the track, to make sure it was Keeva. Then she'd find out who owned Keeva and start the process of shutting down Dedbone's Hole for good.

"How can you do that?" Furgul had asked.

"I don't like greyhound racing," said Jodi. "For every twenty greyhounds they breed, only one is good enough to race. Most of the rest get abandoned or killed. The lucky ones get adopted or come to places like this. But even the greyhound business doesn't allow such abuse as you described at Dedbone's Hole. There are laws and societies for the prevention of cruelty to animals. They'll try to put Dedbone in jail."

"Jail's too good for Dedbone," said Furgul.

"Maybe. But what counts is liberating Keeva and the other greyhounds."

"Can Keeva come here, to Appletree?"

"Of course she can."

"And the other greyhounds?"

"I'll make sure they're well cared for, somewhere. Perhaps I'll give Chuck Chumley another call."

The hope in Furgul's heart was almost painful. "How long will it take?" he asked.

"I'll find out who Dedbone is tomorrow evening. Next day I'll get the society to start an urgent official investigation. It shouldn't take more than a few days."

"A few days?"

"We have to be patient, Furgul, and do this right."

Now Furgul prowled up and down beneath the trees in the dark, imagining what it would be like to see Keeva. Would she recognize him, now that he'd grown so much bigger? Surely she would. Argal had known him. Would Keeva still love him? He hadn't been able to save Eena and Nessa. And Brid was lost, perhaps forever. Would Keeva forgive him?

As he turned these questions over in his mind, he heard a squeal of pain.

His ears pricked up toward the sound. It came from beyond the old stone wall that surrounded the sanctuary. Furgul ran over in the light of the moon, which was almost full. He heard the squeal again—it sounded like a young puppy. He sniffed, but all he could detect was a bitter chemical smell, such as Harriet had liked to spray all over her house, especially the kitchen and the bathroom. Humans thought it smelled like flowers or pine trees, but there was nothing natural about the smell at all. With the chemicals in his nostrils, Furgul couldn't pick up the real scents beyond the wall.

"Who's there?" he barked.

"Help me," cried a little dog's voice. "I think my paw's broken."

The wall was too high for the other dogs, but as part of his training, Furgul had been jumping over it for some time. He trotted back into the field, turned and sprinted forward. At just the right distance he slowed, sprang with all the power in his hind legs and rose up. As he cleared the wall, he saw a little puppy lying near some bushes. His leg was all twisted, and he was crying. Furgul landed nearby and turned to the puppy. The chemical smell was all over the place. Furgul was suspicious. Only a human would spray it. But why spray it just here?

"Please, help me!" begged the pup.

Furgul looked all around but didn't see anything. It didn't make sense.

"Where did you come from?" said Furgul. "How did you get here?"

"I don't know," said the puppy. "Everything went dark, then my leg hurt."

The puppy wasn't lying. The sooner they got out of here, the better. Furgul bent over and grabbed the puppy by the scruff of the neck with his teeth. He picked him up and turned to carry him back to the house. He heard a rustle in the bushes and dropped the pup and started to dodge away. But too late.

He heard a sound: CLACK-CLACK!

Then something hard as steel hit Furgul's skull. He staggered, still trying to get away, trying to open his jaws to bite, but a sack was thrown over his head and he couldn't see. He struggled but there were two of them. He felt ropes wrap around him and tighten, trapping him in the sack. He heard the poor puppy squealing and heard several heavy blows with the steel bar. The puppy fell silent.

Furgul knew there was no point in fighting the ropes. The men would only hit him again and that would make him weaker. Furgul played dead. He felt the two men pick him up. As they carried him away the chemical stink got weaker, and he got a whiff of something he recognized: the rancid odor of Spotty and Tattoo. They dumped him in the bed of their truck, swearing and chuckling with glee. Then they drove away into the night—and Furgul left Appletree farther and farther behind.

Chapter Thirteen

THE CARNIVAL

Spotty and Tattoo were crafty. When they got Furgul out of the sack, they didn't untie the ropes until they'd fastened a choke-collar around his neck. The choke-collar and leash were made of steel chain. They also put a muzzle over his snout. He couldn't bite and he couldn't run away. Furgul decided there was no point in fighting until he had a chance to win. When they pulled on the leash, he jumped from the back of the truck without resistance.

It was morning now, and the scents he'd smelled on the dognappers—cotton candy, hot dogs and engine grease—saturated the air. As Tattoo pulled him along with vicious—and unnecessary—tugs on the choker, Furgul took a look around.

They were on a sprawl of wasteland at the edge of a town.

The wasteland was covered with enormous, dirty machines and with funny little brightly colored shacks full of gimcracks and glitter. In fact, the whole place seemed to be built from color and dirt.

There was a giant wheel festooned with colored buckets. There was a railway that went up and down—over towering peaks and plunging dips—with colored carriages sitting in a row on the tracks. There was a contraption with long metal arms, like a giant spider's, and at the end of the arms were colored coaches with bright red plastic seats. The little shacks were painted with colored stripes and hung with colored balloons. There were colored flags and colored plastic castles and colored fake horses hanging from stripy poles. The colors were so many and so loud, you could almost hear them shouting.

Yet everything was smeared with dirt, and the place was quiet.

None of the machines were moving. And no one was living in the little stripy shacks. A few people mooched around here and there, but they didn't speak to each other. Their clothes were as brightly colored as the machines, and their faces were just as dirty. Furgul didn't know where he was, but he knew he didn't like it.

Tattoo dragged him through the dirt toward a holding pen that was fenced and roofed with wire mesh. At the back was a filthy kennel made of corrugated iron. Furgul's nose detected a gang of dogs. The dogs, like the people, stank of junk food and nasty habits. Bad people and bad dogs were a bad combination. Furgul felt a clench of fear in his belly. He remembered what Argal had said.

When you're scared is the only time you really need to be brave.

Furgul saw the dogs in the cage, and the dogs saw him. They pressed their noses to the wire and checked him out, their black nostrils writhing, their slavering mouths hanging open to reveal rotting teeth. There were four of them, all skanky mutts. They must have been picked for their spiteful and obnoxious temperaments: mixed-up breeds of Doberman and corgi, pit bull and collie, and others too weird to untangle. Dogs who'd been born mean, and whose masters had treated them badly to make them meaner.

Tattoo unlocked the gate of the holding pen and spat curses at the dogs. Mean though they were, the dogs were terrified and cringed away. Tattoo loosened the choke-chain and slipped it from Furgul's neck and kicked him inside. The boot caught him hard on one hind leg. But Tattoo didn't take Furgul's muzzle off. Furgul couldn't use his teeth to defend himself.

"Welcome to the carnival, dogbait," said one of the mutts.

"Give him a break, Gremlin," said another. "The dogbait hasn't had his breakfast yet."

"Neither have we, Lunk," said Gremlin. "But it's just walked in the door."

The gang laughed and slavered, their drool making pools in the dirt.

Furgul didn't respond. These dogs had done this before. Many times before. He could see it in their soulless eyes and smell it on their breath. He had to keep calm and think it through. Argal had given him advice on how to fight in a muzzle.

A muzzle takes away your teeth, but look around—there are teeth everywhere.

Furgul's eyes roved the pen. He spotted a nail sticking out two inches from a fence post. He saw a couple of sharp, rusty edges on the corrugated iron of the walled kennel at the rear. Just in front of the kennel was a stout metal trough on legs, which stank of rancid hot dogs and french fries. Between the roof of the kennel and the roof of the pen, there was just enough room to stand up in.

Turn your enemy's attack against him. Use speed, timing and position.

Furgul felt out the ground beneath his paws. It was slick with drool and other filth. His eyes returned to Gremlin. Gremlin was the type of nasty little rat dropping who liked to talk tough—as long as there were other dogs to do the fighting.

"The masters are always stealing lurchers and greyhounds," said Gremlin. "They've only got one use for you lot—and none of you ever come back."

Gremlin stared at him. Furgul stared back. It was a battle for dominance.

The fight is won or lost before it starts. Never be the first to blink.

Furgul remembered Argal's awesome stare, when they'd first met in the Trap truck. After holding the eyes of the king, looking into Gremlin's hateful little face was as challenging as staring down a hamster. After only a few seconds, Gremlin blinked and turned away. His cronies hooted and mocked him.

"Did you see that, Freak?" crowed Lunk. "Gremlin's scared of the dogbait."

Freak rolled his massive shoulders. "Dog—bait," he mumbled, very slowly.

Freak deserved his name. His yellow coat was shaggy and matted with grime. His big flat head was misshapen, as if a mastiff had mated with a donkey. His teeth were as dirty and yellow as his coat. Furgul guessed that his brain was no larger than a peanut, and that even at that size, half of it had never been used.

"Very good, Freak," said Gremlin. "That's the longest word you've ever learned. And I'm *not* scared of the dogbait, Lunk. I just got something stuck in my eye." Gremlin scrubbed his eye with a paw, but no one was fooled, not even Freak.

"Does the dogbait want to scare *me*?" said the fourth dog.

Furgul looked at him. The fourth dog wasn't as big or as monstrous as Freak, but he looked to be the most dangerous of the four. His eyes were cold, and his spirit was dead, extinguished by countless beatings. All that was left inside him was the need to hurt other dogs, the same way that his masters had hurt him.

"Well, *do* you want to scare me? Dogbait?" said the fourth dog.

"Take it easy, Chopper," said Lunk. "The masters will want the dogbait fit for work. Nothing worse than flesh wounds, remember? Just enough blood to make him tempting to the guard dogs. He's got to be able to run fast."

"I know the routine," growled Chopper. "By the time I've finished, the dogbait will be running faster than a rat on fire."

Furgul had no idea what they were talking about. He didn't bother to ask. He was still staring at Chopper's eyes without blinking. Any second now Chopper would make his move. Furgul decided to provoke him.

"Tell me, Chopper," said Furgul. "Why do dogs who can't fight always have such tough names?"

Chopper hurtled toward him with a growl of rage, his teeth bared and gnashing. Furgul stepped aside and circled behind him. The wind of Chopper's snapping jaws blew through Furgul's whiskers. Chopper tried to halt his furious charge but skidded on the slippery ground. He smashed into Freak, and Freak, without thinking, bit a piece out of Chopper's ear. Chopper snapped back.

"Not me, you yellow oaf!" said Chopper. "I'm fighting the dogbait, not you."

Freak lumbered backward into the fence. "Dogbait," he drooled.

Chopper charged again. Furgul took off across the pen, Chopper's fangs snapping at his tail. The metal trough loomed in front of him. Just before he got there, Furgul coiled his hind legs and powered up into the air. As he landed on the roof of the kennel, he heard Chopper crash into the trough. He glanced down. Perfect position.

"Where is he?" roared Chopper.

Chopper's head was right over the trough, his throat above the hard metal rim. Furgul dropped down from the roof, curling his legs underneath him. He landed full force on the back of Chopper's neck. His weight smashed Chopper's throat down onto the hard metal rim of the trough with a loud crack. Furgul landed on his feet and backed away.

Chopper twitched in jerky spasms. Pink foam spilled from his mouth.

His cold, dead eyes would be cold and dead forever.

Furgul had never killed a dog before, but he felt no remorse. He hadn't started this fight. He was muzzled and outnumbered. And Chopper wouldn't bully greyhounds anymore. Chopper had gotten what he deserved.

"Dogbait!" roared Freak.

Furgul turned as Freak pounded toward him. What Freak lacked in speed he made up for in strength and fury. Furgul glanced ahead at the kennel. For an instant—with a shock—he saw the gleam of deep, dark eyes inside the door. But then they vanished. He glanced back at Freak and waited for the monster dog to come.

"Dogbait!" roared Freak.

At the last moment Furgul ducked sideways, and Freak

lurched after him, trampling on Chopper's corpse. Furgul spun around and stuck his hind leg out, right between Freak's front paws. Freak tripped, tumbled onto his face and went head over heels. His back slammed into the kennel, and a sharp rusty edge of corrugated iron sliced him open to the bone. Freak howled with pain and rage and scrambled to his feet. He wanted to get his teeth into Furgul. Freak charged again.

Furgul ran across the yard but slowed until the brute was right on his heels. Furgul looked up ahead. There it was. He ran straight toward the fence post. An inch away, he braked and skipped to the left, the wire mesh scraping along his flanks. He heard a great clunk, and the whole pen shook and rattled like a giant tambourine.

Furgul turned.

Freak had run headfirst into the fence post, just as Furgul had intended. He stood there panting and growling as if nothing had happened. But when he tried to move he couldn't do it. He shook his head from side to side, and the pen rattled even louder. Freak couldn't turn around. Furgul took a closer look. The nail sticking out of the fence post had driven straight through Freak's forehead. The nail must have missed his brain because Freak seemed as strong as ever. He seemed just as stupid too.

"Dogbait! Dogbait! Dogbait!" howled Freak.

Furgul left Freak to rattle the cage and turned to Lunk and Gremlin.

"Two down, two to go."

Without the big bullies to protect them, Lunk and Gremlin huddled together like the nasty little cowards they were. Furgul panted to cool down. He'd never felt more alive. He breathed deep through his nostrils. Beyond the foul stench of dying dogs, grease and carnival filth, he thought he detected a scent from long ago.

Lunk and Gremlin barked in panic at whoever was inside the kennel.

"The dogbait's killing us! Help!" pleaded Lunk. "We need you!"

"We're sorry we wouldn't let you join the gang!" wailed Gremlin.

Furgul turned toward the kennel. So there was another dog in there.

Just at that moment he heard a "plop!" Freak was sitting back on his haunches, staring at the wet nail in the fence.

"Freak, hurry!" barked Gremlin. "Let's rush him! He can't take us all at once!"

Furgul watched Gremlin and Lunk dart toward him, their sharp teeth bared to nip at his tail while Freak and the mystery dog attacked him. Freak had turned around from the fence post. The leaking hole between his eyes didn't seem to bother him at all. He shambled toward Furgul, smacking his lips. But what bothered Furgul most was the mystery dog. He glanced over his shoulder at the kennel. He felt a ferocious power in there, lurking inside the dark doorway.

Freak, Lunk and Gremlin closed in on him.

"Here she comes!" cried Lunk. "Lend her a claw, boys!"

A thunderbolt, black as midnight, exploded from the gloom of the kennel.

She was fast.

Much faster than Chopper. And almost as fast as Furgul. Furgul's plan was to dodge behind Lunk and Gremlin and tangle them up. As the devil dog closed in behind him, Furgul sprang forward, jumping over Lunk's head. He landed and turned, ready to run, but what he saw stopped him right in his tracks.

The devil dog was a stunning German shepherd, but instead of coming at Furgul, she went straight for Freak's throat and sunk her teeth in. With one savage twist of her head she left Freak panting his last in the blood-slaked dirt. She whirled and sprang at Lunk, who was too shocked with horror to move. A second later Lunk lay dying too. The shepherd turned on Gremlin with the gore of both victims dripping from her fangs.

Gremlin squealed with terror and ran to the wire. He scrabbled at the dirt like a mole deranged, trying to dig a hole beneath the fence, though he must have known he would never make it. The shepherd walked over. As Gremlin whimpered for mercy, she crunched her jaws through the back of his neck, and it was over.

She turned to look at Furgul. She'd changed a lot since last they'd met. Cruelty and abuse, and the company of evil, had changed her. What was most amazing was this: While killing the three cur dogs, she hadn't made a single sound.

Not a bark, not a growl, not a whisper.

She didn't play at fighting anymore.

She was silent death.

"Hello, Dervla," said Furgul.

Dervla didn't answer. She held his gaze.

There was a darkness in her eyes that came from somewhere painful deep inside. Dervla had learned how to hate. She'd become a ruthless killer. Furgul's heart went out to her. Yet despite all she'd been through, despite the many scars on her hide and the scars on her soul, she still seemed lovely to him. She walked past him and poked at Freak's body with her paw. Furgul wondered if she still knew how to smile.

"I don't think he's going to get up," said Furgul.

"You'd better believe it."

She wasn't smiling, but at least she knew how to talk. Furgul had the feeling that she hadn't done even that in a long, long time. She looked at him.

"That was a neat trick, with the nail," she said.

"Something my dad told me. There are teeth everywhere."

Dervla licked the blood from her whiskers. "Hope I didn't spoil your fun."

Furgul laughed, but Dervla wasn't joking. He could see she'd enjoyed the killing. And why not? Dervla was a born huntress. And she'd saved his life.

"Dervla," said Furgul, "I'm very happy to see you."

Dervla said, "I'm happy to see you too."

• • •

Dervla chewed through the strap of Furgul's muzzle. What a relief it was to get it off. Then she made herself comfortable by using Freak's corpse as a bed.

"It's the biggest spot in the yard that isn't covered with slime," she explained.

Furgul thought this was a very good idea. He went over to where Chopper lay and quickly checked his coat for evidence of fleas. To his surprise he didn't find any and grabbed Chopper by the scruff of his broken neck. He dragged him into a sunny spot near Dervla and settled down on top of him. Chopper was a bit bony, but his body was a big improvement over lying in the blood and the ooze.

"They won't start stinking too badly before tonight," said Dervla. "By that time you'll be gone. And I'll never see you again."

"What do you mean?"

"Furgul," she said, "I'm glad to see you're still in one piece. And they haven't broken you inside yet, which is even better. But don't expect me to get close to you. When you leave I don't want to have to care. I don't want to care at all. And you will leave. The masters will make sure of that, just like they did the last time we met. And believe me, this time, we'll never see each other again."

With a sudden sick feeling in his stomach, Furgul realized that Dervla was saying that she had been broken inside. For a moment he couldn't believe it. Then he saw the expression in her eyes. A terrible sadness came over him. He didn't want to think about the horrible things they had done to her. He didn't want to argue with her either.

"Do you know why they called you dogbait?" asked Dervla.

Furgul shook his head.

"Because that's what you are," said Dervla. "You're bait for the guard dogs."

"What guard dogs?"

"Tattoo and Spotty are thieves. Burglars. They break into the houses of rich people, when the rich people are away. Then they steal loot."

"You mean money?"

"Money and things they can sell for money. Jewelry, gold watches, music machines, TVs, even clothes. Anything they can carry. But some of the rich have guard dogs. Like me."

"You're a guard dog?"

Dervla pointed to the strange machines and giant trucks outside the wire.

"Every night they leave me out there to frighten off people who might try to steal from them. Thieves are always thinking about thieving, so they're afraid they'll get robbed themselves. They also expect me to let them know if the cops show up."

"Why don't you run away?" asked Furgul.

"You see that?"

Dervla pointed with her snout. Furgul looked. Just outside

the wire mesh lay five coils of steel chain. Each chain was very long.

Dervla said, "They chain us to the trucks and the machines."

Furgul looked at the bodies of the dead dogs. "They were guard dogs too?"

Dervla nodded. "Tonight we'll be short of staff. But Spotty and Tattoo will just steal some more. Like they stole me."

"How?"

"My mistress left me outside a supermarket while she went shopping. We dogs aren't allowed in shops. They're frightened we might carry germs on our paws." She scoffed. "There are more germs on a single human shoe than on the footpads of a thousand dogs. But humans are frightened of so many things, I think they must enjoy it."

"What happened next?" asked Furgul.

"Tattoo hit me on the head with his steel baton. Then they threw me in their truck in a sack and drove away."

Furgul rubbed the lump on the back of his skull with his hind paw.

"So they want me to help them rob a house," he said.

"You won't have a choice," said Dervla. "The really rich houses—the ones they most like to rob—have fences and gates all around them, and huge gardens or lots of land. They'll throw you over the fence so that the guard dogs will chase after *you*, not them. Then they'll sneak into the house and do their thieving. Most guard dogs are pretty stupid. They'd rather chase a dog than a human. That's why Spotty and Tattoo use greyhounds and lurchers—you can keep the guards running around until they've done their thieving."

"And then?"

"Then they drive away with their loot and leave you behind."

Furgul brightened up. Once he was off the leash, he could escape.

"I know what you're thinking," said Dervla. "But if the guards don't rip you apart, the cops will take you to the pound as a dangerous dog and you'll get the needle."

"I'll take my chances with the guard dogs," said Furgul. "And I'm not going back to any dog pound. Never again."

"Good luck to you," said Dervla. "I mean it."

"But you don't believe I'll get away."

Dervla said, "I don't believe in anything anymore. Except killing."

They lay in the sun on their bony beds, and Furgul told Dervla his adventures. He tried to make them sound funny, but he still couldn't make her laugh. Or even smile. Her ears pricked up the most when he told her the story of Argal and what Argal had said about living and dying and the winds. Her tail even started wagging. But when he told her how Argal had been killed, the hate flared back in her eyes. Furgul realized that the only place where Dervla would heal the wounds to her soul was at Appletree Dog Sanctuary. But Dervla would never get there.

Loud music started pumping from every direction. Furgul felt his chest vibrate and his ears hurt. The carnival filled up with people. They seemed happy and excited to be there. They crowded round the little stripy shacks, where they threw their money away. They ate hot dogs and sticky red apples on thin wooden sticks. They sat in the little colored buckets on the big wheel, and in the coaches of the giant metal spider, and in the carriages of the up-and-down railway. Then the strange machines began to move. The big wheel turned and the spider wheel whirled and the carriages climbed up the steeply sloped tracks of the railway. Then the people started screaming at the top of their lungs.

"Scream! Scream! Scream! Scream! Scream!!!"

Furgul was alarmed. "What's wrong with them?"

"They're frightened," said Dervla. "But like I said, they enjoy it."

"Is it always this weird?"

"Every day's the same until midnight. We'll stay here for a week, then we'll move all the machines to a different town. Different town, same music, same screams."

Furgul shook his head in amazement. He wanted to understand humans. He really did. But at times like this, he doubted that he ever would.

"Look out," said Dervla. "They've come to take you early."

Furgul was disturbed by the tone of Dervla's voice. She

sounded scared. How could a dog of her ferocity be scared? He turned as Spotty and Tattoo approached the holding pen. Tattoo held a tube of steel in his hand. He flicked it downward.

CLACK-CLACK!

Dervla flinched at the sound. The steel tube jumped and became much longer—it was an expandable baton. That must have been what he had used to hit Furgul on the head. He must have used it on Dervla too.

"Watch out for that steel rod," said Dervla. "Tattoo knows how to use it."

She saw the way that Furgul was looking at her. She hung her head.

"You don't understand," she said. "When they muzzle you and tie you up and then beat you with that rod—day after day, night after night—a time comes when you just can't take it anymore. You'll do anything not to be beaten again. Anything at all."

Tattoo and Spotty reached the pen and stared through the wire in shock at the four dead dogs. Then they looked at Dervla and started shouting and cursing and spitting with rage. Tattoo unlocked the door. Dervla ran to a corner and cringed in fear. Furgul was horrified to see her in such a state. In a way it was even more terrible than watching Argal go to his doom. Anger rose within him. How dare these dirty thieves do this to his friend. He felt his lips peel back from his teeth. His chest shook with a deep, menacing growl.

He stood in front of Dervla to protect her.

· Tattoo advanced with his steel rod in his hand. Behind him came Spotty, who was armed with the choke-leash made of steel chain. They shouted abuse and threats. But Furgul wasn't scared of such as these. Not anymore. He snarled.

Harm one hair on Dervla's coat and I will kill you where you stand.

Tattoo and Spotty stopped dead. The curses froze in their mouths. They knew a dangerous dog when they saw one. They murmured to each other as if making a plan. Furgul crouched ready for action. He knew he could take a whipping from the rod until his jaws clamped on Tattoo's throat. But the real danger was the choke-leash. It acted like a Trap's noose—once that was round his neck, Furgul was in trouble. He had to take Spotty out first. He could see by the way that Spotty handled the choke-leash that he'd done this before. These men were experts at handling dogs. But Furgul was faster than a skinny guy with scabs on his face. He'd take Spotty's thumb off. Maybe both his thumbs. Then it would be Tattoo's turn. He coiled his haunches for the attack.

"Furgul, don't!" barked Dervla. "Please. Don't do this for me."

"Stay back," growled Furgul, "I'm going to do them both."

"If you bite Spotty, Tattoo will just run out of the cage and lock us in," said Dervla. "He doesn't care about Spotty. He's a coward and he's sly. He won't stay to fight you. He'll just come back with more men, with clubs and guns."

Furgul studied Tattoo and knew she was right.

"Then I'll do Tattoo first," he said.

"Spotty's even more of a coward," said Dervla. "He'll run too. Please, I'll be fine. I'm the only guard they've got left. They need me. Go with them. Don't sacrifice your chance to escape because of me."

"If we team up now, we can take them both at once."

Dervla looked at Tattoo and cowered. "I can't," she said. "I just can't."

Furgul had never seen such blind terror as was written across her face.

"I can live with a few more beatings," she said. "I couldn't live with knowing that I'd cost you your shot at freedom."

Furgul hesitated. Spotty and Tattoo inched forward to surround him.

What would Argal do?

Argal had possessed the strength and size to smash both men down at once. Furgul didn't. It was time to wait—with the patience of a hunter—for a better time to fight. He let his lips cover his teeth again. He shook the killing fury from his muscles. He walked toward Spotty and offered his neck for the leash. Spotty slipped the slipknot of the chain over his head and held it short and pulled the choke-collar tight. When Tattoo was certain that Furgul couldn't fight back, he thrashed him across the shoulders with the vicious steel rod. Furgul clenched his jaws and refused to whimper. But after five blows he knew why Dervla had broken.

Spotty dragged Furgul from the pen. Tattoo locked the gate.

As they dragged him to their truck, Furgul looked back. Dervla stood at the wire, sobbing with guilt and shame.

"I'm sorry, Furgul!" cried Dervla. "I'm sorry! I'm sorry!"

"Don't give up, Dervla!" barked Furgul. "For we shall meet again!"

CHAPTER FOURTEEN

THE RACE

Furgul was chained in the bed of the truck by his leash. If he tried to jump out as they drove along, he'd be strangled. Furgul sat down on a pile of sacks—which he guessed they used for stealing dogs—and watched as they left the big wheel behind in the distance and the carnival noise of music and screams faded away.

He was hungry, but there was nothing he could do about that. He'd drunk some water in the holding pen earlier on. The ugliness of the town gave way to countryside. In the west the sun painted streaks of vermilion across the blue horizon. They drove past a grove of trees—oak and ash and willow in full leaf—a universe of green shifting this way and that in the breeze. The colors of nature were true. After the fake colors of the carnival, this vision of the wild raised his spirits. Then Furgul saw something so striking that he rose to his feet, his heart thumping.

As the truck swerved around a bend and cleared the trees, a black silhouette emerged against the skyline. It was tall and rugged, thrusting up into the early evening sky as if it wanted to touch the clouds. Furgul had seen that same silhouette as a pup, and he'd never forgotten it. The spirits of Eena and Nessa dwelled inside that stony tomb, along with those of countless hounds who had never known the Doglands. He wondered how many more had since been added to the hill of dead. Back then the shape of the towering rocks had made him think of a dog's head and snout. And it still did. But now, from this new angle, it didn't look like just any dog. With the jaws of its jagged double peak gaping open as if roaring in defiance at the heavens, it looked like Argal.

From now on, thought Furgul, *I'm going to call it Argal's Mountain.*

And if Argal's Mountain was just over there, it meant that Dedbone's Hole could not be too far away. Furgul looked again at the angle of the sun. Brennus had taught him that the sun rose in the east and set in the west. He thought back to that grim day when Dedbone had driven Eena and Nessa to their deaths. He closed his eyes and tried to remember what he'd seen when he stuck his head out of the cardboard box. Yes. That morning the sun had been behind them. That meant Dedbone's Hole lay somewhere to the east of Argal's Mountain. Furgul opened his eyes and looked at the silhouette again. The sun was going down behind it in the west.

That meant the truck—right now—was to the east of the mountain.

Dedbone's Hole was even closer than he'd thought.

He licked his nostrils to make them moist, then raised his nose into the air. He sniffed and sniffed, pointing his snout this way and that. He held his head still as he found it— right there. The scent was faint but unmistakable. The scent of many greyhounds in their crates. One of the earliest scents he'd ever known. The scent of the brutal hellhole into which he'd been born.

Dedbone's Hole.

Furgul looked back at the distant grove of trees. He imagined scraping a line with his paw between the trees and Argal's Mountain. Although he couldn't be sure exactly how far the scent had drifted, he reckoned that Dedbone's Hole lay somewhere near that line. He was that close to Keeva. But he was chained up in a truck.

Frustration rose inside him. He pulled at the chain and the slip-collar tightened up and choked him. The chain of his leash was knotted through a metal ring welded to the cab of the truck. He tried to bite through the steel. And couldn't. As he pulled again in anger, he saw Spotty watching him through the rear window of the cab. Spotty was laughing at him. Furgul stopped pulling. He had to be calm. He thought about what Brennus had told him.

Be patient and wait for your moment.

For your moment will come.

But remember that you have to see it, for it's easily missed.

Furgul turned away and lay down on the sacks. He had a worrying thought. Dervla had said that the thieves had picked him up early. She must have meant earlier than usual to travel to a burglary. And that might mean that the burglary was very far away. Far from Keeva and Dedbone's Hole. But he had to be patient. He had to wait for his moment—and he had to see it.

The truck hadn't traveled much farther when they reached another town. The light was fading, and the streets were full of cars and suffocating fumes. The truck turned this way and that, then they drove into a parking lot and stopped. Beyond the lot was a high brick wall. Beyond the wall rose tall metal stilts. At the top of the stilts was a huge rectangular array of powerful lights. The lights were pointing down at something behind the wall. He heard a loud, distorted human voice squawking words that he didn't recognize. He saw people streaming through a wide gate in the wall. It didn't seem like a very good place for a burglary.

Tattoo and Spotty untied him and took him through the gate.

Inside was a huge open space, bigger even than the carnival ground. People stood in long lines at rows of raised windows with holes in them. They shoved wads of money through the holes, and in return they got a little paper ticket.

These were the bettors putting bets on at the bookies. Beyond the bookies was a large building made of two giant slopes of seats. There were hundreds of people in the seats, chattering and drinking beer from paper cups. In front of the seats was a sandy road that wound around a grassy field in the shape of an enormous oval.

The grass oval was flattened on its two longest sides. The grass was surrounded by a white metal rail on the inside edge of the road. At the end of one of the roads was a long, white, rectangular box. In the front of the box was a row of barred gates. Furgul realized where he was.

This was a racetrack.

A metal bar, with something white and furry stuck on the end, began to whiz around the rail. To Furgul's amazement, the gates of the long white box shot up into the air, and six greyhounds erupted onto the track.

He was watching greyhounds race for the first time in his life. And for the first time he understood why human beings loved to watch them run. It was a sight of wonder and beauty such as Furgul had never seen.

The hounds hurtled down the track in a blur of pure movement, pure power. Furgul fancied himself a fast run- ner, but these dogs were something else. He marveled at the length of their stride, the speed of their footwork, the amount of time they spent in the air with each explosive double gallop. Their pads spent so little time on the ground, it seemed as if they were flying. He watched the way they handled the turn, the muscles bulging from their shoulders as they braked for the curve. Then they picked up speed again as they flooded down the back straight.

Keeva had told him, when he was a pup, that in all the world only one other animal was faster than a greyhound. It was a deadly wildcat that lived in a faraway land and was called a cheetah. Furgul felt a pride in his greyhound blood. He wanted to run with them. Then he became aware of a raucous noise.

The humans in the rows of seats were up on their feet. And they were screaming. Screaming, shouting, cheering, waving and yelling at the dogs as they ran. Each dog wore a colored blanket with a number on its back. And Furgul realized that the humans did not come because they loved to watch the beauty of the dogs. They came only to gamble money on which dog would win.

He imagined what would happen to the dogs who lost. The dogs who weren't good enough. The dogs who were too injured or old. He remembered, as well, that in order to serve human greed, these beautiful animals spent most of their lives in crates four feet long and three feet wide. Even the hellish holding pen at the carnival allowed its prisoners a bit more freedom than that.

Furgul turned away from the track. He didn't want to see who won the race.

The screaming died down, and the distorted voice started squawking again. Tattoo jerked on the leash, and Furgul followed him and Spotty through the crowd. They went to a gate that led to a restricted area called the paddock. Tattoo slipped some money to the man who guarded it. The guard opened the gate, and they went inside.

The paddock was busy with greyhounds in their numbered blankets. The dogs were of many different colors: fawn brindles and dark brindles, white and blacks, reds. Some had already raced and some were getting ready to race. Some discussed what had happened, and some discussed what was to come.

Furgul felt their excitement. They were isolated for twenty-three hours a day in their miserable crates. Who could blame them for being so happy at the track? A race lasted only forty seconds, but those precious seconds were the only real reward they ever got. Furgul felt a stab of sadness. After meeting so many other types of dogs, he realized how gentle greyhounds were. And how easily they were duped and intimidated by humans.

Trainers were checking the feet and muscles of their dogs and securing their blankets. Tattoo pulled Furgul along as he walked among them. By the way he moved his head Furgul knew Tattoo was looking for someone special. Tattoo stopped and called a name toward two men whose backs were turned toward them. Furgul felt a chill down his spine as one of the men turned. He was as massive and evil and bloated as ever, his eyes just as spiteful, his breath just as foul.

It was Dedbone.

Furgul felt the urge to go for his throat. But he controlled it.

Dedbone grinned at Tattoo and beckoned him over. Furgul caught a flash of light from a piece of yellow metal. He looked. It was a brass thumb attached to a human hand. The owner of the brass thumb waved at Tattoo and joined Dedbone. It was the Gambler. They were both here.

Furgul kept cool and went with Spotty and Tattoo. He'd grown and changed so much since he'd been a pup, he was sure neither Dedbone nor the Gambler would recognize him. Then Furgul's heart almost stopped as he saw someone who did. A gorgeous blue greyhound stood at the end of the leash in Dedbone's hand. She wore an orange blanket with a number "1." She was staring right at Furgul with tears in her eyes.

It was Keeva, his mother.

For a moment neither could speak. All the noise and chatter faded to a hum in Furgul's ears. There was so much he had to tell her, and so much that he didn't want to tell her, and so little time in which to do it. A racing muzzle was strapped around her snout. Furgul hated to see it. He couldn't think of anything clever to say, so he said something simple instead.

"So you're racing tonight, then, Mam."

"I'm running on the rail," said Keeva. "It's not my favorite slot, but I've won from there before. Fifteen wins in twenty-two starts this season."

"That's amazing."

"Come here, Furgul," she said.

He stepped closer. Keeva tried to lick his face, but the

muzzle stopped her. Furgul licked her cheek instead. She crooned with emotion.

Tattoo gave the chain a brutal tug and cursed him. Furgul ignored it.

Keeva looked at the shotgun scars on Furgul's body, and the scars on his face left by Tic, the bullmastiff. She trembled, trying not to cry.

"All this time," she said. "I thought you were dead."

"I escaped, just like you told me to," said Furgul. "Just like you said Argal would do. Brid escaped too, but I don't know where she is."

"And Eena? And Nessa?"

Furgul swallowed. "Eena and Nessa have gone."

For a moment Keeva turned away.

"I'm sorry, Mam," said Furgul. "I tried my best."

"I'm not blaming you, Furgul. I'm just so happy to see you alive."

Keeva glanced up at Tattoo. She tried to hide her horror that such an obviously vile man was Furgul's owner.

"Don't worry about Tattoo, Mam," he said. "He won't hold me much longer. And when I get away from him, I'm going to come to Dedbone's Hole and set you free. I've wanted to do it for a long time—ever since Nessa died in the crystal cavern."

Keeva looked even more horrified. "No, no, Furgul. You must never come back to the Hole. There are even more Bulls—Tic and Tac had a litter. The Gambler lives there all the time now. And Dedbone is more vicious than ever."

"All the more reason to get you out. Then I can show you the Doglands."

"Oh, Furgul," said Keeva. "The Doglands are just a fairy tale to make pups feel happy. They don't really exist."

"Yes, they do," said Furgul. "I'm in the Doglands here, right now, because the Doglands are in my heart."

He could see that Keeva almost pitied him for believing in such nonsense.

"It's hard to understand," said Furgul, "but Argal explained it to me."

Keeva stared at him. "You've met Argal?"

"Yes. He told me to tell you that he always loved you."

Keeva struggled to contain the powerful feelings tearing through her.

"We only spent a few hours together, in the Needles," said Furgul. "But he's still with me. He'll always be with me. If I could show you the Doglands, he'd be with you too. He's still out there—on the winds."

"You're talking as if he's dead," whispered Keeva.

"Only in this world, Mam. *A free dog never dies. He only moves on.* He gave his life so that other dogs could be free. Dogs like me and Brennus and Zinni."

"Argal spun those tales for me too," said Keeva. "The winds, the Doglands. No one could tell a story like Argal. That's why I loved him."

"They're not just stories," said Furgul. "If I could show you how to run with the winds, you'd know that."

"I know about the winds," said Keeva. "Racers talk about them all the time. If they blow in your face, they slow you down. If they blow from behind, you run faster. Just like a wet, muddy track makes you run slower than a hard, dry track. Weather conditions, that's all. The winds are just strong air moving though the sky."

Furgul almost wanted to bark with frustration. He'd never convince her here—in the paddock, at the track, in the very bowels of the racing system. Her brain as well as her body was ruled by this system. She'd been born and trained to be its slave. She'd never known anything else. More than anything else she was Dedbone's slave. Argal had been right about Keeva. She wasn't free inside. She didn't carry the Doglands in her heart. She didn't know how to. It made Furgul want to cry.

He also sensed it around him in the other racers. Even though greyhounds could run like no other dog, they couldn't run with the winds. It wasn't their fault. It was the fault of the masters who'd taught them that their only value lay in winning.

Furgul didn't push the subject any further. He didn't know how he'd spring Keeva from Dedbone's Hole. He didn't know when he'd do it. But he'd wait for his moment—for his moment would come.

"I can't wait to see you run—like a cheetah." He smiled. "I hope you win."

Keeva's eyes bored into him, as if something had awoken

in her and she wanted to hear more about Argal and the Dog-lands. Then Spotty took the leashes of both Furgul and Keeva and held them tight while Tattoo, Dedbone and the Gambler walked away toward the other side of the paddock.

"I will win," said Keeva. "But not the way I want to."

"What do you mean?"

"I've seen Tattoo work with Dedbone before," said Keeva. "They're going to pull a scam—a sting. They're going to cheat."

"How?"

"You see that big red?"

Keeva nodded to a superb red greyhound. Dedbone and Tattoo were walking right toward the big red and his master.

"That's Crimson Tide," said Keeva. "Great dog. I raced him once before, and he beat me by his whiskers. He's what they call the favorite in this race. That means the masters think that Tide is most likely to win. So most of the gamblers are betting their money on him."

Tattoo, the Gambler and Dedbone met Crimson Tide's master. As Tattoo shook hands with him, Furgul saw him slip Tide's master a roll of money. They all chatted and laughed. Then Tattoo crouched down to give Tide a pat on the head. As he did so—and as slyly as he'd passed on the money—he pushed what looked like a dog treat into Crimson Tide's mouth. Tide didn't like it and tried to spit it out. But Tattoo clamped Tide's long snout shut so the dog had to swallow the treat down. Tattoo stood up again. He winked at Dedbone.

"Did you see that?" asked Keeva. "They just doped him. There's a drug in that treat that will slow Tide down."

"Crimson Tide's master doesn't mind losing the race?"

"Tide will lose—and so will most of the bettors out there in the stadium. But his master and Tattoo and Dedbone will all win big. They'll bet all their cash on me and make a fortune. It's what they call a sting."

"So they've done this before?"

"Of course. Sometimes Dedbone dopes me. You see, they don't care about winning the race. They only care about winning the money."

Once again Furgul marveled at the craftiness and corruption of the masters.

"They're cheating to be certain you win tonight," he said. "But what if you didn't? What if you lose?"

"Then they would lose a fortune," said Keeva. "And Dedbone would probably drive me away in one of his cardboard boxes."

Dedbone and Tattoo came back and grabbed the leashes. The distorted voice started squawking. Here in the paddock it was even louder. This time Furgul understood some of the words: "Sapphire Breeze."

"I'm on," said Keeva. "When I come back, you won't be here. Tattoo will take you to the bookies window to make the bet with all their money."

Furgul wanted to talk, but Tattoo jerked on his leash while Dedbone jerked on Keeva's. Keeva put her neck on

Furgul's shoulder to hug him. She whispered.

"When you meet Argal again, on the winds, tell him I always loved him too."

Then Dedbone dragged Keeva away into the crowd.

"I love you, Mam!" barked Furgul.

But Keeva was gone.

Tattoo and Spotty dragged Furgul to the bookies windows.

"Sapphire Breeze," said Tattoo.

Furgul saw him exchange a big wad of cash for a paper ticket. By watching other gamblers, Furgul worked out that if they won, then they gave the ticket back and got even more cash in return. The two cheating thieves took Furgul to the edge of the track to watch the race.

"Squawk! Squawk! Squawk! Squawk! Squawk!" droned the disembodied voice.

The crowd got all excited. Tattoo grinned at Spotty and rubbed his hands.

The greyhounds were loaded into their boxes, Keeva in box number one, nearest the rail. Furgul didn't want to see Keeva win a cheated race any more than Keeva wanted to run it. But he'd never seen her fly and he wanted to. As he waited to see her hurtle down the track, the winds blew in from the evening redness in the west. The winds were warm and gentle yet full of mysterious power. Furgul tingled inside. Because they were so gentle, it took a moment for Furgul to understand. The mysterious power on the winds was love.

It was Argal.

Argal, too, had come to watch Keeva run.

The gates shot up into the air, and the greyhounds thundered out.

But this time only five dogs appeared.

And none of them was Keeva.

Foul curses spewed from Tattoo's mouth.

Then Keeva came out of her box. But instead of galloping—she danced. She danced and pranced and spun and cavorted with the winds that wrapped themselves around her. She was dancing once more with Argal, as they'd once danced long ago.

Furgul had never seen her filled with such joy. She was enraptured. The joy filled him too. Keeva had done it. She'd broken the system's invisible chains, right here, on the track—where it should have been impossible—surrounded by a thousand screaming gamblers.

Keeva had found the Doglands at last.

And then something even more astounding happened. As the five dogs reached the first turn of the oval, Crimson Tide looked back and saw Keeva. The big red dog stopped racing.

And he began cavorting too.

It was incredible. It was magnificent. But the spectators did not agree. Great sections of the crowd joined Tattoo in swearing and cursing and screaming.

Then a third hound dropped out and joined the ball.

And a fourth.

And a fifth.

Until only one dog—number six—was left to run down the final straight.

Uproar exploded through the crowd. Even the squawker began to sound hoarse. A small handful of the gamblers were happy—the ones who had bet their money on number six. They whistled and cheered for Six to keep going so that they would win their bets. Six loped toward the finish line.

But Keeva bounded toward Six from the opposite direction—still enchanted by the winds, still entwined with the spirit of Argal. Inches short of the finish line, Six stopped running too. He romped away toward the other dogs and never crossed it.

Pandemonium erupted across the stadium.

Glasses of beer, hot dogs and cigars rained down onto the track. None of the gamblers had won. Not a single one. They'd all lost their money to the bookies. As a crowd of them surged toward the gambling holes, in the hope of claiming a refund, metal shutters crashed down over all the windows. The bookies intended to keep every penny.

Furgul saw a sweaty giant stumble out of the paddock. It was Dedbone. Behind him came a furious mob of trainers, shaking leashes in their fists as if they'd like to string him up. Then a much bigger mob of angry bettors charged the trainers, and Dedbone and the trainers turned around. They sprinted back inside the paddock and locked the gate, with the mob at their heels. The rage of a thousand losers was deafening. It was music to Furgul's ears.

Tonight only the dogs had won. But the dogs didn't care. They were too busy running with the winds.

Furgul didn't know whether to laugh or cry.

It was the most beautiful greyhound race of all time.

Somewhere in the angry crowd, Furgul heard more laughter. Human laughter. A single voice. He scanned the sea of waving fists and flying garbage with his super-sharp eyes. He saw the laughing face. It was Jodi. Of all the people in that seething mob, only Jodi was delighted by the greyhounds and their victory. Furgul remembered: Tattoo had dropped a newspaper at Appletree. Of course. Jodi had planned to come to the track to find out who was the owner of Sapphire Breeze.

"Jodi!" he barked. "Jodi!"

But Jodi couldn't hear him. And Tattoo had had enough. He dragged Furgul out to the parking lot and chained him up in the truck. Tattoo was too enraged to drive, so Spotty took the wheel. Then they drove away from the track to do some thieving.

CHAPTER FIFTEEN

THE BURGLARY

The thieves had stopped the truck outside two tall iron gates. Tattoo and Spotty were doing something sneaky to the lock. Furgul was still chained in the bed of the truck. He listened to a frenzied chorus of barking. They certainly had the lungs of guard dogs. Even a human could hear them from half a mile. But the nearest house was much farther away than that, so the thieves didn't care. Furgul poked his head around the cab to see what kind of trouble he was in for.

Two giant schnauzers stood inside the gate and barked for all they were worth, which—in view of their sleek, wiry coats and their pure pedigree lines—was probably quite a lot. The breed was called "giant" to distinguish them from their relatives, the "minis"—like Mandy, the mini schnauzer at the mall. In fact neither of them was quite as tall as Furgul, though if it came to tooth and claw, he'd have the scrap of his life. Schnauzers were born to fight.

The two dogs—both males—were a dark iron gray in color and were so alike in appearance, they could have been twins. They had deep chests and powerful legs. Their heads were the shape of large bricks. Their masks were dark, almost black, and their eyes were keen and warlike. Most striking of all was their facial hair. Their eyebrows were enormous and bushy and each dog had a bristly mustache. Each had a beard on his chin of remarkable length and splendor.

When they saw Furgul they barked even louder than before.

"Don't you know who I am?" snarled one.

"Never mind him! Don't you know who *I* am?" snarled the other.

"We're going to do you a favor!"

"We'll eat you first!"

"Then you won't have to watch us eat your masters!"

The schnauzers howled with laughter. Furgul remembered what Dervla had said about guards. He decided that these two were barely smarter than pit bulls, and maybe no smarter at all. Tattoo stepped back from the gate. He seemed pleased with himself.

"Good, good, good," Tattoo muttered.

Tattoo had cracked the lock on the gates, but he didn't open them. Instead he and Spotty came back to the truck with their toolbox. They reached inside the cab. Furgul noted that to either side of the gates, a tall fence stretched off in either direction. He also saw that the crest on the gate was shaped like a big golden bone.

Spotty dangled the car keys in Furgul's face. Furgul was about to snap at his fingers when everything went black. The keys had been a distraction while Tattoo had thrown a blanket over Furgul from behind. He struggled to wriggle out, but they jumped into the truck and pinned him down. They wrapped the blanket round and round him.

CLACK-CLACK!

Tattoo's steel rod hammered down on Furgul's head. It didn't knock him out but it stunned him. They unchained the leash from the metal ring and lifted him from the truck. The two men carried him quite some distance, slung between them in the blanket. Furgul's head cleared. Wherever they were going, the barking of the schnauzers followed them closely all the way. The two thieves stopped. Furgul felt himself swinging to and fro inside the blanket.

First one way, then the other, he felt the two thieves swing him higher and higher. At the top of one swing they let go, and Furgul flew up into the air. He was going over the fence. And the schnauzers would be waiting. He kicked at the blanket with all four legs and twisted to land on his feet. The blanket slid from his head, and as he hit the ground he broke into a gallop.

Furgul didn't look back. He didn't need to. He could feel the breath of the schnauzers at his heels. He could have gone faster, but it seemed like his pursuers were at full stretch. If he ran them for long enough, perhaps they'd get tired. One thing was for sure: Furgul felt a whole lot better running—even with two bearded fiends on his tail—than he felt being chained to the truck.

The moon was full tonight, and he took in the rich man's land as he ran.

Furgul ran through an arboretum of exotic shrubs and trees, and then across a nine-hole golf course. He ran along the edge of a silver-plated lake where sailboats bobbed on the water. He passed a big slab of concrete with a helicopter sitting in the middle. Then he reached a huge swath of lawns surrounded by flower beds. At the top of the lawns was a house not much smaller than the stadium he'd seen at the track.

All the while the schnauzers toiled behind him. But if they couldn't go any faster, neither did they show any signs of slowing down, much less of giving up. He could hear them squabble with each other as they panted and ran.

"If you'd stayed out of my way, I'd have had him by now."

"He's making you look like a meatball."

"You'll look like a meatball when this lurcher kicks your butt."

"You won't be saying that when I save your bacon."

"That bacon we had for breakfast was very appetizing."

"You can't beat bacon, it's true."

"I eat a lot of bacon. I'm what you might call a bacon dog."

"The lamb chops we had last night were quite tasty too."

"Wasn't too keen on the lamb chops, too much gristle."

"Nothing worse than too much gristle."

"Gets stuck between your teeth."

"Bacon never gets stuck between your teeth."

"As you say, you can't beat bacon."

"You just can't beat it."

This is getting ridiculous, thought Furgul.

As they approached a lavish arrangement of tennis courts, Furgul opened up a ten-yard lead on the schnauzers. He dodged inside the nearest court and jumped the green net. Then he turned and waited for the schnauzers.

They stopped on the far side of the net and panted for breath.

"Looks like it's time for a midnight snack."

"He looks too gristly to me."

"We'll just kill him, then."

"And leave him for the dung beetles!"

They paused to laugh at their own quips. Furgul sighed and sat down.

"Look, we've worn him out!" said one schnauzer.

"Trapped behind the net!" added the other.

"Lured him in, like a spider into a web."

"No, no, no. Flies get lured into a web, not spiders."

"Says who?"

"Says me."

"What about mosquitoes and bluebottles?"

"Okay, mosquitoes and bluebottles. Moths too. But the spider *spins* the web."

"A moth is drawn to the flame, not lured into a web."

"Anyway, it was me who lured the lurcher into *this* web."

"You can't handle a lurcher."

"I've eaten lurchers for breakfast!"

Furgul stood up and barked so hard that they both jumped back in alarm.

"You eat bacon and lamb chops for breakfast!" growled Furgul.

They looked at him and wriggled their monstrous brows.

"That's a tad aggressive."

"No need to get nasty."

"You're not real dogs," said Furgul. "You're just a pair of glorified pets."

"Pets?"

"Pets!"

"We're professional guard dogs!"

"We're the elite!"

"And we ate the lamb chops for dinner, not for breakfa—"

"Shut up. And listen," said Furgul. "You two live with—I'm sorry, you 'guard'—the richest guy in the universe."

"Well, I wouldn't say the universe."

"Not even the galaxy."

"Do you think they have bacon on other planets?"

"I suppose it depends on whether they have pigs."

Furgul marveled at their stupidity. "While you two are

standing there—bickering like a pair of French poodles—
Spotty and Tattoo are robbing your master blind."

"Where?"

"How?"

"Who?"

"Robbing him blind?"

"But he doesn't even wear glasses!"

Furgul said, "You remember the two men who threw me
over the fence?"

"Of course we do."

"It was me that saw them first."

"But *they* didn't break the rules."

"*They* didn't set foot on our master's property."

"And you did."

For once they just stopped—exchanged a smug smile—
and nodded.

"Spotty and Tattoo are on your master's property now,"
said Furgul. "They're inside his house, stealing all his money—
along with every last slice of bacon in the fridge."

The schnauzers looked at each other. In unison they
roared with panic.

"NOT THE BACON!"

They turned and started to charge out of the tennis
court.

"Not so fast!" barked Furgul.

The schnauzers stopped and looked at him. By now he
had no doubt that they were twin brothers. In their eyes he

saw their dawning realization that Furgul might just be their new boss.

"Tell me your names," ordered Furgul.

"Pumpkin," they said together.

"You're both called Pumpkin?" asked Furgul.

"Well, the master can't tell us apart."

"So it makes it a little easier on him—"

"—if he can use the same name for the both of us."

"He doesn't really see us all that often."

"Though it's not that he doesn't care."

"He works very hard."

"Business commitments."

"Philanthropy."

"What does that mean?" asked Furgul.

The two schnauzers looked at each other. They were clueless.

"You tell him."

"No, it's your turn."

"Never mind," said Furgul. "But I thought Pumpkin was a girl's name."

At exactly the same instant the jaws of the twins dropped open. Their eyebrows writhed. Furgul had never seen dogs look quite so horrified.

"Maybe I'm wrong about that," said Furgul. "I never met a Pumpkin before. Anyhow, it's a pet name. What are your dog names?"

"He's called Cogg."

"And he's called Baz."

"We don't *look* like girls, do we?"

"Do we?"

"Relax," said Furgul. "Cogg means 'war,' and Baz means 'killer.'"

"War?" repeated Cogg. "How about that for a name?"

"It's nearly as good as Killer," said Baz.

"What's your name? asked Cogg.

"Furgul."

"What does that mean?"

"It means you've got to do exactly what I say," said Furgul.

"Yes, sir!" they said together.

"Have either of you ever fought a human?" asked Furgul.

"Well," said Cogg, "there was that time I nipped the chauffeur's ankles."

"And I once gave the gardener's leg a good humping," said Baz.

"Have you ever even fought a dog?" Furgul asked.

"Well, there was that time when the housekeeper brought her Pekingese . . ."

"And I once had a nasty tear-up with—a cat," said Baz.

He saw the expression on Furgul's face.

"A really huge ginger tomcat," added Baz.

"I remember that cat," said Cogg. "Didn't you lose?"

Furgul sighed. "If only you two could learn to keep your mouths shut, you might be quite handy in a fight. Maybe even dangerous."

"You think so?" asked Cogg.

"How dangerous?" asked Baz.

"See what I mean?" said Furgul.

Cogg and Baz opened their mouths to speak—then stopped. They looked at each other. Then they clamped their jaws shut and waited in absolute silence.

"Excellent," said Furgul. "I'm scared already."

Furgul jumped over the net and headed for the house.

"Now think about that bacon and follow me."

As the three dogs stalked around the front of the house without making a sound, Furgul broke the silence with a gasp.

On a stone plinth, surrounded by fountains, stood an enormous bronze statue of a man with a smile of gentle bliss on his face. In one hand he held a large spoon, in the other a bowl of dog food. Around his feet sat a variety of bronze dogs of different breeds, each looking up at him with affection and awe, tongues lolling from their mouths.

Furgul couldn't believe it.

"That's Mr. Chumley," said Cogg, with reverence.

"Everything we are as dogs, we owe to him," said Baz, with wonderment.

"I know who it is," said Furgul.

"Every dog knows Mr. Chumley," said Cogg.

"Mr. Chumley is every dog's best friend," said Baz.

"Wherever a dog is hungry, there Mr. Chumley will be."

"He's the Greatest Dog Lover in the World."

Furgul said, "This is Chuck Chumley's house?"

"It's Mr. Chumley's country house, yes," corrected Cogg.

"He's got another house in the city that's even bigger," added Baz.

"Mr. Chumley's a great man," said Cogg.

"Probably the greatest man in the world," agreed Baz.

"Very possibly the greatest who ever lived," suggested Cogg.

"Why?" said Furgul. "Because he gives you bacon instead of Extra Meaty Dog Feed?"

Baz made a choking sound of disgust. "Extra Meaty Dog Feed?"

"Mr. Chumley wouldn't allow that muck in the house!" said Cogg, shocked.

"The smell alone makes him feel sick!" added Baz.

"And he doesn't want to watch us get fat."

"Or to see us catch diarrhea."

"So what's Chuck supposed to be offering the dogs in that bowl?" Furgul asked. "It doesn't look like bacon to me."

Cogg and Baz stared up at the spotlit statue. They furrowed their brows.

Furgul caught the scent of Spotty and Tattoo. He heard noises coming from the house. "Come on," he said.

The three dogs stalked forward and hid behind a hedge. They spied through the leaves. The pickup truck stood just outside the house. It was half-stacked with loot—including a silver refrigerator that sparkled in the light of the moon.

"They've already got the bacon!" hissed Cogg.

"How can we save it?" whispered Baz.

"Tattoo has a steel rod in his pants pocket," said Furgul. "Don't let him pull it out. And don't attack Spotty—I want him to drive the truck away."

"Drive it away?"

"With the bacon?"

"Why?"

"Shush," said Furgul. "Here they come."

Tattoo and Spotty staggered out of the house carrying a large glass aquarium tank between them. Furgul was puzzled. The tank had no water in it.

"Now they're stealing Mr. Chumley's scorpion farm!" gasped Cogg.

"Over twenty rare species from five different continents," added Baz.

Tattoo and Spotty started down the wide stone steps toward the truck.

"Let's go," said Furgul.

"Why not?" said Baz.

Cogg and Baz tore straight through the hedge in front of them, growling like bearded lunatics. Furgul jumped over and landed just behind them. He saw no reason not to let the schnauzers do their job. They caught the two men just halfway down the steps, the tank still in their arms, Tattoo backing down first in front of Spotty. Cogg and Baz sank their teeth into the calves of Tattoo's legs. Tattoo yelled and lost his footing. As he toppled over, the tank toppled right on top of him. Tattoo's yell turned into a scream as a mass of scorpions skittered over his body.

Spotty started to dash back up the stairs to hide in the house, but Furgul reached the doorway first. He bared his teeth in Spotty's face.

Get in the truck or I'll bite your thieving hands off.

As Spotty reeled back down the stairs, Cogg and Baz seized one leg each of Tattoo's pants in their teeth and heaved, their powerful paws thrusting backward. Tattoo's pants slid right off his legs and ripped completely in two down the middle. The scorpions swarmed over Tattoo's thighs and up the legs of his shorts. They crawled on his head and down the back of his shirt. Tattoo scrambled to the fountains and plunged into the water.

"Help me! Help me! Help me!" screeched Tattoo.

Spotty clambered into the truck and slammed the door.

Furgul jumped into the back and hid among the loot.

As Spotty started the engine, Tattoo screamed from the fountains where he tried to splash the scorpions from his hair.

"Wait! Wait! Wait!" Tattoo pleaded.

But Spotty was too scared to hang around. All he did was toss a cell phone out of the window. Then the pickup's wheels spun in the gravel, and he drove toward the gates. Furgul made room as two bearded lunatics leaped right over the tailgate of the truck. They panted with excitement.

"So this is what a real dog feels like!" said Cogg.

"You were always real dogs," said Furgul, "you just needed to prove it."

"Well, we couldn't leave the bacon unprotected," said Baz.

"Speaking of bacon," said Cogg, "isn't it time for that midnight snack?"

With a speed and expertise that suggested they'd done it before, Baz stood on Cogg's back and popped the refrigerator door. Inside, every shelf was piled with packs of bacon. Cogg's nostrils twitched like a true baconoisseur.

"Oak-smoked, maplewood, hickory and honey, or Cajun-cured vanilla?"

Furgul was starving. "What's the difference?"

Cogg and Baz exchanged a horrified look.

"We've got forty-three exotic gourmet bacons in here," chided Cogg.

"From thirteen different countries," added Baz.

Furgul shrugged. "So why not try them all?"

Cogg and Baz gaped, their tongues lolling out. They looked at each other.

"How come we never thought of that?" said Baz.

"Like I said the minute I saw him, Furgul's a genius!"

"You didn't say any such thing!"

"Oh yes I did!"

"Oh no you didn't!"

As the truck rumbled through the night, the three dogs feasted on the finest bacons in the world. When their bellies were full, they settled down for a nap.

"There's something we've been meaning to ask you," said Cogg.

"Yes," said Baz. "Where are we going, skipper?"

Furgul looked up at the Dog Star, the brightest in the sky.

"Looks like we're going to the carnival."

CHAPTER SIXTEEN

THE MISSION

The strange machines towered in the moonlight without moving. The stripy shacks were deserted. The music was silent. The crowds had gone. Throughout the huddle of mobile homes, where the carnival people slept, the windows were dark. Without the flashing lights, the creaking gears, the roar of wheels on tracks and the screams of passengers, the deserted carnival seemed like the ruins of an abandoned civilization, inhabited only by ghosts and piles of garbage.

Furgul sensed that the fairground was a malevolent place, and not just because of such men as Spotty and Tattoo. Perhaps this spot was the crossroads of a twisted tangle of Doglines. Perhaps something bad had happened here long ago. Furgul didn't know. In any case it gave him the chills.

Spotty stopped the truck outside a squalid mobile home.

He switched off the engine and sat cowering behind the wheel, too afraid to get out even though he wanted to. Furgul jumped off the back of the pickup. Cogg and Baz followed Furgul.

"Let's make him think we've run away," said Furgul.

They retreated into the shadows and waited. When Spotty thought it was safe, he dashed out of the truck and into the mobile home. A light blinked on. They could see his silhouette at the window, rushing around inside.

"Wait for me here," said Furgul. "Don't let Spotty come out of the mobile home. He mustn't get back in the truck. If you have to scare him, show him your teeth, but don't bark or you'll wake the other mobile homes."

"You can count on us, skipper."

Furgul trotted away through the rows of mobile homes, toward the carnival area. He lifted his nose and sniffed about, but the smells were so many and so strong—and so unpleasant—that he couldn't pick up the scent he was looking for. He'd have to depend on eyesight alone. He crisscrossed the fairground in systematic sweeps, checking every shack and machine. Nothing. He spied a section used as a parking lot that was full of the huge trucks that transported the carnival machines. He headed over there.

The first thing that caught his eye was a silver moonbeam flashing on a chain. Then a pair of tormented eyes gleamed from the darkness. Her coat was so black that she was otherwise quite invisible. She emerged from between the wheels of an enormous truck, a long chain clanking behind her.

"You came back," said Dervla.

"I couldn't leave my best friend chained up to a truck," said Furgul.

"You came back for me?"

Furgul grinned. But Dervla's face remained haunted.

"The Dog Who Never Smiles," he said.

Furgul stepped closer. Dervla backed away.

"Don't get yourself in trouble," she said. "Tattoo and Spotty might see you."

"Spotty's in his mobile home. Tattoo's having trouble with scorpions."

"Scorpions?"

"His underpants are full of them—and he's miles away. Let me get a closer look at that collar. Step out into the moonlight."

Dervla stepped out of the shadows. Furgul studied the chain. It was looped around her neck, then threaded through a steel ring that hung from the end of the chain. This created the noose of a slip collar. The harder she pulled, the more the loop of chain would tighten around her throat. He opened his mouth and reached toward her neck.

Dervla shook her head. "You'll never bite through it."

"Just hold your neck stiff," he said. "I've been wearing one of these all day, and I've worked it out. You just can't do it on your own. See, the slip collar works both ways: If *you* pull, it gets tighter, but if *I* pull—"

Furgul grabbed the loop between his front teeth and gave it a steady pull. The chain rattled through the live ring—and the loop got bigger and bigger. Dervla blinked with amazement. She ducked her head backward, and the enlarged noose slid over her ears and tinkled to the ground.

"There you are," said Furgul.

Dervla looked up at the moon. She glanced at Furgul.

"Go ahead," he said.

Dervla craned back her powerful neck. Her jaws opened wide toward the moon. The howl that was torn from her throat froze Furgul's blood, yet at the same time his eyes filled with tears. It started low, from deep inside her, and rose into a cry from the wounds inflicted on her heart. Dervla's howl expressed her rage at being tortured for so long. But it was also a lament of guilt and shame for allowing them to rob her of her dignity. The melancholy howl soared skyward. And when her lungs were empty, it soared on still, as if the cosmos would echo to its sound until the end of time.

And her howl summoned the pack as if from nowhere, as in days of old. Heavy footfalls drummed across the carnival. Furgul's instinct told him who they belonged to, but he couldn't believe it. He turned.

Pounding across the fairground—his paws leaving shallow craters in the dirt—came Brennus. From the blackness beneath the roller coaster came a yap—and Zinni pelted toward them. From somewhere above came a familiar voice.

"It's okay, Furgul!" said Skyver. "I'll get you out of here!"

Furgul looked up as Skyver skipped down from the top of the truck. As he landed in front of Dervla, he attempted a flashy pirouette and fell flat on his face.

"Ooohff!" gasped Skyver. "That usually works perfectly."

Brennus and Zinni hauled up.

"What are you doing here?" asked Furgul.

"We found the poor little pup outside the Sanctuary," explained Zinni. "He told us what had happened. Then Jodi drove him to the animal hospital."

Brennus said, "We figured you were in trouble."

"We've come to take you home," said Zinni.

"But how did you find me?" asked Furgul.

"Easy," said Skyver. "We followed the sweet smell of Chumley's Curry Supreme."

"This is Dervla," said Furgul. "Dervla, meet Brennus and Zinni."

Furgul helped Skyver to his feet. "This is Skyver. He's the scruffiest dog in the world, but you won't hear him brag about it."

"At your service," said Skyver. He tried to get a sniff of Dervla's hindquarters. "You look like you need some tender loving care."

"But you don't look like the one who's going to supply it," Dervla snapped.

Skyver retreated to Furgul's side and whispered, "I think she likes me."

"This is a bad place," said Brennus. He, too, sensed the twisted essence of the fairground beneath his paws. "We should leave."

They reached the mobile home. Furgul introduced Cogg and Baz to the gang.

"Spotty tried to get out," said Cogg.

"But we controlled ourselves," said Baz.

"He can still walk," Cogg reassured them.

"I'd say it's more like a hobble," suggested Baz.

"Let's call it a limp," conceded Cogg.

"Forget about Spotty," said Furgul. "You two can go to Appletree with the others. It's a great place, but if you want to work for Chumley again, Jodi will make sure you get home."

Furgul looked at Dervla. She needed Jodi. Jodi healed wounded dogs.

"Dervla, I want you to go back to Appletree too."

"Where are you going?" asked Dervla.

"I'll follow you later," said Furgul. "Wait for me there."

Brennus said, "So you finally found Dedbone's Hole."

Furgul nodded. Dervla looked questioningly at Brennus.

"It's the slave camp for greyhounds where Furgul was born," said Brennus. He looked at Furgul. "His moment has come. He's going back to Dedbone's Hole—to set the wrong things right."

"Keeva threw the race at the track tonight," said Furgul.

"I know Dedbone. In the morning he'll drive her away in a cardboard box, and she'll never come back."

"What kind of resistance can we expect?" asked Brennus.

"I'm not asking any of you to go with me," said Furgul.

"And I'm not asking your permission," said Brennus.

"Neither am I," said Dervla. "Count me in."

"There'll be at least two men, with shotguns," said Furgul. "Plus a pack of guard dogs who'll protect Dedbone to the death. It's too dangerous."

"Sounds perfect," growled Cogg. "We can prove we're real dogs again."

"We didn't get a chance to do it here," agreed Baz.

"We're all coming, Furgul," piped Zinni. "Whether you like it or not."

"We are?" said Skyver, aghast.

The others looked at him.

"I'll pop back to Appletree and get some more help!" said Skyver.

"You're right, Skyver," said Furgul. "You head on home. Jodi needs you."

Skyver glanced at the others, as if ashamed of himself.

"You're a free dog," said Brennus. "No one here will think the worse of you."

"Good luck, Skyver," said Zinni.

Skyver avoided Dervla's gaze. For once he was lost for words. He turned and trotted away until he melted into the shadows and was gone.

"Well," said Brennus, "looks like we've got us a Dog Bunch."

They all turned at once as the mobile home door swung open and Spotty clattered out, a suitcase in his hand. He stumbled toward the pickup truck, the bloodstained rags of his pants flapping round his ankles.

Dervla took off after him. Like silent death.

Spotty dropped his suitcase and fled for the carnival.

"Dervla!" called Furgul. "Come back!"

Dervla didn't stop. Neither did Spotty. They disappeared.

"Wait here," said Furgul to the others.

He sprinted after Dervla. As he left the mobile home site he saw them.

Spotty staggered toward the big wheel while Dervla trotted in silence at his heels. He blubbered with terror, glancing over his shoulder at the black German shepherd with the pitiless eyes. Dervla could have taken him down anytime she wanted. But she was torturing him with fear, just as Spotty and Tattoo had tortured her.

As Furgul gained on them, Spotty reached the big wheel and climbed into one of the buckets. Dervla sprang after him, and Spotty screamed.

"Dervla!" barked Furgul. "No!"

Dervla stood on her hind legs in the bucket. Her forepaws pinned Spotty's shoulders to the seat. A coward's tears tumbled down his cheeks as he begged for mercy. Dervla stared into Spotty's face, her deep black eyes devoid of pity. She bared her fangs, inches from his throat, and Spotty closed his eyes. He knew he was a dead man.

"Dervla, look at me," said Furgul.

Dervla turned her head. Her gaze met Furgul's.

"Do you remember that day we met? In the park?" said Furgul.

For the first time since they'd met in the filthy pen, when she'd killed three dogs without making a single sound, Furgul saw her soul glimmer in her eyes.

"We played," said Furgul. "We fought. We laughed. We ran. You made me feel free for the first time in my life. It was beautiful, Dervla. You were beautiful."

"That was a long time ago," said Dervla.

"I watched them kill my father," said Furgul. "They starved Brennus till they thought he was dead, then dumped him on a garbage heap. In the morning they're going to kill my mother. That day in the park was a long time ago for all of us."

Dervla blinked. She closed her jaws.

"Spotty's broken," said Furgul. "You've broken him."

Dervla looked at the pathetic, sniveling wretch between her paws.

"He's helpless," said Furgul. "You don't need to kill him. He's nothing."

Dervla looked back at him. And Furgul saw in her face once more the free spirit that had called him across the park when they both were young.

"I want you to run with the winds," said Furgul. "I want

you to find the Doglands, not lose them forever. I want to run with *you* again, Dervla."

With the grace and power that she'd never lost—even when lost in hatred—Dervla leaped from the bucket. She landed by Furgul's side. She heard Spotty whimper in the bucket, curled into a ball. She stepped to a red lever at the base of the machine. She raised a paw and pushed it down. The big wheel groaned and clanked and started to turn. Spotty's bucket rose into the air. He still whimpered, but this time with relief.

When the bucket reached the top of the circle, Dervla threw the red lever again, and the big wheel lurched to a halt. Spotty's pimpled face peeped out, then ducked back.

Then Dervla turned to Furgul.

"I want to run with you too."

The Dog Bunch loped across the carnival as if the moonlight had conjured phantoms from the Doglands' darkest dreams. They crossed the empty roads with their ugly yellow lights, and soon they'd left the sleeping town behind them. Open country beckoned, and they took to the fields.

Furgul led them on at a steady pace with Dervla and Zinni close behind him. Then came Cogg and Baz. Brennus padded along at the rear.

Brennus heard a sound. He looked over his shoulder and grinned.

"Trouble ahoy!" he called.

Furgul glanced back as Skyver galloped up alongside Brennus.

"I suddenly realized, you'd never pull this off without me," panted Skyver.

Brennus gave him a look.

"Okay, so I was scared of the dark." Skyver glanced at Furgul in the lead. "Speaking of which, how does he know where he's going?"

Brennus said, "Because Furgul is the dog who runs in darkness."

PART THREE

THE DOG BUNCH

CHAPTER SEVENTEEN

THE PLAN

As the sun climbed above the easternmost edge of the world, the Dog Bunch topped the crest that marked the craggy northern ridge of Argal's Mountain. They'd covered more miles in fewer hours than any other dogs they'd ever known. They themselves could hardly believe that they'd done it. Only one among them knew what the secret might be, yet he, too, was astonished. They stopped to watch the distant ball of fire drag itself into the sky. It left blood-red claw marks on the clouds.

"Shepherd's warning," said Brennus.

No one else spoke. From the ridge, the rock sloped down toward woods and pasture. Beyond the fields a dirty smudge marred the land, which Furgul knew was the slave camp at Dedbone's Hole.

They descended a hundred feet to a mountain stream, and there they slaked their thirst. While the others drank, Furgul wandered to a ledge and looked down. He saw the dirt track that wound up the hill from the valley below. At the top end of the track he saw the entrance to the cave of death.

He expected grim memories to flash through his mind, but they didn't. Instead he felt dizzy. A strange current flowed up through his legs and through his body. It was as strong as the torrent that had swept him down the river, yet he didn't move. It was as powerful as the strongest wind, yet not a hair on his coat was ruffled. It had no sound. It had no taste. It was invisible. And yet it was there. And he knew that it could tear him apart like a leaf if it chose to.

Furgul shook himself down and stepped back from the ledge, and the strange sensation was gone. When he turned he found Brennus nearby. Brennus had been watching him. Furgul felt safer. He went to stand closer to the old Saint Bernard. Brennus nodded to the stream, where others paddled and rested.

"None of them felt it," he said.

"Did you?" asked Furgul.

Brennus nodded. "Yes. But nowhere near as strongly as you did."

"Do you know why we were able to get here so fast?" said Brennus. "We should still be panting our way toward the far side of this mountain."

Furgul shrugged. "We're a tough, fit, wild bunch of dogs."

"Not if you include me." Brennus smiled. "At least, not the fit part. We did it because you led us along a Dogline. And you didn't even know it. Did you?"

Furgul shook his head. "It just felt like the best way to go. But it felt nothing like that—thing—that just went through me. What was that?"

"I'm not sure. The knowledge of Ancient Dog Lore has almost vanished from our species," said Brennus. "As the human race became more and more remote from its own wild origins—as humans sold the truth of their inmost hearts for TVs and hair products and safety—then so we dogs lost touch with our origins too. We stopped asking ourselves the most fundamental question of life: *What is the nature of wildness?* We stopped asking our mothers and fathers—*What is the nature of wildness?*—just as they had stopped asking theirs. Like the humans, we, too, sold our truth. And for what? For a pat on the head from the masters and a bowl of meat we no longer even know how to hunt and kill for ourselves. We ate our food from tin cans, like they do. We lay down by their kitchen hearthstones and forgot who we once had been. I did it myself, to my shame. And so now, in all the world, there are only a handful of wise dogs left who have any grasp at all of our ancient knowledge. The knowledge we had when dogs owned the earth and humans were helpless as children."

"And you're one of those wise dogs."

"No. Not me. But I met one once, when I was young—and when she was old. She was named Murgen, which means 'from the sea.' But Murgen must be long gone now, at least from the world of blood, bone and fur. No, Furgul, I'm not wise. I just remember some fragments of lore that I was too foolish to value until it was too late. But you could be such a dog."

"Me?"

"Yes, Furgul. You. If you searched the Doglands for long enough—if you sought the answer to the question: *What is the nature of wildness?*—if you were willing to pay the price—you could rediscover the Dog Lore."

"But I don't know anything," said Furgul.

"You know how to find the Doglines."

"I don't really understand what the Doglines are."

"You understand them better than me. I have the crumbs of a few old ideas. But you can feel these things in your bones. That's why you must seek out the Dog Lore."

"What was that feeling I just felt—that force from the rocks that you felt too?"

"The Doglines are the pawprints of the ancestors, first laid down by wolves in the time before long, long ago. But just as a wolf or a dog or any living creature may be right or wrong, a Dogline may be right or wrong. A right Dogline can take you somewhere good—like Appletree—but a wrong Dogline can take you somewhere bad—like Dedbone's Hole. The old ones believed that the Doglines can get tangled—like knots in string—which concentrates their force and makes their fluxions—the flow of power—much stronger. I can't be sure, but I think there are two knots inside this mountain—one right and one wrong. The force we felt was the contrary fluxions—the two knots—pulling against each other."

Furgul had a realization. "One is in the chasm beneath the hill of dead dogs. That's a wrong knot. A wrong place. The right knot is in the crystal cavern."

"How do you know?" asked Brennus.

"Because I've been to both places, wrong and right. I left my sister Eena's body at one knot, and my sister Nessa's body at the other."

"You see?" said Brennus. "Your search has already begun."

"But I wasn't searching. I was just a pup, running for my life."

"No, you were running the Doglines."

Furgul thought back to his escape from Dedbone's Hole, his journey through the mountain and down the river. Brennus was right. It wasn't luck that had saved him. It was the Doglines. He saw the excitement in Brennus's eyes.

"Furgul, you've been running the Doglines—and searching for the Dog Lore—since you were born."

"What else can you tell me?" asked Furgul.

"Only one more thing, the last of my crumbs, but a dark one. The Doglines are powerful—as you just felt better than I. And they give you a choice. Each Dogline is made stronger every time you run it. Some dogs run the right lines, and some dogs run the wrong. And just as you can change the Doglines, the Doglines can change you."

"Did Argal run right Doglines?"

"Yes, on the whole, he did, though he only sensed them. Argal's own natural wildness was so strong, so defiant, that he had no patience for the Dog Lore. He was too busy fighting for freedom. Argal's brother, Sloann, is just as strong, but cooler in temper and more brilliant. Sloann knows exactly what he's doing. He's always chosen to run the wrong Doglines, to harness their strength against the masters. If you ever get wind of Sloann, stay away from him."

Dervla came padding up to the ledge. "We should press on," she said.

Furgul wondered if Dervla felt the Doglines too. He sensed that she did. But now wasn't the time to ask her. It was time to go to Dedbone's Hole and find out if the right was stronger than the wrong.

They studied the layout of Dedbone's Hole from a grove of trees. The main compound was just as Furgul remembered it—a scrubby rectangle of barren land surrounded by a high wire-mesh fence. A fence too high for even Furgul to jump. Inside were long rows of crates, stacked two deep, one crate on another, where the greyhounds lived their miserable existence. On the top row lived the males, and on the bottom the females. In another corner were the whelping cages where Furgul had spent his first days. At the far side stood the troughs where the greyhounds ate.

Less familiar to him were the wider surroundings.

The place still looked like a junkyard. Telephone poles carried paired black cables to Dedbone's house, though it was less a house than a filthy cabin festooned with antennae and TV dishes. Outside stood Dedbone's pickup truck, the one that Furgul and his sisters had ridden as pups. Strewn about the yard were rusting trailers and derelict cars, oil drums, empty bottles and stacks of old tires. A smattering of dilapidated sheds stood alongside a hog pen. Half a dozen billy goats grazed the parched grass. Beyond all this the main road out of Dedbone's Hole rolled away into the distance.

There were no humans to be seen.

"Dedbone must have been stuck at the track until late last night," said Furgul. "He must be sleeping in."

"You'll never get over that fence," offered Skyver, who was licking his travel-worn footpads. "Or under it. We've come a thousand miles for nothing."

To his annoyance, everyone ignored him.

"Which crate is Keeva in?" asked Dervla.

"I don't know. But I didn't come here just for Keeva. I came to free them all."

"Great," muttered Skyver. "While we're at it, why not discover a cure for fleas?"

Down in the compound below, the greyhounds started barking and crooning with hunger. The din grew more and more frantic.

"Breakfast is late," said Furgul.

"Don't we know it?" said Skyver. "I can't remember

the last time I ate. Look, old buddy, I know you're under pressure—and I don't want to make it any worse—but do you have any kind of plan at all?"

"Breakfast is late," repeated Furgul.

"He's lost it," said Skyver. "If you'd listened to me, we'd have already eaten our breakfast by now and be going back to bed, safe and sound, at Appletree."

"Hey, whinger, or whatever your dirtbag name is," growled Dervla, "no one asked you to come along. So why don't you put your feet back in your mouth and stop chirping in my face."

Skyver at once went back to licking his blisters. Dervla looked at Furgul.

"In the dog pen at the carnival I had a lot of time to think about how to get out," she said. "The only weak spot is when the masters open the gate. Like at mealtimes."

"Good point," said Furgul. "And breakfast is late."

"What's their schedule?" asked Dervla.

"Dedbone opens the gate to wheel in the sacks of feed. He may have the Gambler to help him. Tic and Tac will be with him. He locks the gate behind them. After he's filled the troughs, Dedbone opens the crates and lets the hounds out to eat. Then he goes home to drink whiskey. When he returns, he opens the gate, locks it, puts the hounds back in their crates and leaves again, locking up the gate for the rest of the morning."

Dervla said, "Okay, so we strike when he's on his way to

drink his whiskey, just before he can relock the gate. All the hounds will be out of their crates."

"You've never seen sixty greyhounds at breakfast," said Furgul. "While there's food in the trough, they'd rather eat than be free. We'd never get them to leave."

Dervla said, "So we make our move the next time he opens the gate—when he comes back after his whiskey—and before he crates them up again."

"Right," said Furgul. "But even that isn't so easy if you know greyhounds. They've never known anything but slavery—blind obedience—the routine. They're indoctrinated. And they're all too terrified of Dedbone to try to escape."

Dervla nodded. She understood that better than anyone.

"If I could get in while they were feeding," said Furgul, "I could persuade them to rebel. I could also find Keeva. I know they'd listen to her."

"So we're back to square one," cheeped Skyver. "You'll never get over that fence."

Dervla rose to her full height, baring her teeth. Skyver hopped away on his blisters.

"I can get over that fence," piped Zinni.

They all turned to look at her, mostly in disbelief. Skyver opened his mouth—caught Dervla's stare—and shut it again so fast he hurt his teeth.

"See those overhead cables," she said, "with the crows sitting on them? Electrical, or telephone, maybe both? They stretch right over the compound."

They all looked back at the compound. She was right.

Zinni said, "I can walk along them and drop down inside."

"So, what, you were in the circus?" jeered Skyver. He held both paws up to Dervla. "Just a question! Just a perfectly reasonable question!"

"I'm a papillon," said Zinni. "That's the kind of stuff they had me doing in shows and competitions—tightrope walking, somersaults—that's how I got my diamond necklace, for making my mistress look cool to her friends."

"But how will you get up on the wires?" persisted Skyver, one eye still on Dervla.

"If I can walk along wires, climbing on Dedbone's roof is a piece of steak."

"Zinni," said Furgul, "if you can whip up the greyhounds—"

"When they get a load of me, they'll whip up real quick," said Zinni. "I'll lead those greyhounds out."

"Once Zinni's in the compound, our timing has to be perfect," said Furgul. "If it's not, she'll be trapped in there too. The minute Dedbone opens that gate, we have to take him out along with Tic and Tac, the new mastiff pups, and maybe the Gambler too."

Dervla looked at Brennus. He nodded.

"We'll keep Tic and Tac busy," said Dervla. "Cogg and Baz can back us up."

"I'll take Dedbone," said Furgul. "If I can get the key from his hand as he takes it from the lock, he won't be able to relock it."

"All we have to worry about, then, is getting killed." Skyver pointed his paw at Dedbone's Hole. "Speaking of which, no one said anything to me about bullmastiffs."

Dedbone was shambling toward the compound, pushing a wheelbarrow full of feedbags. The Gambler walked beside him with a sawed-off shotgun over his arm. Behind them, enormous and malevolent, slouched Tic and Tac.

"Here's something else we didn't tell you," said Furgul. "You're going in there first."

Skyver cringed. "But, Furgul, after all the times I've saved your life—"

"And before you go in, you're going to douse yourself in goat poop."

Skyver laughed at that one, until he saw the way the others stared at him. The others weren't laughing at all. Skyver suddenly looked rather queasy.

"Goat poop?" he gasped.

Moments later, Skyver was facing a heap of fresh goat poop.

The others watched and waited. Skyver wrinkled his nose.

"I heard rumors that some dogs love to roll around in doo-doo," whined Skyver. "But I thought it was a joke."

"It's not a joke, Skyver," said Zinni. "It's a nice big steamer."

"The Bulls will smell us at thirty feet, even if we stay out of sight," said Brennus. "With you up front—daubed in poop—all they'll smell is goat."

"Isn't there something else I could do?" asked Skyver.

"Sure," said Furgul. "Brennus can be the goat, and you can take out Tic. Or Tac."

Skyver dived into the poop and rolled around until he was covered.

"You've missed a bit around your eyebrows," said Zinni.

"And don't forget your gums," added Dervla.

Skyver gave her a look that said, "You're kidding, right?"

Dervla shook her head.

Skyver grimaced and peeled back his lips—and scooped up a pawful of poop.

"Furgul," warned Brennus. He nodded toward the Hole.

Five more bullmastiffs were mooching around the outbuildings. They were young, but they looked every bit as big and nasty as their parents.

"Tic and Tac's new brood," said Furgul. "Looks like they're allowed to wander about the perimeter at will." He looked at Dervla and Brennus.

"Seven bullmastiffs is a handful, even for us," said Brennus.

"If I can trust my nostrils, that's a smokehouse over there," observed Cogg.

"And a hog pen too," added Baz.

The Bunch looked at them as if they were mad.

"A smokehouse plus hogs equals bacon," explained Cogg.

"Plus ham, jerky, sausage, fatback and other smoked-pork products," added Baz.

"So that's that." Cogg and Baz nodded to each other and smiled.

The rest of the Bunch had no idea what they were talking about.

"What's what?" asked Skyver.

"For that much bacon we'll take any five mastiffs in the world," said Baz.

"In other words, you can leave the five youngsters to us," said Cogg.

"They don't scare us a bit," said Baz.

"Not after fighting that huge ginger tom," agreed Cogg.

"I fought the ginger tomcat!" said Baz. "You fought the Pekingese!"

The rest of the Bunch watched them squabble with amazement. But although Cogg and Baz were maniacs—and absolutely clueless to boot—no one detected the slightest trace of fear in either of them.

"No, no, no, I'll take three, you can have two," said Cogg.

"I'll let you have the two biggest," offered Baz.

"Nope. You can have the two smallest," countered Cogg.

"You mean you want the three biggest? All at once?"

While Cogg thought that one through, Furgul cut them off.

"There'll be plenty for all of us," said Furgul. "This is what we've come to do. Let's do it."

The schnauzers saluted and bounded off down the hill. Zinni, Skyver and Dervla followed. Furgul loved them. Because he loved them he felt a sudden fear. He looked at the impregnable compound. Inside the wire, Dedbone was pouring sacks of feed into the troughs. The sun winked from the Gambler's brass thumb and from the barrels of his sawed-off shotgun. Tic and Tac growled at the greyhound crates for fun.

Furgul turned to Brennus. "Do we have any chance at all?"

Brennus said, *"When leaves die they turn into earth. . . ."*

CHAPTER EIGHTEEN

THE ATTACK

The Dog Bunch crawled through long, scrubby grass to the edge of Dedbone's property. Skyver was prodded along at the front by a series of bloodcurdling threats. They stopped at the edge of the grass and kept their heads down. The first phase depended on Zinni. If she failed, the plan fell apart. Zinni ran the tip of her tail over Skyver's goat-stained cheek to pick up some scent.

"Is that all you need?" hissed Skyver, who was caked from gums to claw.

"You've got to stink for all six of us," said Zinni.

Then she darted out of the grass and into the danger zone.

After locking the main gate behind him, Dedbone had filled the troughs and was working his way down the long rows of crates, opening them one at a time. As the hounds came out, Tic and Tac bullied them into a pack and made them wait. They all had to race for the troughs at the same time. The Gambler did nothing useful. He just stood around, as if the sawed-off shotgun made him special.

Zinni was as fast as a hare and as agile as a sparrow. Her size meant she could hide behind almost anything. She sped from the grass and paused behind a pile of old tires. Tic and Tac were too busy bullying the greyhounds. The five younger Bulls were cocking their legs on the posts of the hog pen and sniffling around the outbuildings. Zinni took off again. Even Furgul, with his hunter's eyes, lost sight of her as she crisscrossed the junkyard.

She reappeared outside Dedbone's cabin. She leaped onto an oil drum. She scanned the terrain she had to climb. She leaped from the barrel to the planks of a scaffold on which stood some cans of paint. She sped along the scaffold and made a leap about five times her own length—to land on the tin roof of an outhouse. From there she jumped, her front paws hooking over the edge of the cabin roof, her hind paws scrabbling the wall to shove herself upward.

She disappeared again.

The next time Furgul saw her she was on the other side of the cabin roof. The two black cables that snaked through the air from the telephone pole were attached to the front of the cabin, a few inches beneath Zinni's feet. Zinni looked over at the Dog Bunch and waved her tail. Skyver began to wave back. Dervla slapped him down.

Zinni stepped out onto the two high wires with her front paws.

The cables swayed this way and that, and the crows turned to gape with amazement. Zinni balanced her weight and then committed one hind paw, and then the other. She was standing in midair. Her tail curled back and forth as the swaying cables threatened to pitch her into the junkyard. For long seconds Zinni's fate—and the fate of the mission—swung in the balance.

Skyver put his paws over his eyes. Furgul didn't blame him.

Zinni's expert tail work steadied the cables. They all held their breath as she inched forward. She crossed above Dedbone's weed-infested garden, then above the pickup truck parked outside. She paused, as if to take in the view, as if she now owned the sky. Below her lay the trash-littered waste ground. She walked on—somehow getting faster and faster—until she passed above the top of the high wire-mesh fence that surrounded the dogs' compound.

No one in the Bunch dared speak. Zinni approached the flock of sullen crows that squatted on the wires in her path. They could knock her off with a single feather if they wanted to. Right beneath the crows, with his shotgun, stood the Gambler.

They couldn't tell what Zinni whispered to the crows, but it worked. They cawed with alarm and took off into the air. As they did so, the Gambler clapped a hand on the top of his head. He swore and started to look up toward the cables.

"Looks like I'm not the only one covered in poop," whispered Skyver.

The flight of the crows caused the cables to swing like a hammock. Zinni froze, trying not to fall and at the same time preparing to jump and run for her life if the Gambler saw her. But the Gambler's eyes saw the crows flap away before he could glimpse Zinni. He threw the sawed-off shotgun to his shoulder and fired. BOOM! BOOM! Dedbone jumped and cursed. The crows sailed away unharmed.

"Grouse! Grouse! Grouse!" shouted Dedbone in annoyance.

"Bicker! Bicker! Bicker!" the red-faced Gambler replied.

Neither of them noticed Zinni, and neither did Tic and Tac, whose nostrils were too far below to pick up her scent. Zinni pressed onward. At last she stopped above the double stack of crates. And there—in midair—she waited.

"What's she doing?" gasped Skyver. "I can't stand it."

"She's waiting until Dedbone has opened the last of the crates," Furgul explained. "Not only does she have nerves of steel, she's smart too."

The starving pack of dogs was held back from the troughs only out of fear of the Bulls. As the last greyhound joined them, Dedbone nodded to Tic.

"Come and get it!" barked Tic.

The greyhounds surged forward in a yowling flood. Zinni jumped down from the wire onto the crates, the sound of her landing smothered by the noise of the pack. In a flash she was out of sight.

The Dog Bunch heaved a sigh of relief. Dedbone and his cronies—Tic, Tac and the Gambler—left the compound and locked the gate. Then they vanished into the cabin to drink their whiskey and eat their meat. For a moment the coast was clear.

Furgul said, "Let's go."

They strung out in a line behind Skyver, whose cowardice made him an excellent point dog. Years on the scrounge had made him as sly as a fox, and as he crossed the open ground and neared the compound, he spotted nooks and crannies that Furgul would not have seen.

"Cogg, Baz," snapped Skyver, "take that hollow behind the empty whiskey bottles. If you lie flat on your sides it'll hide both of you. Dervla—crawl into those garbage sacks. The black plastic will disguise your fur. Brennus—under that old canvas."

Furgul learned fast. He grabbed a perfect hiding place behind a rusting lawn mower. The greyhounds were now just a few yards away, chomping and scrapping at the troughs. He reckoned he could reach the gate in two seconds.

Skyver was peeved. "That was my spot," he hissed.

"Get under the bathtub," said Furgul, pointing with his tail.

"The tub's full of stinking—oh, what's the difference?" sighed Skyver.

As Skyver squeezed beneath the legs of the rotten old tub, it started to leak a foul-smelling slime that drip-drip-dripped on his head.

They were all in position. Now came the hardest part: They had to wait.

Furgul's heart thumped against his ribs. His stomach was tied in knots. But his mind was focused and clear. He wondered how often Argal had faced death. He pictured Argal's tunnel-deep eyes and felt stronger. But for once he didn't have to ask himself: *What would Argal do?* Furgul was doing it for himself.

The minutes crawled by.

The greyhounds finished their breakfast and milled around. Then Furgul saw Zinni emerge from behind the crates. Of all the Bunch, her job was the most hazardous. These greyhounds lived for a single dream: to hunt down something small and white and tear it into tiny pieces. If they detected a whiff of fear, pack instinct would overwhelm them and they'd lynch her. But Zinni faced down sixty greyhounds as if they were a flock of field mice. The big males jostled to get to the front as she spoke. They were mesmerized. And it wasn't in Zinni's character to play any girlie tricks. She just stood tall—even though that was only as high as the shortest greyhound's knees—and told them what it would feel like to be free.

Argal couldn't have done better.

Furgul's eyes scanned the horde of greyhounds for Keeva. He couldn't see her. He caught a flash of dark blue fur here and there, but not her face.

"Psst!" whispered Skyver. "Here they come!"

Dedbone came out of his cabin and rubbed his hands over his bulging belly. He was already sweating, and it must have been from drink, for the morning was still cool. Since the evening before, he'd gained a black eye, and one front tooth had gone missing. The angry mob at the track must have given him a hard time. He scowled and stretched as if his body ached all over. He rubbed his walnut knuckles as if they were sore. Dedbone was a bully and a cheat, but he was hard and tough too. Tic and Tac and the Gambler came behind him.

They started toward the compound.

Furgul would be the first to attack. He had to get Dedbone's key.

"Psst! Psst! Hey, Furgul!"

Furgul glanced toward the bathtub. Skyver trembled underneath.

"Once they've seen you, I don't need to smell like a goat anymore—right?" said Skyver. "So does that mean I can retreat?"

Furgul waved a paw to shut him up. He peered through a gap in the lawn mower. Tic and Tac were sniffing the air and frowning. They were brutes, but they were first-class guard dogs. Furgul could hear their voices.

"Goats are too scared of the dogs to come this near the compound."

"I know goat when I smell it."

"Should we make a fuss?"

"The master hates fuss. Especially after half a bottle."

"Plus the bottle he sank last night."

"It might be the master we can smell. Give his shoes a sniff."

"He hates that too."

Dedbone was almost at the gate. He dug a hand into his pocket and pulled out a key. He was about to slot it in the lock when the Gambler said something.

"Blah, blah, blah," droned the Gambler.

"Spout, spout, spout," spouted Dedbone.

After losing all their money and getting beaten up and drinking whiskey all night long, they were both in a foul mood. Furgul just wanted Dedbone to unlock the gate. Tac took a chance and sniffed at Dedbone's shoes. Dedbone kicked her in the head. It seemed to make him feel better.

Tac yelped and wandered away—right toward the bathtub.

She started snuffling around for the invisible goat.

Skyver's teeth chattered with terror. The bathtub itself started shaking.

Dedbone put the key in the lock. He turned it.

Click.

Furgul heard a suspicious growl. He glanced through the

gap at Tac. Tac was just six feet away from Skyver. Furgul returned his eyes to the key.

Dedbone pulled the key out. He lifted the latch on the gate—a metal bar in a simple slot with a metal knob to lift it up. In a second the gate would open.

Skyver exploded from under the tub with a yowl of pure panic.

Everything seemed to happen all at once.

Furgul lunged for Dedbone, and Dedbone dropped the latch without opening it. He knew dogs, and he was faster than he looked. As Furgul started to jump, Dedbone raised the key above his head—but a little too soon. Furgul put more power into the last of his thrust and jumped even higher. He saw Dedbone's fist come toward him, but he didn't blink. His jaws closed on Dedbone's hand and crunched the fingers. His teeth bit onto hard, cold metal. The fist hit him. He hit the ground and turned.

Furgul had the key. He tossed it through the wire mesh into the compound.

Dedbone could not relock the gate. But the gate was still closed.

Skyver's frantic dash took him right toward Tac's jaws. He braked and spun and ran the other way—right toward the Gambler.

The Gambler fired his sawed-off shotgun—BOOM!—and fur flew from Skyver's butt. Skyver kept going, heading right between the Gambler's legs. The Gambler took aim with the second barrel, trying to keep up with Skyver's speed. As Skyver slithered between the Gambler's knees, Furgul jumped and shoved his forepaws hard into the Gambler's back.

BOOM!

Furgul heard a hideous scream and swerved away as the Gambler toppled over.

The Gambler had shot himself in the ankle.

From above the squirming body, Furgul saw Brennus charge Tac. His shoulder slammed into her ribs and sent her rolling over. Then Tic came at Brennus from behind. Dervla flew across the bathtub in a blur of fury and sank her teeth into Tic's neck. But Tic was not Freak. He matched Dervla's fury and more as he tore himself free and struck back, the shepherd and the mastiff squirming and writhing in a tangle of claws and fangs. Tac came back at Brennus, and she was younger, faster and stronger.

A savage fight to the death began between the two pairs of dogs.

Beyond them Furgul saw the baying pack of young Bulls heading for the fray.

He heard a rousing double bark above the chaos: "FOR THE BACON!!!"

Cogg and Baz charged through the empty bottles to meet the new assault.

The junkyard echoed to a frenzy of dogs ripping and snarling, clawing and barking, squirming and biting.

And though the gate to the compound was unlocked—it wasn't yet open.

For a moment Dedbone was transfixed by the sight of the Gambler. The Gambler wailed with horror in a widening pool of blood. Furgul darted round them both to reach the gate. He'd seen how the latch had worked, when Dedbone had almost opened it. He rose on his hind legs, his forepaws resting on the gate, and pushed his nose against the knob on the metal bar. The metal bar began to rise up from its slot. From the corner of his eye he saw Dedbone grab the fallen shotgun from the ground, but he didn't let the latch drop back. The metal bar clicked up and out of its slot. Furgul shoved on the gate.

Dedbone swung the empty shotgun like a club to smash Furgul's head in. But the gate creaked open under Furgul's weight, and as he dropped to the ground the butt of the shotgun whistled above his ears. Furgul spun around as Dedbone lifted the shotgun to strike again.

For a moment their gazes met. And locked.

Dedbone froze, the shotgun poised in the air.

Furgul saw the change in Dedbone's face—and he knew that the slaver remembered him. Dedbone recognized the lurcher pup—now grown into a dog—that he'd thrown down the chasm of doom so long ago.

"You!" said Dedbone. "You! You! You!"

Savagery flooded through Furgul's veins, and his lips peeled back in a growl.

For Eena and Nessa.

Furgul lunged, and Dedbone swung the shotgun by the barrels. Furgul sidestepped and the shotgun butt caught him in the ribs. Furgul lunged again and sank his fangs up to the gums in Dedbone's belly. Dedbone bellowed with pain and swung the shotgun down on Furgul's head. Furgul landed on his side and scrambled to his feet. Dedbone put finger and thumb in his mouth and whistled. Furgul glanced across the junkyard.

Dervla and Tic were still slashing and wrestling in a whirlwind of blood and fur. Brennus had his back to a rusting trailer and was bleeding from many wounds. Tac hung back with a broken hind leg, but three of the younger bullmastiffs had broken away from Cogg and Baz and were wearing Brennus down bite by bite. At Dedbone's whistle the three young Bulls whirled away and charged at Furgul.

Dedbone turned and bent over the Gambler. The Gambler groaned and held out his hand, but Dedbone swatted it aside and rifled the Gambler's pockets. He pulled out a fistful of shotgun shells and headed for his truck.

With the three bullmastiffs bearing down on him, Furgul looked through the open gate of the compound. Sixty greyhounds were massed behind Zinni like an army whose time had come. Before Furgul could bark, the three young Bulls surrounded him and attacked.

Furgul jumped and twisted in midair as they charged. The first two ran into each other, their heads smashing together like two fat rocks. Furgul landed spraddled on the back of the third. He bit him behind the ears but the bullmastiff's neck was too thick. The mastiff bucked and reared, and Furgul was thrown off. The three young Bulls lined up to attack him again.

"Zinni!" barked Furgul.

Zinni charged forward, and the greyhound army followed her. They roared through the gates in a howling mob and rolled toward the three young Bulls in a cataract of rage. The Bulls stopped in their tracks, their eyes bulging. Then the hounds were on them. As the Bulls disappeared beneath the greyhound flood, a separate pack of hounds, driven crazy by the blood, fell upon the Gambler and devoured him alive where he lay.

Tac hobbled toward the melee to help her youngsters. Brennus rose behind her on his hind legs. While his front paws wrapped about her throat, his great weight smashed down behind her shoulders, and he wrenched her head back. Tac collapsed without a sound. The fight was also over for Tic: Dervla pulled her snout from his lifeless throat. The gang of mastiffs who had policed and terrorized the greyhounds for so long had been wiped out.

Furgul scanned the throng in search of Keeva. Still he couldn't see her.

"Zinni!" he barked above the chaos. "Where's Keeva?"

"She wasn't in the compound," called Zinni. "But when I was up on the tightrope, I saw a cardboard box in Dedbone's truck."

Furgul turned and craned his neck. From here he could see what he hadn't seen before—a big cardboard box in Dedbone's pickup. He realized that Dedbone had never put Keeva back in the compound. When he'd brought her back from the track last night, he must have put her straight in the box. She'd been trapped in there all night, waiting to be killed.

Furgul saw Dedbone wading and kicking his way through the mass of greyhounds. And as he did so, he slotted fresh shells into the barrels of the shotgun.

Furgul went after him, dodging, twisting, shoving his way through the hounds. He saw Dervla head toward Dedbone too. Beyond her, Cogg and Baz abandoned the corpses of the two young Bulls they'd killed, and stumbled toward the truck to reinforce them. Brennus, though exhausted and bleeding, was running in an arc around the milling hounds. He was closer to Dedbone than anyone else in the Bunch.

Dedbone half-turned to look at Furgul, the loaded sawed-off shotgun in his hands. Furgul tensed, ready to try to evade the blast. But Dedbone had something more cruel in mind. He grinned. He turned away. Then he aimed the shotgun right at the box on the back of the truck.

"Keeva!" barked Furgul.

BOOM!

Just as Dedbone pulled the trigger, Brennus, with the last of his strength, launched his great battered body through the air. The blast tore into his broad chest and slammed him into the side of the truck.

Furgul leaped clear of the pack and sprinted for Brennus. Dedbone opened the door of the truck. Then he swiveled, one meaty hand on the bite wound in his belly, as he swung the shotgun with the other.

He pointed the second barrel at Furgul.

Furgul tore straight at him.

As Dedbone locked his aim onto Furgul, a raggedy shape daubed with goat poop and slime shot out from under the truck where he'd been hiding. Skyver threw everything he had into the attack. He crashed his body against the back of Dedbone's knees. As Dedbone tilted backward, waving his arms for balance, the shotgun boomed. One of the electric cables above was blown in two. A shower of sparks fell on the house, and the house caught on fire.

Dedbone stomped on Skyver's neck, just behind the ears. Furgul coiled and sprang up from the ground, his fangs wide, going for Dedbone's face. But the wily slaver rammed the steel barrels of the shotgun into Furgul's throat. Furgul was driven head over heels. He landed on his back. Then Dervla rushed Dedbone from the side, but it wasn't the first time Dedbone had fought a pack of dogs. He swiped her across the skull with the stubby gun barrels and left her stunned and twitching next to Skyver.

Dedbone threw the gun across the seat and climbed into the truck.

Furgul rose again and went back in, hoping to savage Dedbone in the cramped interior of the cab. But Dedbone heaved on the door, which slammed into Furgul's shoulder and bashed him aside.

As Furgul hit the gravel and rolled and found his feet, pain lanced down his foreleg. The leg almost gave way beneath him, but he ignored the pain. He gritted his teeth. As he raised his head, he saw two bearded fiends hurtle through the air in perfect unison.

Cogg and Baz crashed into the windshield with their bricklike heads. A web of cracks whitened the glass, but it didn't shatter. Through the door window Furgul saw Dedbone crack the sawed-off in half. He saw Cogg and Baz, still standing on the hood, butting their heads into the windshield like a pair of hammers, trying to get at Dedbone through the glass.

"Get down!" barked Furgul. "He's reloading."

Cogg and Baz didn't listen. Dedbone snapped the sawed-off shut and fired both barrels. The windshield exploded outward. Cogg and Baz arched backward from the hood in a glittering hail of shards.

Furgul heard the engine of the truck rumble twice and stop. He had to get into the back of the pickup truck. He had to get Keeva out of that box before Dedbone killed her. He swung in a short circle to get the right angle to leap in the back—and glimpsed Brennus still panting beneath the truck.

Brennus was still alive. If the truck drove forward, the rear wheel would roll over his skull. Furgul abandoned his leap and ducked down to Brennus. From the corner of his eye he saw Dervla stagger to her feet, still dazed.

"Dervla! Help me with Brennus!"

Dervla reeled over. There was no time to be gentle. Furgul grabbed a mouthful of skin and fur on Brennus's flank, and Dervla grabbed the scruff of his neck. They heaved together with all their strength, and Brennus shunted toward them six inches. The engine rumbled again. This time it caught and roared. The rear tires spun in the gravel. Furgul and Dervla bunched their muscles and heaved. The enormous Saint Bernard slid toward them, just as the wheel crunched by and missed him.

The truck pulled away in a billow of dust with Keeva still trapped in the back.

Furgul watched it go.

His heart clenched as Zinni sprinted forward. She stopped to stand directly in Dedbone's path. Valiant greyhounds sprang from left and right to follow Zinni's lead. They stood side by side and made a living wall of dogs. It was too late for Furgul to tell them that Dedbone wouldn't hesitate for a second.

The engine roared louder and higher. The truck picked up speed as it plowed right into the wall of dogs. Greyhounds flew to either side, and some screamed as they were ground into the gravel beneath the tires. Furgul choked with horror. But as the truck rolled on, Zinni reappeared between the rear wheels. She was so short the truck had passed right over her.

Furgul turned back to Dervla and Brennus. From beyond the cloud of dust and smoke came a sinister and familiar sound.

CLACK-CLACK!

He saw Dervla's whole body twitch in a reflex of ingrained fear, just as he'd seen her twitch back at the carnival. A monstrous apparition now materialized through the smoke. His face was deformed by scorpion bites. He still wore only his filthy shorts. In his hand he held the dreaded telescopic steel baton.

Dervla tensed again and took a step back as Tattoo spewed a stream of foul threats. He was enraged that Dedbone had just abandoned him. He seethed with his hatred of dogs—and of Dervla above all. Furgul knew that Tattoo was the only creature in the world that Dervla feared. He had used that rod to batter that fear into her every nerve and bone. He was the one man that Dervla could not face.

Skyver tried to stand up off the ground but fell back down.

Furgul coiled to launch himself at Tattoo.

"He's mine," said Dervla.

Dervla hurtled forward into the smoke. Tattoo spit obscenities and raised his baton to beat her down. He expected her to cower, as she'd cowered so many times before. But Dervla's days of cowering were over. As the baton whistled at her head, Dervla sprang and was on him, rearing high, fully as tall as he was. Her eyes drilled holes of fear into whatever it was that passed for Tattoo's soul. Her breath scorched his face with its fury. Tattoo emitted a high-pitched scream as she toppled him flat on his back and showed him her fangs. Tattoo gibbered with terror and pain as his face disappeared inside her maw. His body thrashed beneath her, his arms trying to fend her off, but without success. Dervla's fangs burrowed deeper. The muffled screaming stopped. Tattoo no longer moved.

Dervla stood over his corpse. Her shoulders heaved as she panted for breath. Then she turned to Furgul. He saw her eyes. Dervla would never let a man make her frightened again.

"Furgul."

Brennus's voice was but a husk of the warm, throaty growl that Furgul had come to love. He stood over the buckshot-ravaged giant and licked his face.

"Brennus," said Furgul. "Oh, Brennus."

Brennus heaved for breath. Red foam spilled from his lips.

"Make me an oath," whispered Brennus.

"Anything," said Furgul.

"Seek the Dog Lore. Show us how to find our way home."

"I swear it, Brennus," said Furgul. "I swear it to you."

Brennus smiled, his own blood staining his great, broken fangs.

"You'll find me on the winds," he said.

Brennus coughed and shuddered. He fought for one last breath.

"Now go get Keeva."

Furgul looked at the dust trail that had whipped up in the wake of Dedbone's truck. It was far out of range. Not even a cheetah could catch Dedbone now.

"The Doglines," whispered Brennus. "Run the Doglines."

The mighty heart of Brennus stopped beating.

"Brennus!" cried Furgul. "Brennus!"

Furgul felt as if the earth itself would no longer wish to turn. Grief welled up inside him and paralyzed his limbs, blinded his eyes, fogged his mind.

"Furgul! The Doglines!" barked Dervla. Her voice was harsh. "What did he mean?"

Furgul looked at her. Dervla's strength somehow gave Furgul back his own.

He knew what Brennus meant.

He turned and started to run.

But he didn't try to follow Dedbone's truck.

Furgul's injured shoulder sent knives through his leg with every stride.

He stumbled across the junkyard through the dazed ranks of greyhounds. He hurdled the ravaged corpses of the Bulls. As he broached the parched grassland, he glanced back at the smoking battlefield.

Down the main road into Dedbone's Hole a column of vehicles approached. In the lead he recognized Jodi's truck. Behind her came a convoy of cars and vans, most of them painted yellow with flashing blue lights. Jodi must have discovered Dedbone's human name at the track. She was bringing the cruelty-prevention people, just as she had promised. Dervla and the others would be safe. But Furgul didn't turn back. By the time he persuaded Jodi to pursue Dedbone, Keeva would be dead.

Furgul was the pale dog running.

He had to run.

He had to run like he'd never run before.

Just as he thought he would falter from the pain, he found the Dogline.

And along that Dogline Furgul ran to save Keeva.

CHAPTER NINETEEN

THE CHASM

As Furgul ran the Dogline across the valley—toward the jagged rock jaws of Argal's Mountain—he felt the nature of time and space change inside him.

He didn't feel that he was running any faster than his best—his pace was no quicker, his stride no longer—yet he was covering more distance, much more quickly, than should have been possible. It was almost as if the ground itself was moving under his paws to increase his speed.

Just as mysterious, the crippling pain in his shoulder faded away. He was aching from head to claw from the blows he'd taken, and most of them still hurt just as much as before. But the shoulder—the one injury that would have stopped him—now felt fine. It was as if the Dogline would give him only what he most needed, but no more.

Over to his right, beyond the meadowlands, he could see Dedbone's truck winding around the road that led to the mountain. Though Furgul didn't know how, or why, he knew that the Dogline would help him reach the road in time to intercept the truck. Furgul looked up as rags of cloud raced across the wide blue sky above. As the wind on which the clouds were borne got stronger, the clouds became grim and gray. It was as if the clouds meant to follow him to Argal's Mountain.

Furgul swept through the forest. He couldn't see the truck anymore. He couldn't even see the mountain. The undergrowth was dense with bracken. Yet he wove through the trees without taking a single false step. He broke from the woods into the open. He got nearer and nearer to the road— and to the dangerous leap he would have to take into the rear of Dedbone's truck.

The truck was now bumping its way around a sweeping curve. Billows of rust-red dust smoked up from its wheels. Furgul's own path was straight as an arrow. As truck and dog converged, Furgul saw Dedbone through the shattered edges of the windshield. He was hunched over the steering wheel, using his teeth to wrap an oil-stained rag around his injured hand.

The slaver didn't see Furgul.

Furgul shortened his stride to prepare for the jump. The truck rumbled right in front of him. As he coiled his hind legs to spring, his paws sank into a bright green bed of moss. He drew on every ounce of strength in his haunches. The moss seemed to draw power from the Dogline and acted like a trampoline. Furgul soared through the air. His hind claws scraped the edge of the tailgate as he landed. He managed to slow down before he crashed into the cardboard box behind the cab.

As he panted and recovered his balance, he realized that the bright green bed of moss was the exact same spot where Brid had landed, when she made her escape when they were pups. Had Brid followed the Dogline? There was no time to wonder. He sniffed the box and detected Keeva's scent.

"Mam! Are you okay?"

"Furgul?"

Keeva's voice was muffled by the box. Furgul ripped into the cardboard with his jaws. It was tough and stiff and sealed with thick gray tape, but his teeth were now longer and sharper than those of a pup. In seconds he'd torn a gaping hole. He paused to look inside. Keeva's eyes met his. She still wore the racing muzzle from the track, and Furgul understood why she herself hadn't escaped—she couldn't bite the cardboard. And she'd been trapped in there all night without food or water.

"Come on, Mam. Let's get you out of there."

He took a mouthful of cardboard and tore a great strip right down the box. Keeva wriggled her way out. Furgul chewed through the strap behind her ears, and she shook the muzzle off. He felt the truck slow down as it began the final ascent toward the mountain and the cave of death.

"Jump out of the truck, Mam."

Keeva looked at him, full of a mother's love and a mother's fears.

"Go and find Dervla," said Furgul. "You'll be safe with her."

"Dedbone's an expert dog fighter," she said. "Forget him, come away with me."

"The humans will never punish Dedbone. And he's hurt too many dogs."

"Please," pleaded Keeva.

"You're free, Mam. I'm going to make sure it stays that way." Beyond the roof of the cab, in the side of the mountain, Furgul could see the black hole of the cave. "Go, Mam," he barked. "Go now."

Keeva licked his face. Then she gave him once again the most precious gift he'd ever owned. She said, "Be brave."

Keeva jumped. He watched her long blue body land and swerve about with perfect grace. He saw the dread in her face. Then he turned away.

The truck slowed down and stopped outside the cave.

Furgul looked up the mountainside. The clouds that had scudded across the valley in his wake now collided above the double peak. The wind merged them into a huge black nimbus that blocked out the rays of the sun. The cloud cast a giant shadow over Furgul. Furgul stole up onto the roof of the truck. He waited for Dedbone.

The door of the truck swung open. Dedbone levered

himself out. His greasy head and thick neck and dense, hunched shoulders rose before Furgul's paws. He offered no good target for Furgul's teeth. Furgul held back. As Dedbone turned to the back of the truck, he froze as he saw Furgul on the roof.

Dedbone glanced at the torn and empty box. He nodded to himself, as if he might have expected it. Then he stared off down the valley toward the compound. Furgul followed his gaze and looked too.

Black smoke spiraled into the sky above Dedbone's Hole. The flames of the burning house were yellow and orange. Dedbone's empire of cruelty lay in ruins.

"It's over, Dedbone," growled Furgul. "The dogs are free."

Dedbone turned to look at Furgul. Their eyes met.

Dedbone had enslaved and exploited dogs all his life. They had no greater enemy. Yet in spite of that—perhaps because of it—Dedbone must have known his greyhounds better than any dog lover ever knows his pet. Somewhere in his twisted heart, Dedbone too must have loved his dogs. He had steeped himself in their speed, their grace, their resilience, their trust, their loyalty. Dogs had been his life. And Dedbone had squandered that life by betraying every single dog he'd ever owned.

Dedbone said, *"A free dog never dies. He only moves on."*

Furgul's mind reeled. He understood every word. Dedbone had spoken in dog tongue. Perfect dog tongue. No weapon that the slaver might have wielded could have stunned him so much.

"You're a Dog Talker?" asked Furgul.

"I don't talk to dumb animals," said Dedbone. "I kick them. I breed them. I use them. I kill them. Then I dump them in the garbage where they belong."

His smile was full of malice.

"But if you're asking, do I understand your stupid, yelping, slavering, slobbering gibberish? Of course I do. Because I'm better than you. Because I'm a human being. And you're just a dog."

Furgul felt sick.

He remembered the paddock at the racetrack, where he'd told Keeva what Argal had told him about free dogs. Dedbone had just repeated Argal's words exactly. He must have listened in on every word they'd said. And he must have been listening in for years, eavesdropping and spying on the dogs at the Hole, at the track, in the streets—everywhere. Even Tic and Tac hadn't known.

All the evil that Dedbone had done seemed even more depraved than before. He wasn't just a greedy slaver. He was a snoop. He'd heard the dogs speak—of their suffering, their fears, their hunger, their broken dreams—of their love for their pups and their mates. And he'd used his stolen knowledge of their private thoughts and feelings to make the chains of slavery tighter still.

"Now it's time for *you* to move on," said Dedbone. "The chasm is waiting."

"I've already been there," Furgul snarled.

Dedbone grinned. "Yeah? How many free dogs did you find?"

Furgul stared at him. The faces of Eena and Nessa flashed in his mind.

"Of all the dogs I threw in that pit, not a single one was free," said Dedbone. "There's no moving on for them. They'll never join the winds. They're in a cage that will last forever."

The thought that the dogs would never be free filled Furgul with anger and sorrow. Worst of all, Dedbone was right. They would never roam with the winds. Again he saw the faces of Eena and Nessa. Every muscle in his body clenched with rage.

"Well?" said Dedbone. "What are you waiting for, lurcher?"

Dedbone tipped his head back. He jabbed a thick finger at his own throat.

"Get it while it's hot."

Furgul dived from the roof. The growl that escaped from his chest was so savage that his own ears quailed at the sound. As his paws clawed Dedbone's shoulders, he opened his jaws to go for the veins in Dedbone's thick, red neck.

It was just what Dedbone wanted.

He jammed the meaty edge of his injured hand between Furgul's jaws. His powerful arm snared Furgul's back and crushed him against the hard bulge of his belly. Dedbone squeezed with immense strength, and Furgul's ribs and spine crackled. The air was forced out of his lungs. His neck was bent back.

Furgul thrashed and flailed, but Dedbone was too strong. He tried to twist his head away, to strike again at the throat, but Dedbone rammed the edge of his palm even deeper into Furgul's mouth. Furgul sank his fangs in, but the oily rag protected Dedbone's hand. Furgul bit down until he felt the bones crunch, and Dedbone's face flinched with pain. But Dedbone was tough, and he was crafty. As long as he kept the hand between Furgul's jaws, it acted like a muzzle. Furgul couldn't use a lethal bite. Dedbone had blunted his teeth.

"You fell for it, you stupid mutt," rasped Dedbone. "But you were right about one thing. It's over."

Dedbone carried Furgul into the cave. A familiar and evil stench flooded Furgul's nostrils. Because the cloud above the mountain had blocked out the sun, the inside of the cave was dark. The farther Dedbone carried him into the cave, the darker it got. The only advantage Furgul had was that his eyes could see better in the dark than Dedbone's. *Remember, there are teeth everywhere.* Furgul couldn't move his head very much, but as best he could, he scanned the cave for teeth.

Beyond Dedbone's shoulder, in the shadows up ahead, he saw a sharp spur of rock that stuck out from the far wall of the cave. As they passed it, Furgul wrenched his hind legs from under Dedbone's belly. He twisted his hips and flexed his spine until his hind paws touched the near wall, just opposite the spur. Then he shoved with all the strength in his massive thighs.

Dedbone, caught off guard, stumbled across the cave. The

spur of rock spiked into his cheek below his eye. Dedbone bellowed with pain and he staggered. Furgul broke free of his arms.

He landed on the dark side of the cave. Dedbone stood between Furgul and the daylight. Dedbone ignored the pain of his smashed face and spread his arms out wide. He crouched in the middle of the cave to block Furgul's escape.

But Furgul didn't want to escape. He could have ducked and dodged around Dedbone. He could have sprinted out of the cave. But then Dedbone would still be alive to hurt Keeva and Dervla and countless others. Furgul could not allow that. Somewhere inside Argal's Mountain—he felt sure it was the crystal cavern—Furgul sensed a right Dogline. And Furgul intended to do the right thing.

His memory of being in the box with Eena and Nessa flashed in his mind.

Deep in the cave was another tooth that Furgul hoped he could use.

He skipped this way and that in front of Dedbone. Dedbone bobbed and weaved to cut him off. Furgul faked a whimper of fear and cringed before him.

Dedbone sneered. "Get ready to rot with your sisters on that hill."

Furgul turned tail and went deeper into the cave. He stopped to glance back. Dedbone was peering forward, swaying from side to side, his human eyes straining to penetrate the gloom. Furgul waited for him. The cave was now so dark that Furgul knew the only thing that Dedbone could see was Furgul's pale coat of fur. Just as Dedbone had lured the greyhounds to chase fake rabbits at the track, Furgul now lured Dedbone deeper—deeper, deeper—into the dark. And Furgul was the dog who ran in darkness.

Dedbone spotted his paleness and lunged forward.

Furgul turned and bounded toward the chasm.

He heard Dedbone curse as he blundered onward in pursuit.

Just a few paces farther toward the rear of the cave, Furgul's eyes spotted an area of the floor where the blackness became even blacker. It was the edge of the chasm. He lengthened his stride and picked up speed.

"There's only one end to this race, lurcher!" Dedbone shouted. "And you're about to cross the finish line!"

Furgul's forepaws hit the rim of the chasm. All his weight rocked forward as his hind legs left the ground to coil beneath him. For an instant he was almost falling into space. He powered his hind legs downward against the rock. As his thighs propelled him forward and up, Furgul flew into the void above the abyss.

Up ahead—a foot or so higher than the floor of the cave—he saw a ledge appear from the blackness just before him. The same ledge he had spotted from the box when he was just a pup. For an instant he wondered if he'd judged his leap correctly. Then he landed on the rocky shelf, and momentum carried him on. He gasped but didn't yelp as his shoulder hammered into the wall. He scrambled to his feet. He turned and looked over and down.

He was perched on the opposite wall of the chasm, facing toward the cave. Beneath the ledge the wall disappeared in a sheer drop. He couldn't see the hill of bones. He saw Dedbone's silhouette lumber toward him from the cave. Furgul turned sideways so that Dedbone would see his pale coat.

To get across the abyss to the ledge, Furgul had jumped from a sprint, which gave him the maximum range. But the ledge was too narrow to allow him to build up another running jump. To get back across the chasm again, he'd have to jump from a standing start. From a standing jump he could gain more height—but he couldn't make quite as much distance. Furgul reckoned that he wouldn't be able to reach the safety of the cave again. He was trapped on the ledge—unless he could find a stepping stone to give his return jump a second boost.

Dedbone came closer and closer. His only guide was Furgul's pale shape. And because Dedbone didn't know about the ledge—and couldn't see well in the dark—he thought that Furgul had stopped on the edge of the chasm.

But it was Dedbone who had now reached the edge.

One more step and Dedbone would walk into oblivion.

As Dedbone raised his foot, Furgul barked across the void. "Dedbone! Watch your step!"

Dedbone looked down. He cursed in terror as the emptiness gaped at his feet. He stopped with his toes hanging over the edge of the precipice. For an instant he teetered in panic, his head and shoulders bent forward, his arms cartwheeling backward to regain his balance, trying to tilt his weight to the safety of the solid rock floor behind him.

Dedbone almost made it.

But Furgul judged that his moment had come. He seized it.

His haunches drove him upward from the ledge in a steep, high arc. Alone he wouldn't have made it all the way to the far side. But Furgul used Dedbone as his stepping stone. He stretched out his forelegs, and his paws touched down on Dedbone's shoulders. As he whipped his hind legs in, tight beneath his chest, he dug his claws into Dedbone's broad back and used the slaver's weight as a platform for a second, extra thrust.

As Furgul's takeoff propelled him forward into the safety of the cave, his paws shoved Dedbone away. And pushed the slaver screaming over the edge.

Furgul landed with all four paws on the rim of the cave.

Dedbone plunged headfirst into the chasm.

His last scream faded to a distant, desperate wail as he fell. And fell.

And fell.

Furgul heard a dull, splintering crunch. And then there was silence.

A wave of lemony sunlight rolled through the mouth of the cave and dispelled the gloom. The clouds above the mountain had helped Furgul—they'd made the cave even darker and Dedbone's eyesight even worse. Now that Furgul didn't need them anymore, the clouds had dispersed to reveal the sun.

Furgul went to the chasm's rim. He looked down.

Dedbone lay sprawled on the bones of the hill of dead dogs. His mouth opened and closed, but he made no sound. Crimson stained his lips. His piggy eyes glinted. Broken shards of skeleton, ribs and femurs and jawbones, had impaled him through the back when he landed. He squirmed as the blood-stained greyhound bones jutted out of his belly like spears.

Dedbone tried to get up, but the hill underneath him began to collapse with his weight. The big man's fall had shattered its delicate structure. Now Dedbone sank deeper and deeper into decay—as if the countless greyhounds he had killed were sucking him down into the dust to die among them. Dedbone raised a desperate hand toward Furgul. He was begging for his help.

Furgul wagged his tail and walked away.

Chapter Twenty

THE WIND

O nce upon a time in the Doglands, a pup was born in the slave camp that the dogs called Dedbone's Hole. He'd been born in chains and sentenced to die, yet neither chains nor death had held him. He'd broken their rules. He'd escaped their prisons. He'd defied their guards and their guns. He'd returned and set the wrong things right.

Furgul emerged from the cave and raised his face to the sun.

It was good to be alive.

He knew where he had been, but he did not know where he was going.

The wild and rambling road called him still.

A wind swept toward him from the jaws of Argal's Mountain high above. It bounded down from outcrop to outcrop, then whirled about Furgul in a vortex so strong that it spun him around and around. Furgul grinned.

The wind was the spirit of Brennus saying hail and farewell.

It was Brennus who had rounded up the clouds to help Furgul beat Dedbone. Before Furgul could soak up the Brennus wind into his bones, it was suddenly gone. Mysteriously gone, for he saw no sign of its passing down the valley. No dust stirred, no blade of grass bent, no leaf fluttered on the trees.

A truck drove up the trail. It was Jodi.

The first thing Furgul saw was Skyver. He was strapped to a stretcher. He had a plastic contraption like a giant collar round his neck. The stretcher was fixed to the roof rack. Skyver stared up into space, and he was peeved.

"Is that you, Furgul?" called Skyver. "Do me a favor, will you?"

Furgul jumped on the hood of the truck and onto the roof beside Skyver.

"This is the thanks I get for planning and leading the task force to Dedbone's Hole," Skyver complained. "They won't let me ride inside the car, even though I've got a broken neck."

"Your neck's broken?"

"Jodi says it's just a whiplash, but what do Vets know? And—you'll never believe this—guess why they won't let me inside?"

Despite the fresh air, Furgul detected the overwhelming aroma of goat.

"I've no idea," said Furgul.

The doors of the car opened, and Jodi, Keeva and Zinni climbed out.

Furgul jumped down to join them.

"Furgul?" said Skyver. "Furgul! Tell them to get me off this thing!"

The dogs surrounded Furgul in a festival of sniffing and snuffling. He was glad to see them too. Keeva rubbed her neck against Furgul's shoulder. Tears of relief shone in her eyes. Zinni grinned and gave him her happiest tail wag. Jodi, too, was glad to see him alive.

"Furgul?" whined Skyver. "Are you there, old buddy? It's freezing up here! And I need to cock a leg! Isn't anyone listening? Skyver needs a pee!"

"Skyver told me everything," said Jodi.

"I'm sure he did," said Furgul.

"You must be incredibly proud of him," said Jodi.

"Dogs will tell the tale of Skyver for a thousand years."

"That's exactly what Skyver said."

"Did Cogg and Baz make it?" asked Furgul.

"If you mean the two giant schnauzers," said Jodi, "they locked themselves in the smokehouse and won't come out. Apparently there's a priceless collection of smoked-pork products in there. They said they'd defend their bacon to the last rasher. Chuck Chumley's sending a truck so they can take it all home."

Furgul's spirits soared as Dervla stepped down from the rear of the car.

She watched Furgul from a distance with her dark, haunted eyes. She carried a dozen wounds from the battle. The sadness within her reached out and touched his soul. Furgul smiled. The smile came from deep in his heart. Dervla raised her tail. But she didn't smile back. Despite all that she'd been through, despite her scars inside and out, despite that she was the Dog Who Never Smiles, Dervla was as lovely as the dog he'd played with on that long-ago day in the park.

"The protection society have rescued the greyhounds," said Jodi. "They'll find good homes for them. We're going back to Appletree. Jump in the car and we'll get going."

The dogs all looked at Furgul. He didn't know what to say.

Dervla said, "Furgul's not coming to Appletree."

Furgul saw the way Dervla looked at him. He realized that she was right. She had known it even before he had known it himself. He wasn't going back to the sanctuary.

"Is that true?" asked Jodi. "You're not coming with us?"

Furgul nodded.

"But where will you go?" asked Jodi.

Furgul hadn't thought about that. He looked at Dervla.

"He doesn't know," said Dervla. "He'll find out when he gets there."

Keeva looked at Furgul. She wanted him to stay. Then she saw something behind him. The light changed in her eyes. She trotted past him. Furgul turned.

Two small whorls of dust were skipping back and forth

outside the mouth of the cave. Keeva started whirling around with them. Her face was radiant with joy.

"What's got into her?" asked Skyver. "And by the way, will someone get me off this roof? Anyone? Please?"

They were all entranced in watching Keeva dance. Furgul's heart clenched.

"It's Eena and Nessa," he said. "They're free."

From the throat of the cave came a distant howl, like a pack of greyhounds baying for the chase. The howl rose into an ecstatic roar. Then the ghost hounds hurtled from the cave on a mystic hurricane.

As Furgul felt their spirits rushing by, his own spirit soared. Dervla and Zinni and Keeva felt it too. On the roof of the car Skyver let out a long yowl of fright.

The ghost hounds surged down the slope and through the valley, flattening the grass and bending the trunks of even the strongest trees. In the distance the flames of Dedbone's Hole erupted into an inferno. The buildings were flattened. The junkyard was cleansed. The wire-mesh walls of the compound were torn down. Empty dog crates and eating troughs were blown away like leaves. Then, just as abruptly, the fiery blaze was snuffed out. The phantom hounds galloped on across the sky. And of Dedbone's Hole they left not a wisp behind.

"Hey!" shouted Skyver. He was sniffing his own fur and struggling against the safety straps that held him down. "I'm clean! I'M CLEAN! They blew away all the goat poop! All of it! Honestly! LET ME DOWN!"

For the moment everyone ignored him. They were all too stunned by what had happened. Then one last wind emerged from the cave. Warm, huge, gentle and wise. It was the spirit that had gone into the chasm to free the ghosts of the greyhounds trapped inside the hill of dead. As Brennus brushed by Furgul's cheek, Furgul heard what sounded like a whisper in his ear.

"Seek the Dog Lore."

Furgul looked at Keeva. It was hard to leave her again. He couldn't tell her why he had to go, because he didn't really know. Keeva stepped over and licked his face.

"You know where to find me," said Keeva. "Don't forget."

"Yes, Mam," said Furgul. "I won't forget."

Furgul could feel a Dogline beneath his feet. *The pawprints of the ancestors.* He felt as if they were singing to him, telling him a story he did not yet understand. The story began in the faraway distant past and led toward a faraway distant future.

Toward the Doglands.

Furgul looked at Dervla.

"Have you ever been to the Doglands?" he asked.

"No," said Dervla.

"Dogs like us could find them. If we tried."

"With you, I'll try anything."

Furgul said, "Shall we run?"

"Yes," said Dervla.

And the Dog Who Never Smiles smiled at last.

It was the most beautiful dog smile Furgul had ever seen.

Dervla said, "Let's run."

Furgul didn't hesitate. He turned and loped away across Argal's Mountain.

Dervla ran away with him.

"Furgul!" barked Zinni. "We love you, Furgul!"

"Furgul?" howled Skyver. "FUR-GUL!"

Keeva watched Furgul and Dervla go, her sweet heart aching for her son.

The son she had named the Brave when he was born.

Furgul didn't stop. He had never stopped.

Keeva knew he never would.

Furgul was the pale dog running.

Running.

Running.

Running as if he would run the Doglines forever.

And perhaps he would.

Furgul and Dervla crested the craggy ridge and paused against the wild blue sky.

Furgul looked down at his mother, and for an instant Keeva hoped he might come back. But he turned to Dervla. Together they craned their necks and yip-yip-yarooed a last farewell from the mountain. Then the two dogs galloped away.

And Furgul was gone.

And though Keeva was sad, she was happy.

For she knew Furgul was running to where he belonged.

To where she knew Furgul would always be.

To where dogs would always find him.

Nowhere and everywhere.

Running, always, with the winds.

In the Doglands.

ACKNOWLEDGMENTS

Doglands was conceived during an epic hike along the Kerry Way with my friend and fellow writer David Cox. At every stage—every chapter—of the novel's subsequent composition, David provided the kind of unflagging inspiration, encouragement and faith that constitute a gift far beyond price. This novel would not exist without him, and his largeness of spirit pervades it.

Thanks also to the great Al Zuckerman, who provided expert editorial guidance as well as being the book's champion in the "wilderness of tigers."

There was someone else on the hike that day, sniffing, marking, scouting, sprinting and occasionally—if inadvertently—putting the fear of canine gods into the other dogs we met along the way. This book wouldn't exist without him either, because it was inspired by what little I know of his life. Feargal, an Irish lurcher of mysterious origins, boasts numerous buckshot wounds, several dueling scars *and* an indomitable heart, and is one of the most remarkable individuals I have ever known. This novel may embellish his adventures, but not, I believe, his sensibility and inner beauty.

Feargal was saved from death in the Dublin dog pound by Mary-Jane Fox, creator of Orchard Greyhound Sanctuary (orchardgreyhoundsanctuary.com), and so the book owes its existence to her too. Beyond that, she deserves the thanks, respect and support of all of us for the magnificent work she does in rescuing some of the loveliest creatures on earth from cruelty and destruction.

TIM WILLOCKS was born in the North
of England and became a doctor of medicine in
1983. He has written four novels for adults and
has lived with four unforgettable dogs: a German
shepherd called Gul, a black-and-white greyhound
called Auda, a black greyhound called Lily, and a
white lurcher called Feargal. Tim lives on a mountain
in Ireland.